A NOVEL

LAND
OF
DUST
AND
HOPE

MICHAEL DOWNING

RIVER GROVE
BOOKS

This is a work of fiction. Although some of the characters, organizations, and events portrayed in the novel were inspired by actual historical counterparts, the dialogue, thoughts, and actions of these characters and the events portrayed are products of the author's imagination.

Published by River Grove Books
Austin, TX
www.rivergrovebooks.com

Distributed by River Grove Books

Design and composition by Greenleaf Book Group
Cover design by Greenleaf Book Group
Cover Illustration based on images from Unsplash.com

Publisher's Cataloging-in-Publication data is available.

Print ISBN: 978-1-63299-785-2

eBook ISBN: 978-1-63299-786-9

First Edition

To all who struggle to overcome . . . to the eternal light of
the human spirit that wrestles with the ultimate Mystery of
being, in fear and faith, cowering and courage, humor and hope.

To Charles W. Keller, PhD, intrepid explorer of the truth of
human experience, who, for fifty years, helped countless others
up the rugged mountains of self-discovery, as he walked beside
them across perilous canyons and through the howling winds of
high, jagged cliffs to a new freedom.

To Barbara, in whose eyes the light of love and joy shines
brightly, as bright as the Christmas star.

"*Then the eyes of both were opened, and they knew that they were naked; they sewed fig leaves together and made loincloths for themselves. They heard the sound of Yahweh walking in the garden at the time of the evening breeze, and the man and the woman hid themselves from the presence of Yahweh among the trees of the garden. But Yahweh called to the man, and said, 'Where are you?' He said, 'I heard the sound of you in the garden, and I was afraid, because I was naked; and I hid myself.' He said, 'Who told you that you were naked?'. . . And Yahweh made garments of skins for the man and the woman, and clothed them.*"

—Adapted from the New Revised Standard Version of the Bible, Genesis 3:7-11; Genesis 3:21

DUST

Brother Bob sat in the scorching July sun on the steep concrete steps of the First United Methodist Church of Happy, Texas, watching the high, gusty wind skip tumbleweeds amidst swirls of dust down the worn, red-brick streets laid in 1908. Not far away, on the north edge of town, he could see the weathered sign that stood in the shallow ditch on the west side of Highway 87. Although it was partly covered by drifts of dirt and wilting sunflowers, it greeted travelers going south on 87 across the infinite flatness of the lonesome Panhandle Plains.

From what Brother Bob was told, the tourism development committee had erected the sign in a spasm of civic optimism in 1954, but as a cost-saving measure, they had built it with old posts and planks from a cow barn that had fallen down on a nearby ranch. Now, all these years later, one post had rotted off at the ground, so it tilted forward on the right side. The creaking sign, its white paint cracked and peeling in the sun, swayed at the mercy of the ever-present gusts of wind. Any travelers who drove by could read the bold proclamation, "Welcome to Happy—the Town without a Frown! Pop. 504." The words were painted in black, misshapen letters that sloped downward to the right. The proclamation had been painted freehand by the drunk cousin of a committee member, who agreed to paint the sign for a half-pint of Old Grand Dad and two packs of Lucky Strikes.

Travelers who pulled over onto the gravel shoulder for a rest stop stretch might notice a smaller message in the lower right corner, scrawled hurriedly by a high school boy in the bitter Blue Norther cold and blowing snow on a January night in 1972. The words were difficult to make out now because, apparently, someone—possibly a Baptist, Brother Bob guessed—had been disturbed by the original message and painted over it. However, through the years, the words had managed by some tenacity to fade back through. Now, this was a topic of daily debate among the regulars wearing farm caps at Elmer's Café: it either read "Jessica sucks" or "Jesus saves."

Eight years earlier, the Methodist bishop had sent Brother Bob, fresh out of seminary at Southern Methodist University, to serve the people of Happy. He knew that the people of the community were the survivors, children, grandchildren, and great-grandchildren of the Dust Bowl of the 1930s. He could see that those ominous, dark, rolling clouds of dust had shaped the character of generations of West Texas folks. He had heard the old timers say that during such storms, the dust was so thick that a person could light a match, hold it at arm's length, and not be able to see it. Some infants and children died of dust pneumonia. Scorched crops withered, and the hide-draped bones of cattle and horses could be half-seen in the settled dust that rose to the tops of fence posts and barns. Brother Bob had heard that for a few families, sometimes all there was to eat was cornbread and "water gravy," water flavored with bacon fat.

The drought, the dust storms, and the poverty they brought had made the people stubborn and resilient, yet they were not without kindness, humor, and faith. Faith had sustained them in the Dust Bowl and contin-ued to sustain generations thereafter. They were honorable people. They never failed to help a stranded traveler on the lonely highway or leave food on the kitchen table of the hungry or the grieving. If a farmer died before the family wheat crop was harvested, his neighbors, without fail, would join together to combine the wheat for his wife and children, refusing any payment for their work: "You just bring some iced tea and a couple of your pecan pies to the field about mid-afternoon, and we'll call it even."

Brother Bob had come to know that the people of Happy were down-to-earth and deeply good-hearted. They were the kind of folk who volunteered to sit up with the sick and the dying. They taught their chil-dren to be respectful by their own example and to treat others with charity and forbearance. They were skeptical of the fancy, the newfangled, and the newcomer (anyone who had not lived there more than ten years). They were disdainful of excess and of putting on airs. Few were comfortable with owning a Cadillac unless it had a couple of noticeable dents and had been bought used for a very good price. The one farmer who drove an old Mercedes always did so only when wearing his patched overalls and John Deere cap. The people of Happy would indeed die before they would ever boast, and the idea of making a scene in public was unthinkable, shameful beyond measure in their eyes. Their faces and demeanor reflected quiet dignity and humility. Like the roots of an ancient tree, they were grounded. Brother Bob could see that the Dust Bowl had instilled in them the humbling wisdom that life, with its blessings, is uncertain—and that hopes and dreams are at the mercy of a transcendent Mystery.

Brother Bob was sitting on the steps with his back to the church building, its white cornerstone engraved with "Methodist Church, 1929." Although the church was plainly box-like in shape, he was impressed by the simple, dignified beauty of its deep-red bricks and stained glass windows. For him, the sight of it evoked thoughts of a silent hope amidst the passage of time on the empty plains and a calling to a higher ground. The building did not have the austere fortress-like appearance of the Baptist and Church of Christ buildings. An old elm tree stood adjacent to the steps, its gnarled roots clinging to the unforgiving, hardpan ground. In their stubborn perseverance, the roots had cracked and buckled the thick concrete of the sidewalk, which sometimes caused people to stumble. For more than eighty years, the tree had witnessed much in the lives of the farm and ranch folks who walked the church steps for Sunday services, weddings, and funerals.

Brother Bob looked at the tree, wishing it could tell him the stories of all it had seen. Of course, he had already seen much in his time there as pastor. He had watched more than one lovely young woman in white lace descending the steep steps, waving and smiling amidst cheers and pelting rice, laughing with a blush at the discovery of white shoe polish innuendos on a pickup truck waiting to carry her into a future uncertain. On many other occasions, he'd watched the grim faces of men and women who had weathered the storms of life as they walked slowly down the steps behind a casket being carried by strong, solemn men. Many in the procession could be seen clenching their jaws to staunch their tears, for they were, after all, Dust Bowl descendants. And more than a handful of times, working late on some sermon, he had glanced out his study window to see a teenage boy and girl as they sat huddled in the secret dark of the steps on a cool summer night, enrapt in luscious kisses and breathtaking touches.

Brother Bob squinted into the unrelenting sun as he looked up at the old elm's branches being whipped about, and he saw that its leaves were so withered and curled by the drought that there was little hope they could provide him any shelter. His eyes were stinging from dripping sweat, and his white shirt was soaked as he turned back to watch the dust and weeds blowing down the street past the steps. He thought, *Well, damn, this is a fitting symbol for my life.* A tumblebug near his boot caught his attention as it struggled to carry a sphere of cow manure triple its size up the back of a step. It fell each time it got near the top but, incredibly, would not give up. He watched its many futile attempts, then finally said to it, "Well, good Lord, give it up, Sisyphus. Can't you see it's not worth it? You know you're carrying a big load of bullshit. Besides, as scripture says, 'all is vanity.'"

He knew it was a mighty curious thing for a preacher to be sitting on the steps of his church in the burning July sun, doing nothing but watching a tumblebug and tumbleweeds. For a moment, he worried about his own condition, oddly sitting there, having lost all purpose and direction, especially when he should be making hospital visits and working on Sunday's sermon. But his worry was quickly buried beneath a too-familiar lethargy and emptiness that descended on him and made his body feel like he was sitting at the bottom of a deep lake.

Brother Bob looked up the street and saw a tumbleweed the size of a compact car bouncing down the street toward him, headed directly for the flea-bitten butt of Ecclesiastes, an old, stove-up, three-legger who had adopted the Methodist church eight years before. No one knew why he'd adopted this church over the others. Some conjectured he had been sent as a messenger from God, but no one could figure out what the message could be unless it was that they, the Methodists, were somehow favored by God over the Baptist, Catholic, and Church of Christ folks. However, this theory made many of the congregation—and Brother Bob—uncomfort-able because it seemed lacking in Wesleyan grace and humility, and thus, it was potentially controversial given the smallness of the community. Other folks argued that the dog had been drawn to the music on Sundays, citing the fact that he wagged his tail happily to the old gospel hymns from the Cokesbury Hymnal, ones with phrases like, "Jesus walked the lonesome valley, he had to walk it by himself, you must walk the lonesome valley, you must walk it by yourself." Brother Bob kept quiet about what he suspected was the truth—the old mutt was simply an opportunistic hedonist with no spiritual sense whatsoever whose true motive was to get scraps from the coveted covered-dish dinners in the fellowship hall after church. Brother Bob looked forward eagerly to the meals himself, so he could not blame the mutt.

No one knew how Ecclesiastes had lost one of his legs, but what was certain was that the dog was named by Miss Opal's third-grade Sunday School class as part of the "Name the Stray for Jesus" contest. Miss Opal's class won with the name of "Ecclesiastes." Brother Bob had picked that name, due to its biblical origins, over several other names, including the name "Dick" submitted by the seventh-grade boys. The children of Miss Opal's class had jumped about with excitement like Spring colts when it was announced that they had won, but then they collapsed in moans of sore disappointment when the contest prize turned out to be tiny New Testaments bound in red vinyl, instead of the hoped-for pizza picnic and swim-in at the Ceta Canyon church camp pool.

Ecclesiastes was an aged yet still defiant veteran of many fights. He'd successfully fought packs of coyotes on several occasions, but they had bit-ten off one testicle and gnawed off half of his right ear. On this afternoon, he'd fallen asleep at the foot of the steps, curled up with his butt toward the street, unmoved by the fierce sun, and unmoving except for the occasional flicking of the tip of his good ear to catapult a pesky, biting fly.

Without much feeling or even a smile of anticipation, Brother Bob watched as the tumbleweed bounced closer, aiming for Ecclesiastes. When it struck his butt with stinging ferocity, he jumped up quickly with fangs bared, growling, and snapping at the air as if he were once again in a fight over a female. After he recovered and realized it was a tumbleweed, he looked like he felt—foolish and indignant. Brother Bob wondered what Ecclesiastes thought of him sitting on the steps, just watching the dust and weeds go by. He saw the old warrior staring intently at him now. His good ear was raised up while he turned his head this way and that, as dogs do when they're puzzled.

"What's the matter with you, Cleesy? Haven't you ever seen your preacher sitting in the blazing sun on his church steps before? Well, no, I guess you haven't."

Ecclesiastes lay back down and fell asleep with his back against the tree, and Brother Bob sat a while longer. Dust had gotten under his shirt collar and was now stuck to his skin with sweat. Soon, an unsettling image broke into his thoughts again, and as it did, he felt his heart beat harder and faster. The image was from last Sunday's service. When his choir director, Jen, stood up to lead a congregational hymn, her choir robe fleetingly parted, revealing her lower legs. He had caught his breath at the sight of the smooth curves of her legs. He was distracted during the sermon and, ironically, forgot part of what he had prepared to say about David and Bathsheba. He could see the people noticed that he was not at his best, and they whispered amongst themselves—except for George, an elderly man who was asleep, as usual, on the back pew, snoring peacefully with his head back and drooling from his open mouth.

Brother Bob sat a while longer, but the blood rush of Jen's image came all the more intensely now. He shook his head and thought, *Maybe this heat is making it worse. Jesus H. Christ! Kyrie eleison.* In frustration, he stood to go into his study within the church to work on the prayer he was giving at the Lions Club luncheon tomorrow. But before he did, he scooped up the tumblebug with a twig and placed it in some grass in the shade underneath one of the tall, stained glass windows.

"There, Sisyphus. Sometimes you have to let go of what you want but can't ever have."

The white pine shelves of his small study were full of books on biblical interpretation, theology, philosophy, early church history, Greek and Hebrew grammars and dictionaries, pastoral counseling, psychology, John

Wesley, and Methodism. There was a Greek New Testament, a Hebrew Bible, and various versions of the Bible in English. He also had his favorite books from literature and poetry: Twain, Steinbeck, McMurtry, Dickinson, Cummings, and others.

Brother Bob sat at his desk, holding his pen, staring for a long while at the blank writing pad in front of him as he hoped for some inspiration to write a meaningful prayer. He thought of something one of his professors had once said: "The problem of God is this: How do we find words to talk about God the Transcendent at all?" He also remembered from a chapel sermon another professor's statement: "Faith without doubt is not worth its salt—doubt is inevitably part of faith."

Brother Bob felt he was clinging to a high cliff's edge, precariously suspended over a chasm of doubt. He had gone into the ministry because he wanted to help others, and he wanted his life to matter. He cared about others with genuine compassion. He had worked diligently in the four years of the seminary's rigorous education and training, but now, having a congregation to care for, he felt paralyzed, lost in a deep conflict. He was at a loss as to how to translate the Christian message in meaningful ways that would build people up and give them hope.

For him, the Gospel message—the "Good News" about what it means to be human and who God is—was shrouded in the mythology of an ancient worldview. Because he was scientifically minded, he could not make sense of that worldview with its notions of original sin, divine interventions, blood atonement, resurrection of the dead, and a supposedly loving God who condemns some to eternal torture. He found himself constantly wrestling with what all that meant for modern people, the people he was supposed to serve. He had been aware of this inner conflict when he was in seminary, but now that he had come to know the people of Happy with all their struggles, he was indeed lost. The typical message heard from most pulpits seemed so meaningless and was often such a repugnant propaganda of fear and guilt that it shook him with anger and frustration. So, surrounded by his many books and the empty silence, he sat and stared at the blank page.

Brother Bob enjoyed the Lions Club, which met each Tuesday at noon.

Many were farmers who came in from the fields with dirt, grease, and sweat stains on their shirts and caps. Some were cowboys who wore denim shirts and jeans and boots with spurs that jingled as they walked across the wood floors. The only men in suits were the Baptist and Church of Christ preachers and the undertaker, Digger O'Daniel. Women could join the club, but no woman in the town had ever wanted to join, and Brother Bob knew the women considered the idea of joining as the equivalent of having an abscessed tooth extracted.

The club met in an old stucco building with a steep tin roof. The room had a very high ceiling of water-stained pressed tin and smoothly worn wood floors; it was long and narrow with an open kitchen and low counter at one end. The walls were yellowed sheetrock, unadorned except for a twelve-year-old calendar with a picture of the high school football team and a caption that read, "Go Steers!" thumb-tacked up on one wall. Brother Bob often wondered with bemusement what the unconscious motives were of the town's founding fathers who decided to name their sons' teams the "Steers." Even more curious to him was the fact that the girls' teams were known as "Lady Steers." A small ad under the picture was for Digger's funeral home. Its caption read, "Trust your departed loved one to Digger, the only Happy undertaker."

Brother Bob was fond of Digger in part because he had often seen Digger's kindness to families during viewings and funerals. None of the folks could remember who gave Digger his nickname, as it had been many years since he arrived in Happy as a graduate of the Southwest School of Mortuary Science in Fort Worth. His real name was Seamus Sean O'Daniel, but no one really knew that unless they had looked at the ornate lettering of the black-framed, fading diploma on the wall of his office. Digger was indeed a happy undertaker. He always had a bounce in his step, greeted everyone with a broad smile, and shook hands or hugged them. One of the town's old grouches argued that Digger was only happy to see people because the living reminded him that he had good future business prospects, but everyone else knew he was a truly kind, good-hearted man.

Digger was 6'4" tall and weighed 143 lb. He always wore a dark suit with a brightly colored clip-on tie. His suit pants were invariably three inches too short, and so polar whiteness shone above his socks, especially when he sat down. He typically had an excess of Brylcreem on his flattop hair and dandruff on his glasses that everybody noticed except him. His fingers were yellowed from too many cigarettes and embalming chemicals. People liked him and were fond of him, although they always seemed a little uneasy around him because his presence reminded them of their own mortality.

Few people other than Brother Bob knew that Digger kept a small prayer bench in the mortuary room, and before beginning his work, he would kneel at the bench and pray, "Good Lord, may the labors of my hands show respect for your holy Creation and bring a little comfort to those who loved this person and are hurting."

Brother Bob also knew that whenever any parents experienced the death of a child, Digger never charged them for his services. When Digger prepared an unfortunate child's body for burial, even if he hadn't known the child, he would be overcome with sadness. He would put down his instruments, kneel at the bench, bow his head, clasp his hands, and cry, "Good Lord, we don't understand this life or your ways." It was rumored that he once had a wife and young child but that she left him for whereabouts unknown, and he never got to see his child again. Folks knew he had never remarried, and he told Brother Bob he had not ever dated since the divorce.

In the Lions Club kitchen that day, Brother Bob saw that Ruby had beaded sweat on her face as she fussed over the large fryers and pans of steaming food. She had cooked the meal for the men every meeting for thirty-two years. Ruby, who had considerable girth, was wearing a purple floral-print cotton dress that had gotten a little tight, possibly from the dryer, and a pink apron. Her graying hair was pulled tight into a bun. She always started cooking at five in the morning and was rarely finished with the clean-up until three in the afternoon. She had no one to help her, except during the meal, two skinny girls from the high school Vocational Ed class would walk about the tables, refilling the iced tea glasses. A few of the men would flirt with the girls and make them blush and giggle nervously.

On Tuesdays, the room was always filled with the enticing aromas of country cooking. Ruby's meals were legendary for their deliciousness as well as for their gravity: chicken fried steaks, fried chicken, mashed potatoes, gravy, green beans flavored with ham hock, pinto beans with bacon, peach cobbler with ice cream, iced tea, coffee, and biscuits. The men were especially fond of the biscuits that Ruby baked from scratch, not only because they were delicious but also because they made perfect projectiles during the meeting when any member said anything they deemed foolish. The men would fall into convulsive laughter when a missile-biscuit hit the cap of the man it was intended for, knocking it off his head into his mashed potatoes and gravy. The men also delighted in teasing Ruby. The men sometimes held a formal vote on the quality of that day's biscuits. Each man would solemnly place a biscuit in the palm of his hand and move his hand up and down as if calculating density and weight. Then, a vote was called for a "thumbs up" or a "thumbs down." The vote was a unanimous "thumbs down," with no "thumbs up" ever having been recorded in the thirty-two years. Brother Bob felt a tinge of sympathy for Ruby in this ritual teasing, but he noticed that she smiled each time and seemed to only feign annoyance.

The menu never changed, and that was the way the men wanted it. However, once in 1967, in an impulse of springtime spontaneity, Ruby served Japanese food. She had diligently studied the recipes in a women's magazine while she sat with oversized pink curlers under the large, green, conical hairdryer at Berniece's Beauty Box. When the Lions entered the building that day, their smiles and laughter quickly turned to silence, then complaints, and then revolt, especially by the veterans who had fought in the Pacific. One of the men told her, "Ruby, darlin', we appreciate your effort, but we don't do change."

Brother Bob turned his attention to the club president as he called the meeting to order and announced that there would be a regional Lions Club Golf Tournament in Tulia on Saturday and that two of the members, Pugh and Shorty, had volunteered to represent the Happy Club. They had asked that the club pay their fees, which were ten dollars each, not including any expenses incurred at the nineteenth hole. A motion was brought and seconded to pay the fees. With Pugh and Shorty abstaining, the vote was twenty to zero—*against*. So even the man who made the motion and the one who seconded it voted against the idea. The men laughed heartily until a rotund farmer with red cheeks stood and said with deep solemnity, "Out of a sense of fairness, I believe we as a club have a duty to pay at least *something* for their fees. After all, they are representing us. So, I make a motion that we pay seventy-five cents for each." His motion was seconded and put to a vote, and again, the vote was against them, twenty to zero. The men roared with laughter, and some slapped the backs of Pugh and Shorty, who laughed as well.

After the votes and the Pledge of Allegiance, the president asked Brother Bob to give the prayer. He walked to the podium, and as he looked out over the Lions, he remembered that the people in the community liked him and usually attentively listened when he spoke. Occasionally, he also sensed they wondered why he was still single, being a man in his thirties, but after eight years in Happy, he felt he was more or less one of them. He drank beer with them at the community dances, a scandal that caused the Baptist pastor to visit him one day, lay hands on his shoulders, and pray over him. He remembered with fondness the first time he felt he had gained some acceptance in the town—an old rancher in his church, who in a meeting with the whole church, had told Brother Bob's boss, the Methodist district superintendent, "Reverend, we like ol' Brother Bob—he ain't preacher enough to hurt anything."

Brother Bob nodded, and the men all took off their caps and hats and bowed their heads, and then he prayed: "Loving Creator, we are grateful for this food and the abundant blessings you give us each moment. We are deeply thankful for your grace and for your acceptance of us as we are. Please empower us to love each other. Amen."

He knew folks preferred brevity from preachers, and he knew that the club members liked him to give the prayer because they were hungry when they arrived and impatient to eat, and the aroma of Ruby's cooking made them even hungrier. Unlike the other preachers, he made it a point not to go on about the cross, sin, and the blood of the lamb.

He returned to his table to the meal and to talking and joking with the men around him. As he savored the first bite of the peach cobbler and vanilla ice cream, the image from Sunday of Jen's parting robe and her lovely legs rushed into his mind yet again, and his heart began to race.

LONGING

Jen looked out the open window over the kitchen sink and paused for a moment to look at the sky and feel the breeze on her face. The breeze was cool and fluttered the curtains, which softly brushed against her cheek. The sky was just breaking daylight, and nature had decided to put on a fleetingly glorious show in the east, above the dew-starved pastures and fields. Against a backdrop of the sun's rays slanting through the summer clouds stood the old wooden windmill in the distance. There was a multiplicity of hues of purple, blue, pink, and umber in the clouds. The sun cast a soft light on the white chickens that were pecking in the hard-scrape dirt under the purple-leaf plum tree in a disappointing search for a seed or a roly-poly bug. A newly weaned calf bawled for its mother out past the barn while the cow stood in a nearby pasture. She was looking worriedly over the fence at the calf with her head and ears up, mooing back in response each time the calf bawled. The calf kept running back and forth along the fence, poking its head through here and there, trying in vain to return to its mother. A mockingbird, full of himself, sat on top of an empty Folger's coffee can turned upside down over the exhaust pipe of an old, rusted tractor. The bird was singing as if he was truly happy about the beauty of the sky and the sleekness of his feathers.

Jen briefly closed her eyes and breathed the fresh air that hinted at a distant thunderstorm slowly moving in from the east. As she watched the chickens, she smiled at the thought of her cowboy friend James, who, when he was down on his luck with this or that woman, would say, "Well, Jen, dammit, this one left me too, and so now, by god, I'm just out peckin' with the chickens." She and James had been close friends for a long time, ever since high school.

The radio played Hank Williams' "I'm So Lonesome I Could Cry" as Jen resumed slicing up sausage for Gil's breakfast. Bob Wills's "Milk Cow Blues" came on right after. The song led her thoughts back to childhood because early each morning, as she got ready to catch the bus to school, her father listened to the KGNC radio show hosted by Cotton John, who often played Bob Wills's songs in between the farm reports and the cattle prices at the Amarillo Livestock Auction. Her parents smiled when they told her stories about going to dances where Wills played. Jen used to giggle when they told her he was from Turkey, Texas.

Jen remembered a time when she was young, sitting on her mother's lap, while her mother was singing an old hymn, "I Love to Tell the Story." Because Jen had a very painful earache that day, her mother let her stay home and let her eat breakfast in the living room—something that was never allowed—while she watched Captain Kangaroo on the black and white TV. The bespectacled rabbit and Mr. Moose always made her laugh so hard she would fall over on the couch.

Jen was startled from her reverie when Gil belched as he walked into the kitchen. She cringed and gripped the knife tighter as she washed it; the muscles in her neck and shoulders tensed up and hurt badly again. She kept her back to him. He said nothing as he bumped past her and poured coffee in a cup, half-full. He reached under the sink for the almost-empty half-gallon bottle of Old Crow and filled up the rest of the cup with the bourbon. She knew he was still mad at her from yesterday for giving four hundred dollars to a migrant couple with a baby she saw stranded in town at the gas station. They were out of food and diapers and didn't have enough gas money to get to Dumas, where they were supposed to hoe weeds out of the irrigated maize fields.

Jen told him good morning as she set his breakfast plate on the table in front of him, but he was silent and began to eat aggressively. "You cooked these eggs too done again!" he snapped, chewing with his mouth open as he complained with such intensity that it made his Dekalb seed cap bounce absurdly on his head. At that moment, Jen thought he seemed so pitifully foolish in his anger. No one knew for sure why he got angry so often, and Jen suspected neither did he. Because she remembered when he was happy and caring, the depth of his anger now was inexplicable to her. She turned back to the sink, looked out the window again, and sighed. A realization haunted her—the truth was he was no longer the man he used to be. She longed for the Gil she married, the man whose love, kindness, and charming humor had made her fall in love. She knew that the people in the community were also bewildered by the drastic change they saw in him.

Jen thought back to their first date in 1972. They were both seventeen, and they were parked in his new GMC pickup at the end of his parents' dirt road. They'd sat in the truck with the windows down and the summer moonlight falling on them, watching the lightning in the west flash through the dark in the towering clouds. She'd had such a huge crush on him for so long that she had let him touch her breasts under her bra and touch her between her legs, something which she would never have done with any of the other boys, not even on the tenth date, much less on the first. Gil had taken her breath away back then. Now, in another way, life with him was indeed taking her breath from her.

After his complaint about her cooking, Gil said nothing else. He just chewed his food, smacking angrily, and it appeared that he might utter a growl at any moment. His silence was not new to Jen. These days, whenever he did say anything at all, it usually was that he was angrily opposed to almost everything: Jen being at choir practice instead of home, going on vacation or having dinner out in Amarillo, bonds for the new school, immigrants, Democrats, and gays. He never laughed or smiled. The scowl on his face and his downturned mouth had become permanently engraved on his countenance. He had become a granite monument to anger, close-mindedness, and resentment. Despite his accumulated wealth and good fortune, which Jen knew was due in no small part to government farm subsidy payments, he saw himself as a victim, and so, he was bitter. He often told Jen, "Damn all these changes this country is going through! Everything's turned against guys like me." When she thought of all that they had and how well she treated him, it drove her crazy that he could consider himself a victim.

After he had sopped up the last bit of gravy with a biscuit, he got up from the table but said nothing as he walked out of the kitchen, letting the screen door slam loudly behind him, causing her to flinch and her neck and shoulders to hurt all the more.

Jen finished up the dishes and looked out the window again. She listened as the mockingbird sang an intricately beautiful melody and then puffed out his feathers in pride. Up the dirt road to the east, she saw the silhouette of a cowboy on a black horse against the early morning sky. He was a striking figure. As he drew closer, she saw that it was James. She smiled. He rode up to the house, stopped in the yard in front of the open kitchen window, and flashed a broad grin.

"Hey, good-lookin'. You got any coffee for a no-good cowboy?"

"Well, maybe. It depends on if he's nice to a lady or not."

"Oh, I'm nice to the ladies. *Very* nice."

"No, I mean if you're nice to *this* lady."

"Well, how could I not be nice to a lady as good-lookin' as you? I didn't fall off of a turnip truck, you know. Besides, I'm a damn sight nicer than that sullen rich farmer you happen to be married to."

"Shut up. I'll bring coffee out, and we can sit on the bench under the plum tree. I've got pie too, though you're such a rascal I ought not to give you any."

James was tall, broad-shouldered, and strong, weathered by the sun from spending so much time working on ranches since his childhood. Jen liked how muscular his chest and arms looked in his starched shirts, and she would sometimes steal glances without him knowing it. She also liked how he looked in his jeans and boots, but she often tried to push that image away. James took off his hat when she came out of the kitchen door with the coffee, something he always did in her presence. The mockingbird began to sing again as they sat down on the bench together.

"You reckon your angry husband is going to show up and shoot my sorry ass, seein' as how I'm sittin' here with his pretty wife?"

"No, he left this morning, mad again."

"That man does get eat up with the ass forty-eleven times a day. Is he treating you any better?"

"I don't want to talk about that."

They sat silently for a few moments. Jen savored the beauty of the morning.

"I worry about you sometimes, you know. I'm afraid that when he's in an Old Crow pisser, he'll get his shotgun and shoot your sexy butt off."

"So, you think it's sexy?"

"Well, seeing as how I personally have never had the great privilege of seeing you naked, I can only speculate. But, you know, a feller needs to speculate at times, especially when he's alone on a ranch most of the time. Speculation is essential to happiness. So, I am speculating that your butt is mighty, mighty fine. At least, it has to be finer than Cindy's doublewide."

"Shut up. That's mean. You know how hard she tries—she goes to the gym every day."

"Yes, but it's just to eat the fat-free scones and drink fruit juice and flirt with her trainer."

"Stop it. Her mother had wide hips, and everybody struggles with weight, except for maybe you." She poked him in the ribs with a knuckle and laughed as he flinched. "What are you doing out here, showing up like a scroungy stray dog nobody wants?"

"I was just over at the Campbell Ranch. Mr. Campbell has a prize Longhorn bull named 'Augustus.' He wants me and old Joaquin to load him in the trailer and take him to the Tri-State Fair in Amarillo today so he can show him. He thinks Augustus can win Grand Champion Longhorn. I didn't see any lights on or Joaquin's pickup there yet, so I decided to visit a pretty lady in the hope of getting a kiss on the cheek—and maybe a little dessert."

"So, you're hauling a trailer full of *bull*, is that right? That is so richly appropriate. And I'm not kissing you, by the way, and you're sure not getting any 'dessert.' I'm married."

"Is that what you call it?"

Jen frowned, looked down, and did not say anything. The image of Gil's cap bouncing on his head as he chewed so aggressively came to her mind.

"Are you and Gil going to the steer roping Saturday evening?"

"I don't know yet. It depends on his mood and how early he starts drinking. It's Saturday, so he might start drinking way before daylight to chase the hair of the dog from Friday night." She added with a slight roll of her eyes, "His *remedy* is some pre-dawn Old Crow, crème de menthe, and jalapenos."

"Well, by god, leave his sorry, burning, drunk ass in the barn and come watch me rope."

"It's boring. You always win."

"I take that as a mighty high compliment, missy. But come watch me. It means a lot to me. Besides, all the other women are mad at me."

"You and your girls," she said with a frown of slight annoyance that could not conceal her fondness for him. "Can't you ever learn not to break women's hearts?"

"I ain't learned it yet, I reckon," he replied with a brief, sheepish smile. When he turned to meet her gaze, she saw the playful light in his eyes that endeared him to her. "Women are all so . . . appealing . . . I might say. But, you know, *you* could give me a chance."

"Shut up, you rascal, and eat your pie. By the way, what are you doing with that stupid Band-Aid on your ear? It looks kinda dumb."

"Well, Cindy and I had a little argument the other evening about one of my ex-girlfriends, so when she went and got her .22 Winchester out of the closet, I decided it was time to go to town and get some coffee right real quick. I made it about a half-mile down the road when she shot at me. Damn if she didn't hit me on the first shot. The bullet went through my earlobe. It was real bad luck because I was almost out of range."

"I'd say it's good luck since she didn't shoot off some other appendage you're fond of, and the hole in your earlobe will make you quite fashionable now with the teenage girls. Maybe you can get one to go out with you."

"Naw, I have my ethics."

"Is that what you call it?"

James finished his pie and coffee, and they sat for a while. For a few moments, Jen felt at peace as she looked at the colors of the sunrise in the clouds over the plains.

She felt her mood change when James asked, "How's Cheyenne these days?"

She looked down at her hands on her lap, sighed, and shook her head. "She just got out of the state hospital at Big Spring. She'd quit taking her meds. I think the doctor had her on the wrong ones anyway. I wouldn't want to take Thorazine and those others after what I saw them do to her." She looked up at James. "Which is worse, the meds that make you drool and shuffle when you walk . . . or the voices?"

"Those are some sorry, no-good options."

"I hate it that she suffers so much."

James frowned and asked, "Wonder why she got to be the way she is?"

"I think she never got over not having Mama around. She was just about a year old when she left. Daddy and Molly did the best they could afterward. She started getting sick at about fifteen."

"Poor kid. That's mighty hard luck, Jen."

"Do you remember that time our high school principal called Daddy and told him he didn't want his crazy daughter going to his school?"

"Yes, and your dad went up there and invited him to go with him out behind the school and gave him a genuine ass-whipping. Some of us boys saw it."

"Yep, and the sheriff wouldn't even let the guy press charges and told him to go to hell because he deserved it."

"I remember. Everybody hated that arrogant prick of a principal."

Jen was silent for a few moments as she thought back on her childhood. "You know, not having Mama did something to Cheyenne. It changed her, I guess, forever."

"That's very sad. I reckon any of us could go crazy if life kicks us in the chest hard enough."

Jen felt sadness well up from her chest to her throat, and she almost said, "If you only really knew, James," but she held back.

After a few moments, James asked, "Does Cheyenne still live in your folks' old home place?"

"Yeah, all by herself. She doesn't have any friends. She's too scared. Or she doesn't want them, I don't know which. Maybe both. She just has her dog, Buddy. He's old, but he still follows her every step. I go check on them about every other day and take them food and clean up and stuff."

"You sure have a lot on your shoulders with looking after her and dealing with ol' pissed-off Gil."

"Yes, I reckon I do. It's kind of a rough row to hoe, James."

James patted her on her knee and left his hand there for a minute. They were silent. The gesture made her heart feel warm, and she did not want him to see the tears forming in her eyes, so she turned her face away.

"Well, I better git going along. Old Joaquin and Augustus might be waiting by now. Augustus might get annoyed if he's delayed in getting to show off his fine form at the fair. It's not good to get on the bad side of a twenty-one-hundred-pound Longhorn bull with a ten-foot spread. I appreciate the pie and coffee."

Jen walked with him, and they stood by his horse that had stopped grazing a patch of grass. He now had his head and ears up, intently watching the dark of the distant thunderstorm slowly coming from the east.

"What's your horse's name? I haven't seen this one."

"When I'm mad at him for being too wild and stubborn, it's 'Son of a Bitch.' The rest of the time, I call him 'Blaze.'"

"That fits. He's really beautiful. His black coat shines in the sunlight."

"Yeah, just don't stand behind him. He's been known to kick a feller all the way over into Giles County."

They stood close to each other, face to face, for a long moment without saying anything. James gently brushed a strand of her hair back and touched her cheek. The roughness of his strong hand against her skin felt good to her. She pressed her cheek into his palm. He said, "You're a mighty fine woman, Jen. You deserve better, you know. I hope to see you Saturday."

He got on his horse and tipped his hat to her, then turned Blaze and started up the road. She watched as he slowly disappeared in the distance, riding toward the old windmill silhouetted against the glorious sunrise, now with rays of light illuminating the white spires of the yucca scattered across the darker prairie. For a few moments, she almost forgot the excruciating pain in her neck and shoulders.

———

James rode Blaze the six miles through the mesquite and cedars down the dirt road to the Campbell ranch house, barns, and corrals, which lay on a dry creek with tall cottonwood trees growing along it. Some of the snowy tufts from the trees floated over the corrals. Dust was flying in the corral, and James could hear Joaquin cursing in Spanish. "*Chinga tu madre, toro. Ay, ay, ay! Chinga tu madre!*"

Joaquin and Mr. Campbell were on foot and had Augustus cornered in the corral, but they could not get him to go into the narrowing of the loading chute. Augustus was a magnificent animal with his dappled chestnut markings, large and small patches against a cream background. He was a truly massive bull with rippling musculature throughout his body, especially his shoulders and his powerful, thick neck that supported his grand horns. Each horn extended out horizontally about three feet, then curved at an angle up a foot, then turned horizontally again, extending out in the classic Longhorn look. The sunlight was glinting off them this morning as he butted the air and shook his head. Augustus had deep-fire eyes that reflected a mystery and power for which there were no adequate words. Whenever James saw him, he found himself catching his breath in awe, and now, he stood silently staring, shaking his head in amazement at the bull's power.

Augustus kept turning to fight Joaquin and Mr. Campbell, butting at them and pawing the dirt. With each ground-shaking thud of his hoof, he bellowed deeply. The more they tried to force him into the chute, the more agitated he got until he finally charged at Joaquin, who turned in a flash and ran to jump the fence. Although Joaquin was in his seventies, he was still very strong and agile, more so than many men in their twenties. He had worked all his life on ranches; his father had put him up on a horse when he was four years old. This time, Joaquin was not quick enough, though, for just before he reached the safety of the fence, Augustus hooked his right buttock with the tip of a horn and launched him high over the fence, but Joaquin didn't quite make it over. Instead, he landed with a thud astraddle on the top rail.

"*Ay, cabrón!*" he yelled. "*Pinche puta del diablo!*" He very slowly got down off the fence. Bent over with his hands on his knees, he breathed hard and fast while staring at the ground and spitting. He continued to curse in between breaths and spitting, "*Pinche diablo Toro! Pinche! Hijo de puta!*"

James's initial concern for Joaquin soon turned to bemusement when he realized that no serious injury had been sustained. Mr. Campbell was shaking his head, clearly also amused. He walked over to talk with James, who was standing outside the fence holding Blaze's reins.

"Mighty glad to see you, James," he greeted him. "We sure need a cowboy of your caliber right now. We're having a little trouble with ol' Augustus here."

"Well, no wonder—look who you've got helping you, the *Viejo*."

Joaquin heard James and managed a haughty laugh. For many years, Joaquin had worked for James's father, who was a rancher, so Joaquin had watched James grow up and had taught him much about horses and roping. Joaquin had long thought James was one of the best cowboys in the Panhandle, and James had the same opinion of his teacher.

Mr. Campbell opened the gate to let James and his horse into the corral. Blaze was skittish about Augustus's horns and hesitated to approach, but James calmed him with his soothing voice. "Easy, boy, easy," he said softly. "He's a big-un, but he's no match for you." Blaze was a fine roping horse, but he was also outstanding as a cutting horse. They neared the bull, who bowed his neck and pawed dirt so high into the air that it rained down on all of them. James patiently pushed the horse closer. The bull pawed more dirt and bellowed, but James and Blaze stood firm. Each time the bull charged to run to the right or the left, Blaze was there in a flash to block him. James held the reins loosely because the horse knew what to do. Augustus tried so many runs to the right and left that his tongue was now hanging out, and he was slobbering and panting from the heat.

Finally, Augustus started to charge, but then he suddenly relented, turned and went into the chute. Joaquin ran quickly to slide a cedar post through the chute against the upright posts so Augustus could not back out. The bull's horns were too wide to get past the upright posts, but he somehow knew to turn his head at an angle, this way and that, in order to walk on down the chute. Joaquin poked his rump with a two-by-four all the way down while yelling, "*Vamos, Diablo! Vamos, Diablo!*"

Just before Augustus stepped up into the trailer, he gave one last furious kick that banged the trailer gate but also knocked the board out of Joaquin's hand, sending it flying high and far out of the corral. It hit the windshield of Joaquin's pickup and broke it out.

James said, "I don't think Augustus is very fond of you, Joaquin. Maybe you two could try counseling."

Joaquin spat and said, "*Es El Diablo.*"

Finally, Augustus stepped up into the trailer, and Mr. Campbell quickly shut the trailer gate. James was relieved, although he did not say so. He remembered that Augustus had once gored another prize Longhorn bull, Samson, in a fight over a heifer in heat. Mr. Campbell had sent for a veterinarian, a specialist from Texas A&M, to do surgery. The procedure ended up costing thirty thousand dollars, but Samson died of infection after two weeks. Mr. Campbell had told James that he carried a deep resentment of Augustus yet could not bring himself to sell him—he was simply too magnificent a Longhorn to ever part with.

James asked Joaquin, "Do we need to go look for your *cojones* over there by the fence, *Viejo?*"

"Why don't you reach in my jeans to see if they are still there? I don't think you would mind, but you might get envious."

"No thanks, Joaquin. I don't see too well up close anymore, and things that small are hard for me to find, even by touch." James laughed and patted his friend on the shoulder. "But why didn't you run a little faster? Getting slow in your old age, or did a young sportin' girl ride you too hard last night?"

"I ran fast. I ran very, very fast. No bull has ever caught me before. That bull has special powers from the Devil himself. Look how he was able to break out my windshield by aiming that board at it. No one can outrun him except your fine horse."

The three men stood watching Augustus in the trailer for a few moments. Any time he moved, it shook the trailer and pickup. The bull was sniffing the air now and bellowing mournfully; there were some Hereford heifers in another pen near the loading corral, and he had clearly forgotten all about the fight he'd just put up.

Mr. Campbell said, "Y'all go on and take Augustus to the fair this morning before he decides he doesn't like that trailer and would prefer better accommodations. Tell them fellers at the fair I'll be along later to do the paperwork and pay the fees. Before you get to the fair, stop at that car wash on Amarillo Boulevard and wash him off right real nice so that he looks his best."

Joaquin and James looked at each other, then at Mr. Campbell. There was a long silence.

Joaquin said, "You want us to wash him at the car wash?"

"Yes."

There was more silence before Joaquin continued, "The one where you hold the wand or the one where you drive through with the brushes?"

Mr. Campbell thought for a minute. "Probably the one with the wand, I reckon. I think he would prefer that over the brushes. Come to think of it, wash off the trailer, too, and shine it up a little. A king don't ride in a grimy carriage."

James and Joaquin looked at each other again and smiled but didn't say anything as they got in the pickup.

James drove them down the ranch road with the pickup and trailer kicking up a dust cloud behind, and then down the county roads until they pulled up onto Highway 87 and headed north toward Canyon and Amarillo. They had driven for a while, and James noticed that Joaquin seemed preoccupied; he wasn't as talkative as he usually was on their trips together.

James finally said, "Did losing your *cojones* back there knock all the words out of you?"

Joaquin didn't smile. He sighed, looking worried. "It's Angelica."

"Your granddaughter."

"Yes."

"Now, which one is she? I'm sorry I get them mixed up. The one in California?"

"No. You remember my daughter Ana left her mother in Mexico and moved to Antigua, Guatemala, to work in an orphanage there? It was over twenty years ago now."

"Yes, and she died in childbirth a couple of years later. Oh, shoot, I remember now, Angelica is hers."

"Yes. Angelica was born there and grew up there. She was raised by her father until she was sixteen, then he ran off to Spain with a woman he met on the internet, and we haven't heard from him since. Although she was raised without a mother, she did well in school, made As, even learned English—was never in trouble. She's been on her own and is nineteen now. She's an independent girl. She has a flower shop and a boyfriend who's good to her."

"So why are you worried now?"

"She usually calls me each Sunday, but I haven't heard from her for three weeks now, and she doesn't answer her phone."

"I hear young people often get busy with their lives. Maybe that's it."

"No, I've been dreaming about her. That's a sign that something's way wrong. I've been hearing from some friends that the cartel gangs are bad there now—they kidnap and rape people to keep their power and their place in the drug business. Even kill them. Many of the police work with the gangs. I'm worried about her. It's not like her not to call me."

"Well, damn, Joaquin. I sure hope she's okay. I bet she turns up soon."

"I hear that if they manage to escape the Guatemalan gangs and make it to the Rio Grande, the coyotes do terrible things to them."

James was quiet for a few minutes and felt himself clenching and unclenching his jaw. "You know, I think any man who would do those things to a woman is a spherical bastard."

"What's a 'spherical bastard'?"

"I was told it's a feller who, when you hold him up in the air to the light and turn him all around, he is still a bastard any which way you turn him."

"*Es verdad, mijo. Es verdad.*"

"You just holler if you get any news and you need any help. I can run down to the border with you if need be."

They drove on in troubled silence until they got to Amarillo. They crossed over the overpass that straddles the Santa Fe railroad, drove on through downtown, and then turned right off 87 and drove east on Amarillo Boulevard.

As they neared the car wash, James said, "I don't recall ever washing a twenty-one-hundred-pound Longhorn bull at a car wash before."

"Me neither."

There were several cars and trucks already in the bays. People stared curiously at them as they waited there with the trailer and the immense bull. A bay opened, and James pulled in. He pulled quarters out of his pocket as he studied the machine.

He asked, "Should we do regular soapy or extra soapy?"

"He's pretty dirty from our fight this morning, so I recommend extra soapy."

James aimed the nozzle through the trailer's slats and began to spray down Augustus with the soapy water. Augustus was not happy. The fire in his eyes shone more intensely. He snorted and butted at the spray as if to scare it off.

"I reckon this fine bull holds to the principle same as you, Joaquin, that a feller should only bathe on Saturday evening before going out. And today ain't Saturday."

Augustus butted at the spray so hard that the whole trailer and pickup rocked, even though it was a one-ton truck. People gathered around to watch, but they all jumped back when they heard the bang of his horns and hooves hitting the trailer sides.

James tried to focus on the task at hand, but Joaquin, who stood on the opposite side of the trailer as James, with his arms folded over his chest, shook his head. "*Este gran toro no está feliz,*" he said gravely. "*Está muy enojado.*"

Augustus butted the trailer even harder, and then he reared up, and it looked for a moment as if he was going to try to jump out over the top of the trailer. A few of the onlookers scurried to get in their vehicles, and some sped away.

"*No es una buena idea. Es una idea muy mala.*"

A stream of dirty water was running out of the trailer. Augustus was now covered in soapy water.

"Do you think I should wash his *cojones* too, Joaquin?"

"Well, I don't think he has a date tonight for the fair, so no."

James got Augustus rinsed off, and when he turned off the spray, he noticed on the panel that there was a carnauba wax option.

"Joaquin, do you think we should wax him too, so he would be really shiny for the show? The wax on his horns would make them really shine, and it might increase his chances."

"*No, mijo. Es loco,*" he said, getting into the passenger side of the truck.

James pulled the trailer out of the car wash with some of the crowd still watching and drove on down Amarillo Boulevard toward the fair, with the immense bull drip-drying in the wind, in what James knew was a very bad mood.

DARKNESS

As Angelica lazily woke from a pleasant dream, she felt the warmth of the early morning sun on her face and a fresh, gentle breeze coming through the door that opened onto her small balcony. She noticed the sunlight shimmering softly on her waist-length, black hair spread against the pristine-white sheets. She moved her hand to hold the silver crucifix that lay on her chest, touching its intricate chain and feeling the comfort of its presence. She was filled with gratitude for her life and its blessings. She looked over at Mateo, who was still sleeping peacefully next to her, and she thought how much she adored his freckles and the crinkles about his eyes, etched there by his habit of smiling so often. Her little dog, Paco, was sleeping contentedly on top of her bare belly. When Angelica sat up in bed and stretched, a startled Paco jumped up quickly, trembling as if he'd just been rescued from an icy lake. As usual, his eyes were bulging as he nervously studied Angelica's face.

She gazed out her balcony door, which opened onto the street that led to the Santa Catalina Arch. Through the arch, she could see the volcano, the *Volcan de Agua*, far in the distance. There was a band of white fog circling the gray volcano halfway up, and some black birds with outstretched wings were silhouetted high up against the clouds. The air was fresh, and the peaceful beauty of the morning made Angelica smile with contentment as she patted Paco on his trembling head and admired Mateo's handsome form. Her heart seemed to overflow with love for him and for Paco, more and more each day.

In the kitchen, Angelica ground coffee beans that were picked on the hillsides not far from her apartment. She sat out on the balcony at an old wooden table with a brightly-colored tile top as she ate her breakfast of scrambled eggs, grilled banana, black beans, and tortillas. When she finished, she lingered for a while to savor the coffee and look at the volcano. A ruby-throated hummingbird darted down from the blue sky to hover in flight about a foot from her face. It remained there for at least a minute, looking intently into her dark eyes as if it knew something. She could feel the air on her face from the beating of its wings, and the sound of its stationary flight was loud yet pleasing to her. Angelica greeted her visitor, "Good morning, beautiful. Are you trying to tell me something? Did you fly all the way from Happy, Texas, from my grandfather's ranch to say hello to me? Tell me now, did *mi abuelo* send you? Well, when you're back up north in Happy, tell my grandfather that I love him very much."

The hummingbird, now seemingly satisfied, flew to the next balcony over to a planting box of white nun orchids and brilliant cardinal flowers arrayed up their long stems.

Before she left to go to work, Angelica kissed the sleeping Mateo goodbye and kneeled to pet the still trembling and worried Paco. "You're okay, silly Paco. No one is going to hurt you. Mateo and I will protect you from the big, bad world."

Angelica walked the several blocks to her flower shop near the plaza, past storefronts that were painted in various shades of blue, red, and yellow, colors that shone brightly in the sun. She passed the vendors' carts, which were shaded by large colorful umbrellas. The street was beginning to bustle with traffic, shoppers, and women carrying large baskets on their heads, balancing them with their bounty of fruit, vegetables, fabrics, and handmade toys. From her shop, she could see the *Catedral de San José*.

Angelica was happily humming as she was unlocking the door to her shop, but then she sensed someone very close behind her. Every muscle in her body went rigid as she felt a large, rough hand forcefully cover her mouth and nose, and the cold steel of a knife edge pressed hard against her throat. Her heart pounded furiously, and her body was quickly covered in sweat as she tried to scream, the muted sound haunting her ears. She began to struggle, but the man was tall and strong and gripped her tightly. His rank odor reminded her of dead animals. He shoved her through the door and onto the floor. When she looked up, she saw he had eyes devoid of any feeling, as if there was no light of a soul behind them. She thought, *He has dead eyes.* She saw that the number "18" was tattooed in black on his forehead, and some tattooed tears in red trailed down from his left eye. On the other cheek, there was a black "69". Two other men stepped into the shop and locked the door, but she could not see them clearly as the sun was behind them.

The dead-eyed man slowly lit a cigarette. He stared at her for a long moment and said, "We have come to get acquainted with you, *bonita*, and to work out a business agreement. Your shop is on our street, so from now on, if you want to continue selling your flowers, you will have to pay us a fee. We will come by at closing time every day to collect."

"Who are you? You have no right to do that. You can't demand that of me."

"Oh, but you're wrong. You see, we have all the power. Besides, we are fair and only require five hundred *quetzales* each day."

"I'll tell the police."

He grinned. "That's really funny. You make me laugh. Ha, ha."

"Your demands are crazy, impossible. I don't even make that much. I make just enough to live on."

"You're lying. We've been watching you and we see many people who come in and out of your shop. You are a very popular florist. People love your work. They say you're creative. We know that you're a resourceful young woman and that you will find a way to pay us."

"I'm not going to give you any money at all, so get out of here."

The man's gaze grew even more reptilian, so much so that the hair on the back of Angelica's neck stood up. The man took a long drag from his cigarette, exhaled the smoke through his nostrils, and pulled a photograph from his pocket.

"I think you have a good friend you grew up with. Daniel—is that right?"

"Yes. How did you know?"

"Oh, we have ways. Your friend was invited to join our group, but he refused. We tried to persuade him very politely, but he was stubborn, like you. Too bad. This is how he ended up for refusing our kind request."

The man showed the picture to Angelica. She first noticed Daniel's face, but then her eyes grew wide in horror, and she shuddered in revulsion. She covered her mouth to avoid vomiting. The picture was of Daniel's tortured and mutilated body.

When she recovered enough to speak, she said, "Go to hell, you pigs. I'm never going to give you any money. Rot in hell for all eternity for killing Daniel!"

The man stood and studied her with his dead eyes. "We'll see," he said, shrugging. "By the way, I hope you sleep well at night."

Over the course of the next few days, Angelica had Mateo come to the shop to be with her when he was not in his pre-med classes at the university. She felt a sense of sickening dread, but she hoped and prayed that the man was bluffing. She did not have the money to pay the gang anything at all. Her nights were filled with fitful sleep and bad dreams, some of demons chasing her.

Several nights later, Angelica was jolted awake by the crash of her apartment door being kicked in. Three men with guns and machetes rushed in, grabbed Mateo out of the bed, and pinned him to the floor face-down with his arms behind his back. One held a pistol to the back of his head. Paco was barking furiously and biting their ankles, so one of them kicked him across the room into the kitchen, where he fell silent and motionless. Angelica was screaming until the man—the one who had "18" tattooed on his forehead—yelled at her to shut up or they would shoot Mateo.

"*Puta*, now you'll pay us when we come to your flower shop tomorrow."

"Yes, okay, please, just don't kill Mateo. Come to my shop tomorrow."

"You swear you're going to enter into our business arrangement?"

"Yes, I promise on the Virgin Mary, but please just don't kill Mateo."

"Okay, but just to be sure you'll keep your part of the agreement, we'll seal it with this."

He nodded to the man who was holding the gun to Mateo. The man then shot Mateo in the back of his head. Angelica flinched at the gun blast, but then froze in shock, unable to move or speak. She could only stare blankly up at the corner of the room near the ceiling, where she now felt herself to be, looking back on herself sitting in the bed. She did not notice the men as they stepped over Mateo's body and went into the kitchen.

Finally, she forced herself to turn her head and look at them through the open bedroom door. She watched as they kicked Paco's body out of the way and searched the cabinets and refrigerator, taking some bread and ham and mango slices. The silence was broken only by the sound of their smacking and chewing. One of them eventually said something, and the others laughed, but the words sounded like gibberish to her and seemed as if they were coming to her from the end of a long tunnel. Time had painfully slowed down; Angelica remained on the bed, numb and frozen. After the men finished eating, they threw their plates on the floor and casually walked out of the apartment back into the dark.

After what seemed like a couple of hours—though she could not be sure—Angelica recovered enough to move. She could not look at Mateo and shuddered as she stepped over his body to go outside. Although she felt numb and that she and the world were no longer real, she managed to call her friend Gabriela and tell her what happened.

"Gabby, Gabby, Gabby," she said breathlessly when her friend picked up on the third ring.

"What, Angelica? What is it? Tell me."

"Gabby, oh Gabby. They did it. Mateo and Paco are dead. Come quick."

By the time Gabriela arrived, Angelica had made her way outside and was sitting on the curb, slumped over with her arms on her knees and her face buried in them. Gabriela sat down and put her arms around Angelica, gently rocking her back and forth while stroking her hair. With Gabby's touch, Angelica slowly felt herself coming back to the present from being, in her mind, back in the room near the ceiling, looking at herself stunned and motionless on the bed.

"Oh, Angelica. What should we do now?"

"I can't stand to go back inside. Let's go to the police station. They'll help us."

Gabriela helped her up, put her arm around her waist, and they started walking to the police station. The station was in a run-down part of the city, a one-story building with bars on the windows that stood at the end of a dark, narrow street. The dull light from its windows cast an ominous, lurid presence into the night. A sergeant at the front desk, who wore a wrinkled khaki shirt that was too tight around his belly, grinned at them when they walked up to his desk.

"What can I do for you two lovely women?"

After all she had witnessed, the long walk to the station had taken the last bit of strength from Angelica. "The blood," she managed to say in a barely audible, monotone voice. She cleared her throat and tried to speak more loudly. "All the blood."

"What? I don't know what you mean."

Angelica gathered her strength. "The Gang 18 killed my boyfriend and my dog. Just a little while ago. Please help me."

"The who?"

"The gang . . . Gang 18."

The officer's grin turned to a cold glare. "Well now, you *say* they did, but we here at the station are not so sure."

"What? That's crazy. Their bodies are still there on the floor in pools of blood."

"Well, you say the bodies are there, but we have no proof."

"What? Don't you understand? Just come look!"

"How do we know you are not lying?"

Overwhelmed by this madness, Angelica screamed in rage as she lunged at the sergeant, but Gabriela grabbed her and struggled to hold her back.

"Calm down now, *puta*. You're making a public disturbance. We are going to have to arrest you and your friend for assaulting a police officer."

"What? Why don't you go arrest the gang? You're crazy!"

"Shut up, *puta*!"

The sergeant and a guard grabbed Angelica and Gabriela by their arms and dragged them down a long, narrow hall and a flight of stairs to a cell in a dark basement. They shoved them in and locked it. The damp basement smelled of feces, urine, and mold. Angelica kept screaming in rage until the officer opened the cell and knocked her down with a club to her temple. She saw stars amidst the spinning room growing darker. Gabriela rushed to Angelica and held her as she fought to stay conscious.

The sergeant kept them locked in the cell for three days with no food and only a cup of water a day. They were forced to urinate and defecate in a corner as there was no toilet, and they had to sit on the concrete floor as there was no chair or bed. They could not sleep much at all because the floor was wet, and there were cockroaches big as lizards. Occasionally, a starving rat would scurry into the cell and linger, staring at them with gaunt, beady eyes and intermittently baring two long, yellow teeth while sniffing them. If they happened to doze off, they could not keep the roaches off themselves, and they were afraid of the rat, so they took turns trying to sleep, usually to no avail.

Finally, on the morning of the fourth day, a guard opened their cell and took them back upstairs to the front, where a captain interrogated them in a small room. The walls were painted a drab gray, which made it seem even smaller and more sinister. It smelled of stale cigarette smoke and the captain's sweat—Angelica started to feel she could not breathe.

As the captain nonchalantly inspected his fingernails, he said, "Now, ladies, what was your complaint?"

Angelica's body began to tremble with raw outrage. She could see Mateo and Paco lying on the bloody floor, and she thought of the cruel humiliation she and Gabriela had suffered in the cell. The sight of the captain so causally picking at his fingernails and speaking as if he was bored flooded her with adrenaline and rage—she would have clawed out his eyes if she could have. She made an effort to force herself to speak calmly. "The gang called '18' murdered my boyfriend, Mateo, and my dog," she told the captain. "They did it because I couldn't pay the extortion fee for my flower shop. They also told me they killed a friend of mine. They showed me a picture of his body."

"I see. I'm sorry about your dog. People should not be cruel to dogs. You know, little *puta*, you cannot say these things in this city. You cannot make such allegations, even if they are true. So, you see, there was no murder. Obviously, you hallucinated. If you keep saying such things, then something worse is going to happen to you and to your friend here. You can either keep quiet or we can have you relax in the nice cell again, perhaps until you are too old to have children. Or, since you hallucinated, we can put you in a hospital for the mentally ill and never let you out. I hear it is rather nice there, except for the shock treatments."

"I'm never going to keep quiet. Never, ever. You're the police. Why don't you help me? Don't you have any shame?"

The captain didn't answer and only glared at her. He snapped his fingers for the guard and told him to take them back to the basement cell.

As they were being pushed down the hall, they passed another small office where Angelica saw one of the killers, the one with the "18" on his forehead, sitting with his feet up on a desk, smoking and laughing with the sergeant who had first thrown them in the cell. The men both grinned when they saw her and Gabriela. The gang leader made a "V" with his fingers, held them to his mouth, stuck out his tongue, and moved it rapidly up and down between his fingers. Angelica thought he looked like a vile, disgusting lizard. Upon seeing his friend's gesture, the sergeant laughed loudly and began to mock her in the same way. The sergeant laughed as he yelled, "*Tengo algo muy duro para las putas.*"

Angelica spent innumerable days and nights in the cell without being let out, but the guards started feeding her and Gabriela twice a day and gave them more water. At night, there was only one guard in the building, a man that the others called "*El Gallo Flaco,*" because, in addition to being very skinny, he had a long neck with a prominent Adam's apple and a beak-like nose. At night, he would stand outside their cell and touch himself as he leered at them, often turning on the light above them to see them better. The light was a solitary, bare bulb in a white porcelain base dangling on a braided, black cord from the open electrical box in the ceiling.

One night, before El Gallo came down the stairs at his usual time, Angelica pulled Gabriela close and told her of her plan for their escape. "If we stay here any longer," she said, "they're going to rape or kill us. We've got to try to get out of here tonight."

When El Gallo arrived, he turned on the light, stared at them, and began to touch himself again. Gabriela stood up, unzipped her jeans, turned her back to him, and slowly pulled them down just below her bare bottom. Smiling seductively, she turned back to face him, pulling her jeans and underwear down to her knees. With a lascivious grin, El Gallo stroked himself faster and faster. Gabriela pouted her lips and motioned for him to come into the cell. He hurriedly unlocked the cell door and moved toward Gabriela. Just as she was kneeling before him, Angelica, who had been watching everything from the corner of the cell, sprang onto his back, wrapped her legs around his waist, and jerked the light and cord down. She smashed the bulb in his eyes and, with gritted teeth, began strangling him with the cord. He fought back by grabbing her long hair and jerking her head forward several times, but she did not let go of the cord that she kept cinched tightly around his neck. Gradually, the man weakened, stopped his struggling, let go of her hair, and dropped to his knees. He toppled over, unconscious on the floor, where he lay still with the black cord about his neck and blood dripping down his blue face.

Angelica grabbed his keys, ran out of the cell, and locked it behind them. With Gabriela right behind her, she fled up the stairs and down a long hallway leading to a door that opened in the alley. As they rushed out the door into the night, Angelica tripped over a drunk man who was lying passed out by the door. She fell face down on the gravel, but as she got up, she saw that the back of the station was across the alley from a bar, where she could hear the lively music and the laughter of the revelers. She and Gabriela held hands as they ran on down the alley in the darkness and through the streets paved with ancient stones until they came to the *Catedral de San José*. They rushed past the ornate façade and went around to the back where the cathedral's crumbled walls stood. They hid, shaking and breathless, in the dark amidst the ruins.

FIRE

Brother Bob looked around at the many people who were settling into the bleachers all around him. The Ray Baker Memorial Steer Roping was held each year in August at the rodeo arena on the southwest side of town out by the cemetery. Roping cowboys came from all over the Panhandle to compete, but it was a no-frills venue—the bleachers were made of rusting steel supports with unpainted wooden planks that sometimes gave people splinters in their nether regions, and the public address system was dependably temperamental so that the announcer's voice was often intermittent with static and wavering echoes. But there were plenty of coolers of beer carried in from pickup trucks and horse trailers, so the people usually had a very good time. The announcer told the crowd that Brother Bob would do the invocation after Raylene Baker sang the national anthem.

Brother Bob knew Raylene and her family well. Raylene was in the Methodist Youth Fellowship, a high school honors choir student, and the granddaughter of Ray Baker, for whom the roping event was named. He'd been a very promising young cowboy and the youngest to ever win the national bull riding title. The night he won the title, he celebrated raucously with his fellow bull riders in an eastside Albuquerque bar until 2 a.m. but later died in a head-on crash into a utility pole on the remote U.S. 60 east of Vaughn, New Mexico. The highway patrol found his championship buckle in the weeds by the pole and returned it to his wife, Raylene's grandmother, in Happy. Brother Bob liked that Raylene wore it on her belt on this special occasion to honor her grandfather.

Raylene stepped up to the microphone, and the crowd stood and grew silent. The men took off their cowboy hats and caps and held them over their hearts as they all solemnly faced the flag on the east end of the arena. The sun was setting, and so the colors of the stars and stripes stood out brightly against the darkening eastern sky. Before she started to sing, Raylene told the crowd, "I want to first recognize that we have with us one of our Gold Star mothers, Wanda Watkins. I dedicate the anthem to her and to all those like her whose sons and daughters gave their lives so that all God's children might live freely and in peace." Wanda had lost three sons in World War II: one on D-Day at Calais, one on Guadalcanal, and one in a B-29 shot down near Tokyo.

Like the others in the crowd, Brother Bob was touched by how beautifully Raylene sang, and he sighed with relief that for once, as if by divine miracle, the PA system cooperated. He watched as some of the veterans fought back tears as she sang. There was perfect stillness in the crowd, except for a young mother in frayed denim shorts on the top row of the bleachers who was thumping her seven-year-old twin boys on their heads for pinching each other, giggling, and snorting during the anthem after one of them belched loudly.

Brother Bob moved to the microphone to give the invocation. He felt awkward because he had received no instruction in seminary on spreading the Gospel through giving invocations at steer ropings. He had decided to give a brief prayer that reflected his best understanding of the heart of the Christian faith. But just at the moment, he'd finished saying "Gracious Creator," a drunk cowboy standing next to him dropped his beer bottle, which smashed loudly on the bleachers two rows below. The beer splashed up onto the newly fixed, blue-tinted white hair of an elderly lady who was overly bedecked in a bright red shirt, starched jeans, and very large turquoise jewelry. The lady yelled, "Shit! My hair! You son of a bitch shit-kicker!" so loudly that it was picked up by the microphone and broadcast over the PA system to the crowd. Brother Bob couldn't help himself—he laughed along with the crowd for several minutes.

Once everyone quieted down, he resumed the prayer: "Gracious Creator, with incomprehensible grace, you have given us this beautiful life, with all of its joys and sorrows. You held us in love in the infinite time before we were born. You *will* hold us in love in the infinite time after we die. And you hold us *all* in love *now*. Even in our despair and doubt, we live and move and have our being in You. May we live our lives with trust in your love, and may we live in love and kindness for each other. Help us to dance life's dance with grateful joy. Amen."

One of the men who sat not far from where Brother Bob stood clapped and announced to all those sitting around him, "Damn, we oughta go to his church. He doesn't go on promiscuously about all that religious crap."

But the man sitting right next to him, who was clearly offended by the prayer, said to his wife, "Did he just talk about dancing? He knows us Baptists are not supposed to dance."

His bemused wife replied, "Well, you know the old joke. You hard-shell Baptists don't have sex standing up for fear that others might think you're dancing."

"Smart ass."

Jen was in the crowd and had listened intently as Brother Bob spoke. She thought, *Oh wow, I like that . . . "Dance life's dance with grateful joy."* She turned her eyes toward the arena pens, where the men on horses were waiting their turn to rope. She saw Blaze with James astride, a rope ready in his gloved hand. He was grinning and laughing with the other men.

The roping continued for three hours, with the contestants all vying with fierce determination to win. It was an exciting thing to see. Jen watched as the steers and then the horses exploded out of the gate at furious speed, with the cowboys whirling the ropes high and fast before throwing the loop with great speed and precision at the horns of the racing steers. The roping went on longer than usual due to a delay when one of the steers suffered a broken neck from the sudden stop and sharp jerk of the taut rope. The crowd moaned in unison when they saw what happened. Jen closed her eyes, flinched at the sound of the gunshot, felt sick to her stomach, and covered her mouth. She kept her eyes closed until the unfortunate steer could be dragged outside the arena by two cowboys on their horses. She tried to push that disturbing image out of her mind by focusing on James. Although she had seen him rope before, this evening, she found that she had a keen interest in his every move.

———

James felt happy that he had won the roping again, with much faster times than the other contestants. For a moment, he wondered if his father had been looking down from heaven, watching him compete. Ropings like this one always made James remember him with deep gratitude because his father had, along with Joaquin, taught him his skills. He'd grown up on his father's ranch, which lay east of Happy, off the Caprock of the Llano Estacado. From the time he was six years old, he'd had been on a horse, working cattle beside his father, who had also been a cowboy all his life. James loved his work and couldn't imagine doing anything else.

James knew that when he won a roping, it was because his father was a hard man. When he reached seven years old, each day after he got off the school bus at the end of the long ranch road, he had to get his rope and go out by the barn. There a set of heavy, forged steel steer horns sat on top of two hay bales. James's father would not let him come into the house until he had successfully roped them twenty-five times in a row. The weather never interrupted this ritual. Whether it was cruel heat, freezing rain, or blowing snow, James was out there practicing every day.

With each year that went by, his dad's expectations went up, as did the number of throws he had to complete before he could come in the house. By the time he was fifteen, James had to complete one hundred throws in a row. He sometimes resented having to be out there practicing instead of being in town with his buddies, hanging out in the parking lot of the Kreme Kone, and flirting with girls, but his desire for his father's scant approval was very deep. The first time he completed one hundred throws successfully, his father did not smile or pat him on the back. He simply nodded, turned his back, and went into the house. That acknowledgment made James try harder. When James once proudly told him, "Dad, I hit one hundred again today," his father replied, "I don't respect a man who brags. You know you can do better."

The death of the steer in the arena this evening troubled James more than it had at past events when it had happened. He thought back to one day when he was sixteen and was helping his father in the corral with a young sorrel mare a neighbor had sold to them because she was too hard to break. She was so wild that the neighbor couldn't even get a rope on her. She hadn't been handled at all because she had been raised on a large ranch in the Canadian River Breaks north of Amarillo, where she had been allowed to run free by an elderly rancher who had gotten too old, tired, and stove-up to deal with her.

James was on foot and roped her on the third try, but he was having great trouble getting the rope cinched around an upright post fast enough to hold her. He was gripping and pulling with all his strength, but still, the rope was slipping through his hands and from around the post. The mare was wild-eyed as she jerked back. James's father came running up to help him hold the rope, but just as he did, the mare turned away from them and kicked violently with both hind legs, striking his father squarely in the chest. The force knocked him back several feet, and his hat flew even farther. He fell on his back, moaned once, sighed, then lay silent and still on the ground.

James yelled, "Dad!" and dropped the rope to run to his father, who had lost all the color in his face. James dropped to his knees, grabbed his father's shoulders, and shook him several times.

"Dad!" he cried. "Dad! Wake up! Don't die on me! You can't die! Don't you die!" He saw that his chest was crushed inward within the sweat-stained denim shirt. The light had gone out from his eyes. He was gone.

James gave up trying to rouse him. He leaned across his father's body and laid his head on his shoulder. He could not stop sobbing and did not move for a long time. As the sun was getting low in the west, James raised himself up, looked at his father's face, patted him on the shoulder, and stood up. He picked up his father's hat and began the long walk to the house to call the deputy sheriff. Through all the years, James kept the sweat-stained hat hung up on a peg next to his father's worn rope in his barn.

James called the sheriff's office and spoke with Curtis, the deputy.

"Dad got killed out here. That wild mare we were breaking kicked him."

"What? W. T.? Oh no, James. So, he's gone? You don't need the ambulance?"

"No, sir. Dad's gone."

"I'm so sorry. Well, God damn it. That's just pure-dee terrible. Your dad was a good man. I'll be out there as fast as I can get there."

By the time Curtis finally arrived with Digger following his pickup in the hearse, James had managed to get the rope off the mare's neck, but she was still pacing wild-eyed in a circle around the corral fence. They walked up to James, who was standing at the corral gate. Digger put his hand on James's shoulder, but he shrugged it off.

Curtis asked, "Do you want me to shoot that mare?"

James was watching the mare pace the corral. He didn't turn to face Curtis as he spoke. "No. Not at all. She's just being who she is. She's determined to be free, and I can't blame her. Damage is done—won't do no good now to kill her."

"Are you sure, son?" Curtis asked.

"I'm sure," James answered. "I'm going to turn her loose. I'm never going to break her. She can run free here on the ranch. I reckon some spirits just aren't meant to be broken."

James threw the gate open and gave three sharp, loud whistles. "Git! Git! Git!" he yelled. The mare shot through the gate past the men and disappeared over the rise, head held high, mane flying, kicking up dust as she ran.

Digger pulled the hearse into the corral alongside W. T.'s body. Curtis, Digger, and James lifted his father onto the gurney and into the hearse. Digger placed a sheet over the body, and then James watched as the deputy's pickup and the hearse drove down the dirt road toward town. He turned to look up at the moon and the stars. The breeze was cool on his wet face as he stood with his arms draped through the corral fence. The palms of his hands were rope-burned and bleeding. He kept looking up at the night sky until daylight began to break in the east.

As the crowd and cowboys gradually left the arena grounds, Jen waited for James at his pickup and trailer. She sat on the tailgate, sometimes swinging her legs as she waited, often glancing up at the vacant arena and pens. It was dark now, but the arena lights were still on. Before long, she saw him leading Blaze from the pens toward the trailer. His shirt was sweaty, and his jeans and boots were dirty. When he looked up and saw her, he grinned and took off his hat.

"Well, looky here. Good lookin', so you did come out to watch me. I reckon you couldn't resist seeing such a good thing."

"Oh, I could resist *you*. I just didn't have anything else better to do, and it was more boring at home with Gil drunk-cussing cats in the barn than it was watching you win again."

They both smiled. After he put Blaze in the trailer, he sat on the pickup tailgate next to her and pulled some beers out of the cooler. Although the day had been a scorcher, the night was cooling off with a breeze and a lovely moon. The parking lot was now deserted, so they were alone. Jen slowly swung her legs back and forth as they drank and talked. James had a cow dog, Jesus, who came running in from the pasture adjacent to the arena where he had been hunting rabbits all evening. The dog had found a soft spot in Jen's heart from the moment she had gotten the unusual call from Slim, who Jen knew worked at the landfill a few miles from her house.

Jesus had been a starving stray and had actually once been euthanized by animal control and then taken to the landfill for Slim to bury him in what everybody called the "dead dog pit." One morning, just after arriving at work, Slim noticed that the dead dog pit pile of dirt was moving. With some alarmed astonishment, he watched as something slowly emerged, clawing its way out from beneath the pile of dirt and trash. The dog made it happily into the air and sunshine, shook the dust off in a cloud, and wagged his tail. Dust was still flying off him as he sprinted toward Slim. Slim bolted for his pickup and jumped inside, but before he could get his window rolled up, Jesus leaped through the window into his lap and started licking his hands. Once Slim realized that the dog was friendly and not some Cerberus escaped from Hell, he relaxed and started petting him.

"That's unbelievable," Jen had said when Slim had told her the whole story—down to his fear of a Hell-beast—over the phone.

"Yep, he seems mighty happy to be alive on this pretty day," Slim told her. "I know I'm supposed to take him back to animal control to get killed again, but it don't seem right."

"I sure agree, Slim. You're a good man."

"Louise, over at the city hall . . . I gave her a call because I wasn't sure what to do with him. She told me to call you, that you rescue animals, and you might be able to help find him a home."

With a story like that, Jen couldn't refuse—she went and got him and brought him to James that same day.

"Where'd you get that dusty cow dog?" he asked, rubbing the friendly animal's head.

"The landfill. He was dead and buried, but he rose again."

James paused, then said, "You're joking, right?"

"Nope. True story. Dead, buried, raised again. 'Up from the grave, he arose,' as we sing at Easter. I guess Johnny with animal control is half-dosing those euthanasia shots to save money, or this is one tough dog."

"Well, it's plain this dog prefers to be aboveground. You know, I could use a good cow dog, and it appears he doesn't have a lot of quit in him."

"What do you think we should name him?"

"I reckon we have no choice—we'll have to call him 'Jesus.'"

Jen replied, "Sounds right. Besides, 'Lazarus' is a weird name."

That night at the arena, Jesus jumped up into Jen's lap, knocking the beer out of her hand and splashing it all over James's shirt. "Now remind me again why I agreed to take you on," James scolded with a laugh. Jesus licked Jen's face excitedly, then jumped about in the bed of the truck, running in circles as if he was chasing his tail.

"Makes sense that your unmannered dog would splash beer all over you. He doesn't have any better manners than you do."

"Well, at least beer smells better than sweat and steer manure."

"You didn't smell so bad. I kind of liked how you smelled being all sweaty. And now you just smell a little like Coors."

Jesus soon settled down and went to sleep under the truck. James took off his wet shirt. Jen impulsively put her hand on his bare chest, pretending to see how drenched he was, as she said, "Oh my, you're soaked." He was firm and strong, unlike Gil, who had gotten soft all these years from riding in a pickup and sitting on a tractor. At her touch, James pulled her closer.

"Whoa, James, I can't. The beer got to me, and I shouldn't have put my hand on . . . James, I'm sorry, I can't. I can't. I just wanted to feel your chest for a second. Just for a second and . . ."

James kissed her, and she fell into the kiss effortlessly. Deep feelings that she thought were long gone flooded her. For a few years, she had felt that her spirit and body had died. But here, with James in the moonlight, being held firmly against his bare chest by his strong arms, she felt herself falling deeper and deeper into the kiss and into him.

"I'll get a blanket." He stood up and went to the trailer, where he opened a compartment and got a blanket. "Come here."

"In the horse trailer? Wow, aren't you a classy charmer?"

"I reckon I am. I'll put Blaze in the front half and shut the mid-gate, and we can lie down in the back. That way, if any high school kids come out here to party and make out, they can't see us."

Jen walked back to where he was, and he held her hand to help her step up into the trailer. She lay down on the blanket with him, and they began kissing. Her hands fumbled with his belt buckle. James pulled her skirt above her waist and pulled her thong aside. Soon, Jen felt herself falling into a deep, warm, and mysterious sea. She was merging with a mystery she could not name, an ancient mystery in which she knew she had always belonged and to which she was now returning. She'd forgotten what it felt like to be truly alive.

After a while, they lay still, and Jen listened to their still-rapid breathing. Her body felt so weak that she thought she wouldn't be able to ever move again. At some point in the fever of the moment, she had put her right leg up on the trailer wall with the boot sticking through the slats, but neither of them had noticed. When she tried to move her foot, she realized it was stuck between the slats.

"James. James, I'm stuck."

"Well now, that's a new one—I never heard it called that."

"No, I mean, I'm *stuck*."

"What do you mean you're stuck?"

"My boot. It's caught between the slats."

James sat up, and when he saw her predicament, he busted out laughing and couldn't stop.

"James, It's not funny! I'm half naked with my damn foot stuck in the side of your horse trailer in public."

James smiled and said, "Well, it's a mighty fine sight to see. Seeing as how you are naked and already in that position, you know, we could take advantage . . ."

"Stop it, you rascal. Get my leg loose."

James tried to turn her boot this way and that to get it loose, but each time, she cried out, "Ow, James, ow!" and so he had to stop. He tried moving her closer to the trailer wall, but that hurt her too. They tried to slip her foot out of her boot, but her boots were brand new and still too tight.

The commotion had awakened Jesus, who jumped up in the trailer and began licking Jen's face again. It made her scrunch up her nose and laugh, but she pushed him away, irritated. "Stop, Jesus. Stop." He lay down next to her, and from the serious look in his eyes, it seemed like he, too, was concerned about the next step.

James said, "I'll get my pry bar and pry up the slat." He went to his pickup and got the pry bar, but he could not pry the slats apart wide enough to get her foot free. "I guess I bought a pretty stout trailer." James sat down by her and again started laughing. She got tearful and lightly punched his arm.

"It's not funny, James. It's getting really late, and if Gil is not passed out by now, he'll be wondering where I am, and I'll catch ol' Billy hell from him."

"Oh, that's right, I forgot. You *are* another feller's wife."

James was quiet for a moment, then said, "I'll call Danny with the volunteer fire department. He can go by the station and get the jaws of life.

We can pry open the slats with those, for sure. He's a good friend. He won't tell anyone."

After about twenty minutes, Danny arrived in the rescue truck with what Jen hoped truly were the jaws of life—she'd be good as dead in the morning if they weren't. Danny pulled up to the trailer and stepped out.

"James, what have we got here?" Jen could hear him asking.

"Jen's stuck in the trailer."

"Stuck? Gil's Jen?"

"Yes."

"How'd she get . . .?"

"Don't ask."

Danny stepped inside, where Jen was lying on her back with her foot stuck through the slats. "God almighty, Jen! It's good to see you. This is by far the prettiest wreck I have ever worked. Don't worry none. I'll get you out."

Danny wedged the jaws of life through the slats and pried them apart. Jen pulled her foot out. She stood up, the pain in her ankle making her limp a little, but she was alright. They all laughed with relief.

James said, "Thanks, Danny. I appreciate it."

"You betcha. No step for a stepper. Anytime."

"You didn't say anything on the radio to the other boys about this, did you?"

"Naw, I did what you said and didn't radio any of the other guys for help. I knew if you called me, you needed help. I won't say nothing to nobody. You've got my word."

As Danny was about to leave, Gil's black Denali pickup with its bright lights on entered the parking lot at high speed and raced toward them. Gil was swerving as he drove and screeched to a stop just before crashing into the trailer. The dust swirled like fog in the headlights as he got out yelling, stumbling as he walked up. Jesus growled and curled his lips up in a snarl.

"Jen, goddamn it! What's going on? What are you doing out here with this worthless shit-kickin' goat roper?"

James said, "Well now, I'm mighty happy to see you too, Gil."

"I was just talking to James and Danny after the roping," Jen said defiantly.

"Danny, what are you doing here?"

"James had a dead battery on his truck, so he called me to give him a jump."

"Get in the Denali, Jen. We'll come get your car tomorrow."

"Gil, you've got no business driving," James said. "It looks like you've had one quart of Old Crow too many. You and Jen'll get in a wreck . . . though it's not you I'm worried about."

"Shut up, cow shit. Get in the truck, Jen."

Gil kicked at Jen's bottom as she walked by him, but he missed and almost fell down. She turned and glared at him, then gave James a goodbye glance. He was clenching his jaw, and it would only make matters worse if she dragged this out. She walked over and got in Gil's truck without saying anything. With a lump in her throat, she watched the men through her open window.

With clenched fists, Gil came drunk-strutting up to James. "You wanna tell me what you're doing out here this late with my wife, you son of a bitch?"

"Absolutely nothing, Gil. Nothing wrong, that's for sure. And you're a sorry mean-ass bastard even when you're not drunk, which is as rare as a July snowstorm in Lubbock."

Gil took a roundhouse right swing at James, but he deftly dodged it. James then punched Gil in the face so hard that it knocked out three of his bottom front teeth—Jen saw them fly up in the air—and landed him out cold, flat on his back in the dirt, with his arms out wide so that it looked like he was beckoning the moon for pity.

Jen gasped—it made her legs weak, and she felt like she was going to come again. She was astonished at James's strength. She had heard stories of how hard he could hit, but she had never seen it. She had heard that he was once in a fight with three men who were beating a horse and that he left them all on the ground, unconscious.

Jen got out of the truck and walked over to where James and Danny were standing over Gil. She looked down at Gil and his bleeding mouth and said, "I'm going home." She got in her car and slowly drove away.

James watched the receding taillights of Jen's car as she drove away. He felt bad about the trouble he'd caused her, but then again, he didn't. He wondered if this would be the last straw and maybe she would leave Gil, but, knowing Jen as he did, he doubted it.

Danny broke him out of his wishful fantasy. "What do you suppose we should do with sorry ol' Gil here?" he said, kicking the toe of his boot in the dirt next to where Gil lay.

"Let him be. He'll likely come to about daylight. I didn't hit him hard enough to kill him. He may have trouble successfully eating corn on the cob now, though. If he's still out here in the morning and anyone sees him, they'll just assume he passed out drunk and busted his face on the bumper."

Jesus came over and was now sniffing around Gil's motionless body. He sniffed Gil's crotch where he had wet himself, then hiked his leg and peed on his face. James said, "Jesus, that's what a lot of folks around here think of him too these days."

Danny had left, and James got in his truck to go but hesitated, then he got back out and started looking through his toolbox. He found some clean rags and wet them down with water from a white plastic gallon jug he kept wrapped in wet burlap held in place with baling wire. He went back to the still unconscious Gil, kneeled, and, with some disgust, carefully wiped the urine and the blood from his face. "There, you damn fool. Don't you see? Don't you see, Gil, what you've got? You're the luckiest man in the world, by god."

JOURNEY

Angelica knew Gabriela was right, but getting up and getting on the move seemed like an impossible task. Gabriela tugged gently at her arm. "We have to leave these ruins before it gets to be daylight," she urged. "It's the only way to lessen the chance of the gang or police catching us."

Angelica nodded and rose to her feet, unsteady at first. They walked quietly south of the cathedral for several blocks to Gabriela's house, where they drank water and had some food. Though she knew it would strengthen her, Angelica was only able to eat a few bites. She hoped a shower would help her feel better, but once she stood under the running water, she found herself too weak to stand and wash herself. With her back to the tile wall, she slowly slid down and sat on the shower floor, letting the warm water run over her. She let her eyes focus on the blue of the tiles. It could be an ocean, she imagined, some big stretch of open water to lose herself in forever.

How long she sat like that, she didn't know. By the time Gabriela found her on the floor of the shower with the water still running, the water had gone cold. Gabriela helped her out, dried her off, and put clean clothes on her, but then Angelica went to the kitchen and sat cross-legged under the table. She shut her eyes and rocked back and forth, whispering to herself, repeating something Mateo had told her: "You're my precious beauty and I'm going to love you forever." It was the only thing soothing her in that moment from the images flashing through her mind. Gabriela coaxed her out from under the table and got her to lie down on her bed. Angelica slept for a few hours, and when she woke up, she felt a part of herself had been restored.

Later in the evening, they sat at the kitchen table, talking about what to do next.

Gabriela said, "What are you going to do? There's no way you can go back to your shop. The gang will be watching and looking for you. And you've lost everything."

"I know. My life here's over—Mateo and Paco . . ." She was unable to talk for a moment and just looked down. "I can't believe it. We were so happy. It all doesn't seem real, and I don't even feel like myself now."

"I can't believe it either."

"Even if I move way out into the country to some remote village, the gang will find me. They have people everywhere."

"That's true. I've heard many stories about people being *disappeared*."

"But Gabby, what are you going to do?"

"I have family in Costa Rica. I think it's safer there. My cousin works at an expensive resort and makes good tips from the American tourists. She's been trying to get me to come work there and live with her. I think that's what I'll do."

"All your students at the school . . . you'll miss them."

Gabriela got tearful. "Yes, very much. I hate to go and leave them. It makes me terribly sad. They're so eager to learn and have so much promise."

"I know they all adore you, but you can't stay here and get killed. I'm so sorry that I've put you in danger by calling you to help me. I shouldn't have called. I've ruined your life."

"You haven't ruined my life. You and I are survivors, you know."

"But Gabby, the gang knows you now, and they may kidnap you and torture you to try to get you to tell them where I am, or force you into prostitution. They never relent."

"It's not your fault. The gangs are everywhere, and we now know how the police are. There's no law anymore. So, don't feel bad. But you have to come up with a plan."

"After the gang came to my shop and threatened me, Mateo and I had talked about going to Texas. So, I'm going to walk north. I'm going to go to my grandfather's place there in a little town called 'Happy.' I'll be safe there. I don't think this gang knows that I have a relative in America."

"Walk? All the way to America? That's kind of crazy. Why not take the bus or fly to northern Mexico, then cross over?"

"The gang could be watching for me at the airport, and the bus station and some of the ticket agents and security might work for them. I sure couldn't trust the police there to stop me from being kidnapped."

"Even if you walk to the border, the U.S. won't let you in, will they? They've gotten so strict. A lot of them think all of us people trying to cross the border are murderers and rapists."

"I know. But I have to hope that's mainly the politicians who stir people up to manipulate good Americans. I don't think most Americans think like that. I think most are good-hearted people, like my grandfather and all his friends there in Happy."

"I hope you're right."

Angelica added, "Look at how many Americans died in World War II fighting for others."

"Yes. Over four hundred thousand. I teach that in my classes."

"But I'm worried because I know their government won't let me in, at least not at first until I can get asylum if I ever can."

"I know you were born here, but your mother was born in Texas, right?"

"Actually, no, she was born in Mexico. My grandfather had been working there for one winter on his uncle's ranch. He met my grandmother at Mass in her village, and, later he asked her to a dance. They fell in love and had a baby—my mother. But my grandmother couldn't stand to leave her parents and family in Mexico and wouldn't go with my grandfather to Texas, so she never left even though he begged her. He said his life's dream was to buy a ranch in Texas and that there was a young boy there, his friend's son, who was like his own son. So, he told her he couldn't help it, but his heart was in Texas."

"That's so sad for your grandparents."

"Yes. I think she died still loving him. I think it was hard for her to see him when he visited my mother as she grew up."

"I wish God hadn't made love so painful."

"And there are other reasons I can't cross into the U.S. legally. The American laws are so complicated."

"I wish it was all easier."

"Once I get to the border, I can pay men to sneak me across the Rio Grande, and I should be less likely to get caught. If I can just get to Happy, I'll be okay."

"I don't know," Gabriela said while taking Angelica's hand. "Your plan worries me a lot. I've heard that it's dangerous at the river, especially for women."

She held Gabby's hand to her heart. "I know. I've heard that too, but I can't stay here, and I've got nowhere else to go."

"Okay, but then how are you going to get from here to the border with Mexico without the gang catching you?"

"I could only walk at night."

"But they're out watching all the roads—day *and* night."

Angelica thought for a moment, then said, "Maybe you could help me come up with a disguise as a man."

"Now *that* is going to be tricky, making *you* look like a man with your shiny long black hair." Gabriela reached out and ran her fingers through it as if to prove her point. "We could cut it shorter and hide it up under a cap. And we'd have to wrap your breasts and get you some boy clothes that fit well."

Angelica sighed. "I can't think of anything else. It's all I've got. I've got nothing else."

"Then we'll work with what we have," Gabriela said with a weak smile. "I'll walk to the men's shop that's a half-block from here and buy some jeans and a shirt and belt. Oh—and a cap and some work boots."

"I'll come with you."

"No," Gabriela said firmly. "It'll be easier to recognize us if we go together. You stay here. Pick out some food from the cabinets to take with you."

When Gabriela came home with all the items she had purchased, Angelica felt a surge of relief go through her.

"Why are you crying?" Gabriela asked, her face full of surprise as she set the bags down on the kitchen table.

"I'm sorry," said Angelica, wiping her face. "I'm just glad you're back. It's like I'm constantly waiting for the next terrible thing to happen. I can't let it go."

Gabriela went to Angelica and wrapped her arms around her. But there was no time to waste, so they began the process of making Angelica look like a man. Gabriela wrapped an elastic bandage around Angelica's chest.

"Very tight," Angelica insisted.

"Okay, but make sure you can still breathe!" Gabriela told her. At first, she tried to pin Angelica's hair up under the cap, but it was impossible.

"There's no way this will work."

Angelica said, "Okay, cut it all off."

"Ah no, I can't bring myself to cut your beautiful hair. I've always admired it."

"Go ahead, cut it boy short. Better short hair than the cemetery."

"Okay, but not boy short."

Gabriela grimaced as she made the many cuts. When she finished, she pinned up Angelica's hair, put the green cap on her, and then backed away at arms' length to study the look. "Well, my friend, not bad. And the cap has a John Deere logo on it, and so maybe the gang will think you're a farmer." Above each of her shoulders, underneath the shirt, they taped a folded washcloth to give her shoulders more of a masculine shape. The disguise was completed with a pair of Gabriela's large sunglasses.

Gabriela fussed with the positioning of the sunglasses. "Now I'm just worried that all our efforts will be in vain," she said. "If anyone looks too closely, they'll easily see you're not a man. I'm envious—you're so pretty, even as a dude."

"Don't fret. I know you've done your best to help me with the disguise," Angelica said. "At some point, we have to just trust that it'll be enough. We've got no other choice."

Angelica decided to wait to leave the house until it was dark. Gabriela fixed her a backpack with food and bottled water. The police had kept Angelica's wallet with her ID and her credit card. They had also kept both of their cell phones. Gabriela gave her what cash she had hidden in a shoe box at the top of her closet.

When the time came for Angelica to leave, Gabriela asked if she could pray for her. They kneeled on the living room floor, and Gabriela embraced her as she prayed: "Gracious God, please go with my dear friend on her long journey. I'm afraid she'll face many dangers, but please send down your angels to protect her every step of the way. May the light of your love guide and protect her through the darkness of the valleys of death she will be walking through. May your peace come to her in her sufferings. And may your justice and mercy flow down like waters to heal our broken land. We pray in Jesus' name. Amen."

They stood and held each other for a long time. Angelica wiped away Gabriela's tears, smiled, kissed her on the forehead, turned, and walked out the door into the night.

Angelica's heart was racing as she made her way north through the old city streets. She had to fight the impulse to run—she knew that would make her more conspicuous, so she walked at a moderate pace. She passed various people who had no idea of the danger she was in as they went about their own lives: a group of drunk college kids laughing and singing as they swayed and staggered arm-in-arm; a young woman walking briskly with her daughter; a dour priest; a white-haired, old crone with scoliosis who was pushing a stroller with a Chihuahua in it that was wearing a pink tutu; a dead-looking homeless man lying on a picnic table in a park; and on another picnic table next to his, two lovers lying in a feverish embrace. Two men in expensive black suits and bright ties glanced at her curiously as they passed by, but she avoided their gaze and pressed on.

After a while, Angelica passed the *Catedral de San José*. She stopped to rest for a few minutes in the dark on a secluded bench in the plaza nearby. She looked at the grand façade of the cathedral and thought of the ruins just behind it and hiding there with Gabriela. Soon, a kaleidoscope of images and sensations began to flood her mind: red blood dripping down on a man's blue lips, a rat's yellow teeth, a black cord, the sound of a man choking, a cell door clanging shut, and the smell of urine. The images made her hyperventilate, and she couldn't feel or move her body. She panicked at the thought that she was going to remain paralyzed on the bench until daylight and would be discovered. She sat for a while, trembling and tingling with terror, but gradually her breathing slowed, and she could feel her body again. She recovered enough to resume her walking.

As Angelica continued on north, she tried her best to stay in the shadows and avoid being under the streetlights. She felt her skin crawl as she passed by her apartment. She wondered if Mateo and Paco were still there, and it made her sick to her stomach. *No,* she told herself firmly, *don't let yourself fall apart here.* She blinked back stubborn tears as she looked up at the balcony and thought of waking up that morning with the soft sunlight and the breeze and seeing the sleeping Mateo next to her. She thought of how beautiful it all was. She was no longer the same happy, innocent person who sat on the balcony watching the hummingbird. *Was this what the hummingbird was trying to tell me?* She walked on through the Santa Catalina Arch and made her way past the *Iglesia de la Merced.* She remained hyper-vigilant as she walked and kept up a steady pace.

As she was walking down the street toward the volcano, Angelica saw that a few blocks ahead on the right was a group of men who were smoking and talking, standing outside of a bar. Their faces appeared lurid in the flickering light from the bar's neon sign. As she got closer, she saw that one of them was tall and had tattoos on his face, and another was very skinny with a long neck and a large nose and a bandage over one eye. She felt the adrenaline rush through her heart, arms, and legs, but she knew if she suddenly stopped and turned around to go back the way she came, such a move would call attention to herself.

A few yards before she reached the men, she casually moved to the other side of the street to go past them. She kept her head down and turned left down the next side street that she came to. As she did, she could tell from her peripheral vision that the men were studying her. Soon, one called out to her, "Hey, *cabrón,* what are you doing wearing those sunglasses when it's dark?"

Angelica's body went cold as she recognized the voice as that of "18." She acted as if she had not heard him and continued walking down the side street. She furtively glanced back and saw the men still watching her. Hatred and disgust and fear welled up in her—they were like hyenas stalking a young gazelle. She kept walking but then heard their quickening footsteps and knew they were running to catch her, so she broke into a very fast sprint down the street. It curved slightly up ahead, and she went around the curve and ducked into someone's backyard. She quickly hid in some large thorn bushes next to the street. She crouched down and then pushed some leaves aside to watch for the men. From her vantage point, she could only see the men's legs and feet in a blur as they raced past her down the street, cursing as they ran. She sighed with some relief, but then, one of the men turned and trotted back, lingering in front of the bushes, leaning over them, and looking into the backyard. She could have reached out and touched his legs.

Angelica held her breath and shut her eyes tightly as she felt him moving the branches above her. Her heart pounded in her neck. The man cursed as the thorns scratched his arms, and three droplets of his blood landed on her hand. After a minute, he moved on to the next house and looked into that yard as well, then gave up and rushed on to join the others. Once she realized he was gone and that the others must now be far down the street, she started breathing again and wiped his blood on her jeans. She wondered if she should go back toward the bar, but that didn't seem wise. She looked at her watch and thought, *I'll wait twenty minutes, and if they don't come back, I'll go on.* She waited, but soon she heard the men drawing near, walking back toward the bar. She held her breath again. She heard "18" say, "*Esa era la florista bonita.*"

Yes, she thought, *that is what I once was. A pretty flower girl.*

Once they were well past her, she got up and quietly but quickly continued down the side street.

Angelica walked for another hour down the *Calle San Isidro* until she came to Highway 14, which led out of town toward Mexico. The adrenaline was still coursing through her body as she walked in the deep ditch along the shoulder of the highway. She watched the headlights of the cars making their way through the darkness and felt the roar of the trucks that shook the ground as they thundered by her. There were fewer and fewer buildings and more open spaces and fields.

She walked for quite a while, thinking she was well hidden by the darkness since there was no moon, but a truck slowed down, pulled over on the shoulder, and stopped near her. She darted out of the ditch, up a small rise, and into some brush and trees, but the truck didn't move and sat idling with its lights still on. The driver got out and walked slowly around the truck to stand by the passenger door. He kept looking toward where she was. She noticed that he walked stiffly and was bow-legged. A child appeared in the passenger window and was also looking toward her. Angelica could see that it was a very old farm truck, and she could see through the slats of the panels on the truck bed that it was hauling some pigs. She crawled through the brush, trying to get a little closer so she could get a better look. The man seemed to be older.

Angelica cautiously walked out of the brush and back into the ditch. After she took a few steps closer, she saw that the driver was indeed an older man with the weathered face of a farmer and kind eyes. She also saw that the child looking out the window was a girl who appeared to be about six or seven years old.

The man smiled and said, "*Amigo*, I didn't mean to scare you. I just wanted to see if you need a ride. Plus, I could use some company."

"I don't know. Maybe."

"Where are you going, walking way out here in the dark? There is nothing ahead for miles. You'll get blisters on your feet if you don't have them already."

"I want to end up in Mexico, at Tapachula, near the border."

"Well, I'm going in that direction. I can take you most of the way to the border if you don't mind riding with me and my granddaughter. And my pigs."

"Oh, I've had a lot of dealings with pigs these past few weeks. I don't mind the kind you have."

The man chuckled and nodded but said nothing more to convince her.

Angelica studied his face some more, then looked at the long, dark expanse of the lonely ditch by the highway. She hesitated for a moment but then decided to get in the truck. As she climbed up into the cab, the girl moved over to the middle next to her grandfather. She stared at Angelica and smiled. It was a very broad smile that revealed her missing front teeth. Her hair and eyes were dark and lovely, she had on clean clothes, and she seemed well-cared for and quite happy. As she smiled at Angelica, she took a bite of a half-eaten candy bar.

"I'm Esperanza," she said proudly. "I hate boogers."

Angelica smiled. "Me too. They're gross and annoying."

"And scorpions."

"Definitely. We hate scorpions."

Esperanza held up the slobbery end of her candy bar. "Do you want a bite of my candy bar? It's yummy."

"No thank you, Esperanza. That's very nice of you, though. I want you to keep it just for you."

"This is my grandfather. I love him. Do you have a grandfather?"

"Oh yes, I have a grandfather. I love him very much too."

"Where does your grandfather live?"

"In Happy, Texas. That's in America."

The girl giggled and said, "That's a really funny name for a town."

"Yes, it is."

"America?"

"Yes."

"It must be so wonderful there."

"I hear that it is. I hope to find out."

With some curiosity, the farmer and the girl watched as Angelica unbuttoned her shirt, reached inside, undid the metal clip on the elastic band, then pulled it free and stuffed it in her backpack. Next, she took off her cap, undid the pins in her hair, and shook her head to let her hair fall free again about her shoulders. She noticed that they were both initially surprised and confused by what they were watching, but, with a slowly dawning recognition, both smiled a toothless grin at the same time at the sight of her. The man put the old truck in gear; it lurched forward, and they began the journey on toward Mexico.

NEON

It was Christmas Eve, and the snow was blowing furiously across the fields and pastures. From her kitchen window, Jen was watching a scrawny jackrabbit shivering behind a pile of tumbleweeds that had blown against the corral fence. She saw, too, that Gil's truck was still not parked in front of the barn. She bit her lip and shifted her gaze to where the rabbit had been, but he was no longer there.

She had not heard from Gil for five days and did not know where he was. He would not answer his phone, and no one in town had seen him or heard from him. She had been looking forward to Christmas, hoping he would be happier this year and not ruin the holiday. She had enjoyed shopping for him for Christmas and had packages for him under the tree. For a few days now, she was unable to sleep through to the morning, and in the middle of the night, she would find herself waking and drifting back to memories of her childhood. Even now, as she stared out the window, scanning the snowstorm for the rabbit, a winter day from her childhood came to her.

It was the rabbit and all the snow that made her remember.

Before the school bus was to pick her up to take her to kindergarten, Jen was sitting on the couch next to her father, who had his arm around her shoulders. Her one-year-old sister, Cheyenne, was sitting up in her playpen, babbling happily and patting her stuffed bunny. It was a bitterly cold winter morning with a gray sky and wind howling from the north. Jen looked out the picture window across from the sofa, where she could see the dry snow blowing sideways across the fields and the road. The cattle had their backs to the wind and their heads down, battling the cold snow that was covering their hides; some had small icicles hanging from the fringe of their bellies.

Jen looked down at her small backpack, which she had packed and ready at her feet. It contained a small doll she carried everywhere. She called the doll "Sunbeam."

"Sunbeam and I are going to school."

Her father pulled her closer by his side. "Yes, Jen," he said, "you and Sunbeam are going to school."

She wanted to ask her father the question, but she also didn't. She looked up at her father. His face looked older to her than it had just yesterday. She decided she should ask.

"Where did Mama go, Papa?"

"I don't know, sweetie."

"Is she coming back?"

"I don't think so."

Jen hid her face in her father's side and cried. He patted her and stroked her hair.

"We'll be okay, Jen. We'll be just fine. The good Lord will help us."

"I'm sad. Sunbeam is sad too."

"Yes, Sunbeam is very sad. I'm very sad too. Sometimes mommies leave, and we don't know why."

At school, Mrs. Black noticed Jen's sadness and pulled her aside as the other kids were filing out to the gym for recess. Mrs. Black leaned down and said, "Come with me, Jen. Let's you and I go in the back and sit on the story rug and have a talk."

Mrs. Black took her by the hand and led her back to the rug, where they sat down.

"What's the matter?" she asked. "You look very sad today."

"Sunbeam is sad. But I'm not sad."

"I see. Did something happen to Sunbeam?"

"Sunbeam's mother left her. She didn't want her."

"Oh no."

"Yeah, but I have my mama. She's gonna be home when I get home today. She wants me. Sunbeam's mama doesn't want her. Her mama thinks she's bad."

Mrs. Black hugged Sunbeam and Jen and held them close for a long time.

"Someday, Jen, someday Sunbeam will feel better. Someday, she won't feel so sad."

"No, Sunbeam will feel sad forever."

Jen's mother never called or came back. Jen's father eventually married a very good-hearted woman named Molly when Jen was thirteen. Molly had a wonderful laugh and was kind to everyone. She worked as an RN in the Canyon hospital; her patients loved her.

Jen once asked Molly why she didn't have any children. "Oh, I guess the good Lord didn't have that in mind for me."

"Doesn't that make you sad?"

"It did for a long time. Then I realized that I have you, and I love you deeply." Hearing this at age thirteen made Jen feel warm inside yet very uncomfortable because she wanted too much to believe it.

Jen kept Molly at guarded arm's length for three years. Molly was patient, and that irritated Jen all the more. She often thought, *I don't want her to be my mom.* Even the sound of Molly at the dinner table quietly chewing her food grated on Jen's nerves and made her angry. Sometimes, when Molly said something to her, Jen would roll her eyes with searing contempt. She stiffened and pulled away anytime Molly tried to hug her until Molly finally stopped trying, but that felt even worse to her. Jen was starting to love Molly—and it hurt.

On prom night, when Jen was sixteen, Molly got home late from work at the hospital. Jen was crying in her bedroom in the dark when Molly knocked and opened the door. Jen was lying face down on the bed in a pretty blue dress with her face buried in the pillow. Molly sat on the edge of the bed.

"Do you want to talk to me?"

"No!" But then Jen turned over to face Molly and saw that Molly's eyes brimmed with tears. At this moment, Jen's walls crumbled with the realization of Molly's deep compassion, and that experience released a surging flood of sorrow Jen had held in for far too long, ever since her mother had left.

"Oh honey," Molly said, "what's the matter?"

Jen was crying so hard she couldn't talk, but after the storm within died down, she was finally able to say, "There's a boy at school I really like. His name is Gil. I've liked him a long time. All the girls want him. He's handsome and cool, and he's a football star and in the Honor Society and he goes to church."

"That doesn't sound like something that would make you cry. Is there more you want to tell me?" Molly glanced at the dress Jen was wearing and the heels that Jen had kicked off at the foot of the bed.

"He'd asked me to go to the prom tonight, so I waited at the end of the driveway by the mailbox for over an hour, but he never showed up."

Telling the story of Gil's betrayal and seeing the understanding kindness in Molly's eyes caused Jen to be flooded anew with pain, so she began to sob deeply again. Molly put her hand on Jen's shoulder, and Jen didn't push her away.

"Oh my, Jen. Some boys will break your heart—even the good ones."

Years later, Gil would tell her how he almost showed up to take her to the prom. He had stopped down the road from her house and pulled his pickup into a pasture next to the dirt road. He had a bottle of tequila under his pickup seat, and so, for some courage, he had taken several shots. He could see Jen in her pretty dress, waiting by the mailbox. He reached his hand up to the ignition several times to start the truck and drive on to her house, but each time, he lowered his hand and felt the twenty-dollar bill in his pocket that his friends had given him as a dare for him *not* to show up at her house.

Of course, none of that mattered that night as she stood waiting. As the appointed time came and went, Jen's smile slowly left her. She looked up the empty road one last time for a long moment. She unpinned the white orchid corsage her father had bought for her, dropped it to the ground, turned, and walked back inside the house.

Jen got up from the bed and said, "I'm going to go wash my face and go to bed." Molly stood up too. Jen hesitated for a moment as she stood in front of Molly. Molly held out her arms and said, "Come here." Jen moved toward Molly, and she wrapped her arms around Jen and held her tightly. Molly's tears fell on the back of Jen's prom dress. As she lay her head on Molly's shoulder, Jen saw Sunbeam sitting on her pillow. Sunbeam was sad.

Jen roused herself from these memories and took one last look out the window toward the barn where Gil's truck should be. The snow on the pastures made her feel all the more alone. Later, around noon, she tried Gil's phone one more time, but he still didn't answer. She slumped to the floor by the Christmas tree and watched the twinkling lights.

———

Gil was sitting in his Denali that was parked in front of Earl's Paradise Lounge on east Amarillo Boulevard when he saw Jen calling him again. He started to answer, but then he tossed his phone on the seat where it bounced off and fell on the floorboard. He stared at the marquis sign above the door of the bar. The wind had blown some of the letters from it, so it read, "Nude g rls ins de . C me on in. Get lucky. O en 6 a.m." The building was faded-blue stucco with no windows, and it had been built in the glory days of the boulevard in the late 1940s. Gil's grandfather had told him how, back then, the boulevard was a striking, neon ribbon of Route 66 crossing Amarillo on its way from Chicago to L.A.

Earl's Paradise Lounge stood across the street from the long-shuttered, once-elegant Aviatrix Ballroom. "What was it like in the Aviatrix, Grandpa?" Gil had asked years ago.

His grandfather's eyes had twinkled at a memory. "Oh, it was fine. Mighty fine. Your grandmother and I used to go dancing there. All the folks were dressed up fine in tuxedos and gowns. And everybody was drinking French 75s and Sidecars—nobody drinks those anymore. Come to think of it, nobody has class like that either now. It was quite a sight, people laughing and dancing to the big bands. You know, like Harry James, Woody Herman, and others. Boy, howdy, *those* were the times."

Now, the boulevard was a faded, sad symbol of lost glory. On his many trips to the bar, Gil had driven past the abandoned tourist courts with their crumbling-down brick walls and caved-in roofs. He saw that the spaces for the cars between each room were now full of tumbleweeds, empty beer bottles, and plastic bags. Scattered among these ruins were run-down liquor stores with bars on the doors and windows, transmission shops, pawn shops, and tattoo parlors.

As Gil walked toward the bar, the wind whipped dry snow around and underneath his truck, and the sky was gray and overcast with an ominous, darkening blue from the approaching Norther. The lounge was dark inside, mostly lit by the neon beer signs around the walls. The carpet smelled of rank beer, cigarettes, and oilfield chemicals from the steel-toed boots of the many oilfield workers who would come down from Borger on Friday nights to get drunk and have a big, loud time. Sometimes, of course, the big time ended with fist fights in the alley at 4 a.m. in arguments over one of the dancers.

Gil's eyes had not yet adjusted to the dark well enough to see that there was the small, tattered aluminum Christmas tree with tiny red ornaments that Earl had set up on one of the tables, just like he had done each Christmas Eve since 1966 when he bought it at a garage sale for a dime. The bartender, a plump seventeen-year-old girl with tattoos and pink hair, shaved on one side, had made a creche and placed it in the middle of the bar. It annoyed Gil as he sat down at the bar because it was in front of his usual spot, so he asked her about it.

"That manger thing is new, isn't it?"

As she poured him his first shot of what he called his "old dependable," she said proudly, "I made the manger myself. Me and my mama started going to a Pentecostal church and so I got the idea after the preacher kept screaming at us that we need to be spreading the word, or something like that. I don't know what that means exactly, but I thought, okay, I'll do my part. I made it out of popsicle sticks I'd been saving for months. I like grape-y popsicles a lot."

Gil patiently listened as she told him all the details. She had painted the stable a royal purple. The wise men, Joseph, and the baby Jesus were small dolls she used to play with when she was a little girl, but she had had to use a Barbie for Mary. He stared at the poorly dressed Barbie. She explained,

"I put a doll shirt on her that was loose fitting so that there's less boob happening. I don't think Mary would have shown her tits off like Barbie does."

"No, I reckon she wouldn't have, being Jesus's mother 'n all. But who knows, maybe Jesus worries about more important things than showing boobs."

"Oh no, our preacher is very much against that. He said that it's in the Bible."

"Where does it say that?"

"I don't know. It's what he said."

"Some preachers are scoundrels."

"He keeps badgering me to come for an office visit so he can counsel me."

"Don't go. I'm not sure he means *counsel*."

"Do you have a preacher?"

"Yeah. Guy named Bob."

"Do you like him?"

"Can't say I *like* him. Oh, he's a good guy, I guess. My wife's real fond of him. He doesn't seem fake like a lot of them. I hear he doesn't scream or preach that judgmental, hellfire shit that makes people feel more guilty than they already do."

"I feel bad after church, but I know I'm supposed to go."

"Maybe you need a different church. Myself, I don't go—all that stuff doesn't make a lot of sense to me. I don't know what the word "God" means anymore, but I know I feel close to something bigger when I'm out in the fields on a tractor in the early mornings."

The young woman started cutting up limes and washing last night's glasses. "Christmas Eve rush, later on," she explained.

After a few moments, Gil said, "My preacher keeps pissing me off because he's always hassling me to go to rehab like he's worried about me. Honey, pour me another one. This one evaporated on me."

She frowned as she poured Gil another generous shot. Because it was early, the bar was largely deserted. Gil moved to sit at the low bar adjoining the stage when he saw Sapphire walk out. He ordered four more Old Crow shots to help him get in the Christmas spirit. Gil sighed and rolled his eyes with irritation when Sparky, a scruffy little man with gaunt cheeks, smoker's face, and no teeth, sat down by him. He was wearing a dirty Santa hat, a red and green Christmas sweater with an embroidered upside-down Santa whose legs were protruding from a chimney, and plaid pajama pants with holes in them. Every time Gil had gone to Earl's, Sparky was there. As he hoisted a celebratory beer, Sparky boasted that today was his twenty-fifth consecutive Christmas Eve there. Gil didn't know for sure how Sparky got his name, but he had heard that he'd gotten fired from being an apprentice electrician and that there were rumors about a lawsuit filed by a family for the sake of their deceased grandmother.

Gil and Sparky watched Sapphire on the stage as she swung around the brass pole. Each time she swung her legs out and around to flash her ample bottom, the pole shook, and it appeared it might break loose from the black ceiling and smash the silver disco ball on the stage. The last time he was in the bar, Gil had asked her about her favorite song to dance to, and she told him it was Tom Jones singing "She's a Lady." She had proudly described how she had practiced for an hour on a special pelvic thrust to accent each beat of the song. She then happily showed Gil the specific movement.

Gil had first met Sapphire the night he stood Jen up for the prom. After watching Jen go back in the house, he drove to Amarillo, hoping to distract himself from a troubling urge to cry and the image of Jen in her blue dress. He started racing his loud, shiny pickup, weaving in and out of cars and tailgating others while making the drag up and down Polk Street, where all the teenagers hung out Friday nights. He saw Sapphire standing with her girlfriends by their cars parked in the turn-around parking lot, so he skidded up close to her with his window down.

"Hey, blonde girl with pretty blue eyes. Don't you know smoking is really bad for you?"

She took another drag on her cigarette, leaned in, and slowly blew the smoke in his face. "So is driving down Polk Street like your nuts are on fire, especially when your bloodshot eyes are screaming 'I'm drunk off my ass.'"

"I ain't drunk," Gil said defiantly.

"Yeah, right, and I'm a movie star. What now? Are you going to tell me you've been crying over some girl?"

"Us men don't cry."

Gil remembered that moment as the start of their on-off casual connection and seeing her at Earl's from time to time through the years made him feel a little less down, somehow.

Like Amarillo Boulevard, Sapphire's beauty had now faded. She had been homecoming queen at Amarillo High, but the years since had been filled with a string of men who hit her, cheated on her with her best friends, and then left. Now, the corners of her mouth turned down so that, even when she was momentarily happy, she looked sad or angry. She wore clunky, red stripper heels, and she had pendulous breasts with tattoos of puppy paw prints that descended to her navel. On one inner thigh, there was a small tattoo of a red heart broken in two by a black arrow piercing it.

Gil started tipping her a one-hundred-dollar bill after each dance—it was Christmas Eve, after all, and he wanted to make her smile. He also knew that her live-in, Chance, never worked and was fond of being couch-bound, playing video games, smoking pot, and eating pork skins. Sapphire had told Gil that she stayed with him only because he had unique lingual abilities and could make her squirm in pleasure until she passed out for a few seconds in melted relief from her life.

Sparky told Gil a joke about a man tormented by a recurring dream of a goat that winked at him. Gil was sullen and did not laugh, so Sparky laughed loudly and slapped Gil hard on the back for comedic emphasis. The blow caused Gil's temporary dental bridge to fly out on the dance floor just as Sapphire was finding new energy with "Highway to Hell." She rolled her eyes and stopped her dance, looking especially irked that she was interrupted. Gil's face grew crimson with rage and embarrassment.

Sparky said, "Aww, man. Sorry, buddy. What the hell happened to your front teeth?"

Gil's voice trembled with anger. "Some dumb-shit cowboy got in a sucker punch on me this past summer. The bastard blind-sided me. But I fixed his ass. I kicked his sorry ass, and he was begging for mercy, I'm telling you."

With a look of disgust, Sapphire got a cocktail napkin to pick up the bridge, pitched it back to Gil, and then resumed spinning on the pole. This time, she clasped the pole between her legs tightly while she hung upside down; her high heels knocked dust from the black ceiling tiles.

Sparky grinned his toothless grin, saying, "You look kind of funny with those front teeth missing."

"Sparky, if you're such a damn smart ass, why don't you fill me in on what happened to your damn teeth?"

"It was genetics."

"Genetics?"

"Yeah, all my folks lost their teeth early. We were never big on what they call 'oral hygiene.' Though I did get my teeth cleaned once when I was thirty, but then that dentist told me I never needed to come back to his office again, so I didn't."

Sparky reached into his pants and began to scratch his crotch vigorously. "Say, you ever had the crabs? Those suckers will make you scratch Ol' Blue during Mass in front of the Pope."

"I never had them, and I don't want them. Can those suckers jump?"

"I don't know. When my buddy Spud was in the Navy, he got the Singapore crabs. That's the meanest kind. He thought they wouldn't migrate north to his beard, but by god, they did. His wife quit him when she caught them from him. She was a good-un' too. Made ol' Spud sad. He ended up shootin' hisself. Didn't die, though. Ended up in a nursing home on one of those tubes."

"Sparky, damn, you have such a gift for making Christmas Eve so much brighter."

Gil moved over two chairs and tipped Sapphire another hundred. As the afternoon and evening wore on, Sparky had gotten too drunk, and about 9 p.m., he groped Sapphire as she was kneeling before him while pushing her breasts in his face. She stood and kicked furiously at his head. She just grazed the side of his face, but she hit a Lone Star beer bottle as she kicked, sending it flying across the room, where it broke the Christmas lights draped on the mirror behind the bar. Gil spun in his chair to watch as the big bouncer came over, grabbed Sparky by the scruff of his sweater, dragged him across the floor, and threw him out the door into the dark and onto the snow-blown asphalt. Being dragged across the floor had caused

Sparky's pajama pants to be pulled down to his knees. Sparky was indignant and yelled, just before the door closed, "You sonofabitch! Just go straight to hell, you goddamned, goat-humpin', fat rat bastard!"

Gil continued to do shots, so by 3 a.m., the spinning room was blurry, and the late-shift dancers were revolving in his vision. The hours spent in the loud music made his ears ring and his head hurt. He sank deep into his own thoughts and let everything else fade into background noise.

The puppy prints on Sapphire's breasts made him remember when he was five years old, and his mother had given him a blue heeler puppy that he named "Jack." Jack slept with Gil each night, nestled under his chin, and licked his face when he coughed or whimpered due to a bad dream. When they walked the pastures together, Jack would chase cottontails, only to be faked out by their sudden darts and turns which made him go tumbling. Sometimes, Gil was a cavalryman in the Old West, exploring the Great Plains with Jack as his faithful scout. Jack would hunker down with Gil behind a mound of dirt as Gil lobbed dirt clods at the incoming warriors. Jack played along as he lay on his belly, barking and snarling at the attackers, trying to harm his friend. In the early summers, as they walked through wheat fields, Gil watched as Jack would appear and disappear, jumping about with ears up and eagerly pouncing after lizards or mice.

Early one morning, Gil's father shook Gil hard, jolting him awake. His father was very angry, and his voice felt like cold steel.

"Your damned mutt got in the hen house last night and was getting the eggs. I won't have no egg-sucking dog on this place. I have my rules."

Gil sat bolt upright and rubbed at his eyes. It took him a moment to realize it wasn't a bad dream he was having. His father was going to kill his dog. "Daddy," he said, "you can't do that."

"Dammit, Squirt, see if I can't. And don't backtalk me. I said I won't have no egg-sucking dog on this place. You know the rules. I'm getting my shotgun."

"No, Daddy, no!" The terror coursing through Gil's body made him feel weak and faint. He felt like he was going to vomit. He cried again, "No, Daddy, no!"

But his father was heartless and headed for the gun rack in their den for his 12 gauge. Gil screamed and pleaded as he ran to his father and wrapped his arms and legs tightly around his father's leg.

"No, Daddy, no! Please. Please! I love Jack. He's my friend. He's my best friend!"

His father drug Gil a few steps and then knocked him to the floor with a fist to the top of his head. "Let go, dammit, you crybaby."

His father got the gun and went out, slamming the door behind him. Gil was frantic. He ran and hid under his bed, clenching his teeth. His pajamas were wet with tears and urine.

He waited.

He clenched his teeth harder and shut his eyes so tightly his head hurt. He put his hands over his ears. There was an eternity of sickening silence.

He waited.

Boom! Boom! Gil flinched each time.

Silence. Gil waited, listening. *No God, no, no God no.* He prayed that he would somehow hear Jack barking, that Jack would run into the house and jump into his arms as he had done so often. Gil prayed that it all was not real. He kept his eyes shut, trying as best as he could to pretend it was all a dream.

Gil lay still with an unbearable aching in his heart that went to the depths of his soul and body. He could not talk. He lay under his bed, numb, with a blank stare for several hours. His mother finally came home from work and found him there. Gil listened as his father explained that he had shot Jack for sucking eggs. His mother was livid.

"I've never hated you more," Gil heard her say. "I wish I could have killed *you* instead."

She came into Gil's room, kneeled by the bed, and looked underneath. Gil saw her kind, worried face. "Come on out, Gil. Come on out now from under the bed." Gil finally crawled out and climbed in her lap, but he could no longer cry, and he only stared off—he wanted to be as far away from all of this as he could.

His mother held him and stroked his hair. "Come on. I'll wrap Jack up in his blanket. I'll help you dig a grave out by the pine tree."

For months after, Gil would come home from school and go sit by Jack's grave under the pine. He would sit there till dark, thinking of all the good times with Jack. Sometimes, he would tell him about his day at school. He developed an occasional stutter, usually only on proper names that began with "J." He got teased at school about his stutter. The other children would call him "Jupid" and "Jutardo." He would feel his face go hot, and he wanted to die.

His stutter had continued on into adulthood. That was why he rarely mentioned Jen's name; he usually just referred to her as "my wife." Throughout childhood, Gil kept a small photo on his dresser that his mother had taken of him and Jack in the wheat field. Even now, he still carried the photo in his wallet, though it was faded and crinkled.

When Jen first saw the photo, she asked, "Gil, this is you with the dog, right?"

Gil said, "Oh, that's when I was a kid. He was just some mutt we had. Daddy said he had to shoot him because he got in the chicken house and got the eggs—said he wouldn't have an egg-sucking dog on the place."

Jen had gotten tears in her eyes. "What was your poor dog's name?"

Gil hesitated. "Aw, I don't really remember. It don't matter."

Many years later, his father told Gil—in what Gil saw to be an obvious effort to relieve his conscience just before he died—that the day after he shot Jack, he saw a skunk going out a hole in the back wall of the chicken house where a plank had rotted. He realized then that it had been the skunk getting the eggs—not Jack. Gil said nothing in response, turned his back on his father, and walked away. Gil thought, *I guess the old coot can just die with his guilty conscience, so to hell with him.* One thing he knew for sure— he was not going to his funeral.

Gil left the bar once he had gone through the three thousand dollars he'd brought with him. He stumbled in the dark as he walked to his Denali. He reached under the seat and pulled out a Smith and Wesson .44 magnum revolver and one shell. He put the shell in a chamber and walked to the weedy lot behind the bar. The snow was still whirling. The storm had arrived now in full force, and the wind was howling fiercely. The brutal gusts were raising up the corrugated tin roof of the bar so that it made a creaking sound as if it were mocking someone. Gil was alone in the dark.

The neon from the lounge cast a yellow aurora into the darkness behind the bar, making the dumpsters and the tall weeds seem surreal. Gil yelled, "I'm coming to join you, J —Jack!" He spun the gun's cylinder and shoved the barrel of the gun into his mouth until he gagged. Click. He spun again. Click. Click. He paused, pulled the barrel out of his mouth, and this time he yelled, "Here's to you, Daddy!" He pointed the gun at his face. Click. Click. Click . . . Boom!

The sun blinded Gil as he came to. He was on his back in the weeds behind the bar, shivering and half-frozen. His hands were blue and numb, and his feet felt like they were being stung by a thousand needles. He lifted his hand to his head, where he felt some pain, and pulled it away to see blood on it. He realized the bullet had only grazed the left side of his head. He couldn't hear out of that ear, and his other ear was ringing. When he rolled over, a devil's claw scratched his face, and so his cheek was bleeding too. He flung the devil's claw toward the dumpsters, where it hit a starving stray mutt that was sniffing around for food.

Gil managed to sit up, but he hurt all over. He had a silver flask in his pocket, so he took a very long swig and started to feel some warmth. He realized his Rolex was gone. At first, he thought he'd been robbed, but then he remembered he had given it to a waitress named Crystal. He'd thought she was really pretty, and her face had reminded him of Jen's when they first met. She told him she was going to Amarillo College and studying to be a paramedic. He had taken the Rolex off and given it to her and said, "I might need you someday, sweetheart. I'll be the drunk lying in the middle of I-40 at midnight, trying to get run over by an eighteen-wheeler."

When she saw that it was a Rolex, she screamed, "Oh my god," threw her cocktail tray across the bar, kissed Gil, and then flipped off the bouncer, who Gil knew had been hitting on her for months. She ran out of the bar, yelling something about how she was going home and not coming back.

The sun was starting to warm Gil up some. He touched his blue lips and found he had lost his temporary bridge again. He began to crawl through the weeds and snow on his hands and knees, looking for it. He scratched around in the snow here and there. The snow made his hands hurt more. "God damn it," he said. "God damn it." He finally found the bridge behind a discarded, well-used adult diaper. He brushed the bridge off with his numb fingers and put it in his pocket. "There."

Finding it made him feel better, and since it was Christmas, he took another long swig from the last of the flask. He shouted, "Merry Christmas, Jen!" as he held up the flask to toast the cold sun in the gray sky. The neon lettering of "Earl's Paradise" was now flickering in the bitter cold.

NIGHTS

Angelica reached into the pocket of her jeans for the silver ring. She held it in her palm, admiring its simple beauty in the moonlight. Esperanza, the old *campesino's* granddaughter, had given her the ring that she now slowly slid on the little finger on her left hand. The girl had told her that the ring had been blessed by the Virgin Mary and that as long as she wore it, the Virgin would send down the angels to protect her on her walk to America. Now, standing alone on the dirt road, she looked up to see Esperanza, leaning half-out of the truck window, enthusiastically waving, beaming her toothless grin, as her grandfather turned the truck around with its load of sometimes squealing pigs.

Angelica smiled and waved back, then blew the girl a kiss, who pretended to catch it. She watched the taillights gradually becoming tiny points of red in the darkness until they disappeared altogether. She remembered how, as she reached for the truck door to get out, Esperanza had wrapped her arms around her waist so tightly and with innocent affection, not wanting to let her go. The child's warmth toward her— warmth Angelica knew came so freely and naturally to children—reminded her of Mateo sleeping with his arm draped across her chest, and of trembling Paco's adoring yet worried eyes, and of Gabriela holding her close as she prayed for her safety.

When she turned to look north, Angelica could see the lights of Tapachula not far across the Mexican-Guatemalan border. Silhouetted in the lights were tall palm trees, an elegant white church with two small gold domes, and, closer to her, the high pavilion of the checkpoint that spanned the road. *I shouldn't risk it*, she thought. The farmer had told her he'd heard that there was a large, open-air immigration prison in the town, with thousands of refugees held there. As he gave her his pocketknife, he patted her hand and told her, "*Tenga cuidado.*"

She decided to walk through the low mountains to the east of the city in order to cross over. She remembered her promise to Gabriela that she would walk only at night and try to rest and sleep during the day, doing her best to avoid the cities and even the bigger towns. She got the elastic bandage out of her backpack, unbuttoned her shirt, wrapped her chest again, then pinned her hair back up under her cap. She adjusted her backpack, kissed the silver ring, and, with a deep sigh, started toward the mountains. *Maybe I'll be safe in their arms.*

A few nights later, hungry and tired, but on the other side of the mountains, she walked just a few yards off the deserted road to rest before continuing on. With aching arms, she dropped her backpack then sat down on it and began rubbing the length of her sore legs. When she glanced back down the road toward the mountains, she noticed a road sign, and although it was dark, she was able to make it out: "Tapachula 257KM/160MI." *No wonder my feet hurt.* Although she was hypervigilant as she made her way through the dark nights, she hadn't encountered anyone who was threatening, except once.

The night before last, as she was passing through a quiet village about midnight, a man bolted out of an alley in a dead run chased by two *federales* who almost knocked her down as they passed her. She instantly felt the adrenaline flood her body. One glanced back over his shoulder for a second but kept running. She turned down the next alley, made her way to the edge of the village, and took off running through some fields until she felt safe. When she'd been able, in the daytime, she had hidden herself among trees and slept on beds of leaves, but now her legs and back were covered in ant bites that itched badly. Her feet were already hurting badly, and she wondered how, at this rate, she would ever make it to the border. She stood up, pulled on her backpack, and trudged north down the road.

Several miles and a few nights later, Angelica sat shivering in the pre-dawn cold with her back against a tree, her knees up, and her arms around them. She could see her breath cast out into the night air as she rested. She was sorely wishing she had thought to pack a jacket. Her stomach was growling and hurting—she had eaten the last of the food Gabriela had packed two days ago.

Fortunately, a few hours earlier, she'd come across a garden with no one around and snuck away with an ear of corn and a palm-sized, ripe tomato. She shucked the corn but struggled to cut off the conical end that held a brown-mottled wiggler, protesting its exposure. *Yuck!* she thought as she tossed it away from her. When she bit into the tomato, she felt the juice spurt onto her fingers and drip down her chin. She closed her eyes and moaned in sweet relief as she savored its richness and then licked the juice from her fingers.

Soon, she heard an owl's haunting sound, which made her feel even more lonely. She looked up through the leafy canopy to see the bright, full moon and imagined that at the same moment, her grandfather was out in his corral tossing hay to his horses under the same moonlight.

With dawn approaching in a couple of hours, her thoughts turned back to the clearing. Earlier, when she arrived in the grove, she had spied a clearing just beyond the trees that caught her interest. She pushed some leaves aside to look out and saw that off in the distance, right in the middle of the open expanse, there was a tall shed with its sloping, moonlit tin roof, and further out in the clearing, there were several black cattle slumbering. She was puzzled that there was no farmhouse nearby. She thought, *I'll watch this shed for a while, and if nobody shows up, I'll sleep there today—this cold's killing me.* She studied the shed and its surroundings, scanning the areas beyond for any signs of people. There were no roads leading to the shed that she could see, except it looked like there might be a path that led out the other side of the clearing.

Although her surveillance of the shed did not fully ease her apprehension, she reasoned, *I better go now before it gets daylight. I wish the moon weren't so bright tonight.* As she made her way with hurried steps across the open pasture to the shed, she scanned all around her. She noticed her hands shaking as she reached for the leather strap handle. She breathed rapidly as she slowly opened the creaking door and peered into the darkness.

Although it was quite dark, a little light came through a small window on the side and from between gaps in the planks so she could see there were some bales of hay stacked inside. Two shovels and a pitchfork leaned against one wall. She stood at the door for a couple of minutes, straining to see and listen. When she grew satisfied that no one was in it, she entered. *I'll hide myself up on top of the haystack to sleep.*

She closed the door behind her, approached the haystack, and saw that there was a way to get to the top. Just as she put one knee up on the first bale, she felt something brush against her lower leg. She jumped aside and stood perfectly still without breathing, with the hair on the back of her neck standing up and goosebumps all over her body. After a few seconds, she heard purring and felt more rubbing against her leg. She whispered, "Damn, you mouser, you scared the breath out of me!" Her fear and irritation subsided, so she bent down and gave him a few pats on his scruffy head.

She climbed the bales up to the top, where she lay down, using her backpack for a pillow. The tomcat followed her up, lay across her chest, and stared at her face while contentedly pushing his paws rhythmically onto her breast. She whispered to him, "What, so you think my chest is softer than the hay or that you're claiming ownership of a new friend? Okay, you can lie here and protect me from rats." She went to sleep with the sound of his purring and the gentle, alternating pressure of his paws.

Angelica was startled awake by the jolt and pain of the tomcat launching himself off of her and the sound of him bounding down the haystack to land with a "thud" on the ground. Her wide eyes instantly focused on the steel tines of a pitchfork gleaming in the moonlight, only a hand-width from her face.

She dared not move and cried out, "No, no, don't, please don't!"

"Did he send you?"

"Who?"

"My husband."

"No, no one sent me. Please don't kill me."

"Wait . . . you're not a man."

"No, I'm Angelica. I'm alone. Please take the pitchfork away."

The woman threw it off the haystack, and it stuck standing up in a bale below. Angelica was able to breathe again.

"I thought Javier sent you to kill me or force me back. Someone's been following me."

"Your husband wants to kill you?"

"He shot at me and tried to run over me with his Mercedes. And beats me. He's crazy with jealousy, but I'm not a flirt—I've never cheated."

"That's terrible."

The woman squinted her eyes to study Angelica more closely. "What are you doing here?"

Angelica sat up. "A gang in Antigua murdered my boyfriend and my dog in front of me. When I told the cops, they locked up me and my friend. We thought they weren't ever going to let us go or were going to kill us, so I strangled the guard, and we escaped. I'm walking north."

"To America? Me too. I'm Reina. I'm from Tapachula."

Angelica was gradually able to see her better as the soft sunlight began filtering in. She saw that Reina seemed to be in her forties and appeared strong, fit, and well-dressed. But she was shocked to see that her pretty face, with its fine features, was badly bruised and cut.

Angelica frowned, "He hurt you. Why didn't you just get a divorce instead of running away?"

Reina looked amazed at her innocence and laughed at her. "You haven't ever been with a man who was crazed with jealousy, have you?"

The image of Mateo came to her as she said emphatically, "No, I've only had one boyfriend, and he was wonderful to me."

Reina asked, "He's the one the gang killed?"

Angelica nodded. "Mateo."

Reina made the sign of the cross. "I'm sorry," she said.

Angelica looked down at her hands resting on her lap. "I loved him deeply."

"My husband's not in a gang, but he's a big attorney and has powerful friends in our city—police, prosecutors . . . judges. He told me if I ever left him, he'd send someone to kill me. Every time I filed charges, they'd never arrest him even though I had photographs and records from the ER of my fractured cheekbones and broken arm. When the judge would throw out the case, I'd catch hell even worse, so I stopped reporting it. There's no place for me to be safe in Mexico—he knows so many people and has ways to find me. Just now, I was sure his man, Carlos, had found me—that's why I almost stabbed you in the face with the pitchfork."

"Don't you have family you can go to?"

She shook her head. "He'd find me. I'll only be safe if I can get to Dallas. I have a friend there that he doesn't know I have."

"Why is he so jealous? It doesn't make sense—you're faithful to him."

"Javier's not just jealous in a normal way. He burns with possessiveness. But it's complicated. He forces me at gunpoint to be with other men while he videos it. Then he sells the videos to his friends, the police, and prosecutors and puts them on the internet. If I don't submit, he'll kill me. One time, I shoved this guy off me and jumped out of the bed, but just as I reached the door, Javier grabbed my hair. He choked me until I passed out—I thought I was dying."

Angelica thought of her own experiences. "I never knew that men could be so cruel. Until recently."

"Time changes how you see things. We lose our innocence as we learn the ways of this world."

"I don't feel the same as I did a few weeks ago," Angelica said quietly. "I feel I've lost me."

"Javier controls me with his cruelty, but it doesn't make him happy. When he's not forcing me to be with other men, he lives in the constant torment of his fear that I'll be with other men."

The information about her husband was making Angelica nauseous with disgust and revulsion. She couldn't imagine being with any man other than Mateo. And she knew he would have been crushed if she had ever been unfaithful.

"I don't understand how your husband could be that way."

"It's about control—and fear. But also, he *enjoys* hurting me. His eyes light up when he does it, and he smirks. He won't let me leave the house without him. The house has cameras and alarms, and he has a tracker on my phone. I threw it in the bushes as I escaped. He keeps Carlos there to keep me from leaving the house when he's at work or when he's out cheating with his women."

"He cheats on you?" Angelica asked incredulously.

"Yes, frequently. I see the hickeys, smell their perfume, and he's given me STDs. He harassed all my friends so badly, he scared them off. He lets me talk to my mother on Sundays for fifteen minutes *if* I have it on speaker phone, and he listens in."

Angelica, still bewildered, asked, "Was he that way when you met him?"

Reina shook her head. "Not at all. We talked for hours. He was super nice and respectful—he'd open doors for me, hold my hand when we walked, pull my chair out for me at expensive restaurants, pretty flowers, little notes each day before he left. What guy does that?"

"Mateo was so good to me," Angelica said with sadness in her voice.

"One night, out of the blue, Javier surprised me by telling me he was taking me to Barcelona the next day." She reached into her shirt and pulled out a diamond necklace. "When we got to the hotel there, he gave me this."

Angelica remembered the lovely mahogany jewelry box Mateo had spent days making for her in his friend's woodworking shop. At this moment, she could see his proud, happy smile when he surprised her with it. How she wished she would have been brave enough to go back into the apartment to get it the night she walked past it, leaving Antigua.

Angelica had never seen such a necklace. "Wow, that's really beautiful."

"It's ugly to me now, so I'm going to sell it. I've never really cared that much about expensive gifts and stuff. It's that we had so much fun together. And he was so handsome. I felt he really loved me—he told me so many times—and I fell for him and knew in my heart he was The One."

"But now it's like you're a possession?"

Reina nodded. "I'm a *thing*."

Angelica, still quite stunned by her story, asked, "Do you have children?"

Reina's countenance darkened. "No. I was pregnant once and happy. Then he punched me in the . . ."

Angelica moved closer and put her hand on her shoulder. "Oh no, not *that*."

Reina brushed her hand away. "I'm okay now, but I don't like thinking about it."

"I'm sorry I asked you. How did you get away?"

"Three nights ago, he got really drunk and beat me again, as you can see. But afterward, he started swallowing hydrocodone with his top-shelf vodka. When he fell out of his chair onto the floor and didn't move, I grabbed all the money from his wallet, and since Carlos wasn't on duty, I was able to run out of the house. I just started walking."

Angelica climbed down from the top of the hay and sat on a hay bale on the ground as Reina joined her. Dust particles were floating about in the rays coming through the window. Reina frowned, put her hand to her chest, and, with some difficulty, took a deep breath. She reached into her pocket and brought out an inhaler. Angelica raised her eyebrows as she watched her. "This hay dust . . . my asthma."

Angelica nodded. She felt herself being drawn to Reina—despite having a toughness, she seemed like she had a genuine goodness about her. Angelica found her easy to talk to, so she told her more about Mateo's murder, Paco, Gabby, and the escape from the cell. As she told her story, she could see the compassion in Reina's eyes and the flashes of anger, and so she knew that Reina knew what she had suffered.

As Angelica was talking, suddenly, there was tapping at the window, which caused them to jump up instantly and hide behind the corner of the haystack. But then it stopped.

Angelica peeked around the hay to look and gasped when the tapping started again, but then it stopped once more. With her thoughts racing, she waited, watching and listening for a few moments, but then came the deep, thunderous bellowing of a bull. Angelica looked at Reina in relief, walked to the window with Reina behind her, and carefully pulled the tattered burlap curtain aside. When she wiped the dust from the window, she was met face-to-nose with a large brass ring in huge nostrils pressed against the pane. She shrieked and jumped back, making Reina laugh.

The black bull stared in the window at them with his ears forward and eyes intense. Then he backed away and turned to sniff the air with his head held high, mouth open, and tongue out. When he did, it made the nose ring stand straight up, and he gave four short bellows, each ending in a higher pitch. Angelica crinkled up her nose, pointed, and said, "Ewww, his thing is out, and it looks like a really long carrot. Creepy. I didn't know that's what they looked like." The bull's penis protruded far out of its sheath, and his incredibly large, elongated *huevos* were swinging as he humped the air.

Reina joked, "He and Javier must be twins."

Angelica smiled and said slyly, "And I thought he only wanted this hay."

"And I thought Javier only wanted to love me," Reina mused.

As they turned away from the window, Reina winked at Angelica and said, "I guess his priest didn't tell him that that behavior would make him go blind," which made them bust out laughing. When they sat down on the bales, Angelica's thoughts became serious again. Night would be approaching soon.

"So, what happens with you now?" Angelica asked.

"I'm supposed to meet a man in the next town, in San Felipe. I've made arrangements to pay him to drive me to the border and help me get across the river without getting caught by the Border Patrol. Someone across the river will then pick me up and take me to Dallas. What are you going to do?"

"I'm going to continue walking to Ojinaga, then cross to Presidio, and go on to my grandfather's ranch at a town called 'Happy.'"

Reina looked skeptical. "Do you have money?"

"A little bit left that Gabby gave me, but only enough now for a day or two."

"But it's almost seventeen hundred miles to Ojinaga, isn't it?

"That sounds right."

"And food and water?"

"I get food from gardens and fill my bottles from water faucets, and sometimes I get stuff from women street vendors."

"When you walked to and from the window, you were limping."

"My feet hurt from all the miles."

"Let me see."

Angelica unlaced and then pulled her work boots off, saying, "Ow!" as Reina slowly peeled off her socks. She watched as Reina inspected her feet closely. "You've had some very large blisters that popped, and now they're bleeding. But the big problem is your feet are getting infected. You're going to have to doctor them, or they'll get worse."

"How can you tell? I thought they were just blisters."

"No, see where this pus is starting? It'll get really bad. I used to be a nurse before I met Javier."

"Nothing's going to stop me getting to my grandfather's. I can handle the pain."

Angelica saw that Reina was frowning. "You're going to come with me. I have some money. We'll walk to San Felipe tonight, and I'll get something from a pharmacy to doctor your feet, then I'll meet with the guy who's going to drive me to the border. I'll pay him for you to go with me."

Angelica said, "I feel bad accepting your help. I can't pay anything. I'll just walk."

"Shut up. You're going with me."

Angelica hugged her. "You must be one of the angels a little girl told me about."

Reina waved her hand in dismissal. "Nope. I'm no angel. I just try to do the right thing."

When it got dark, Angelica opened the shed door and looked around the pasture. There was no one in sight as far as she could see. They began the walk to San Felipe. When they got to the edge of the town, Reina said, "You wait here behind this tobacco shop. I'll go find a pharmacy and then meet that guy where he told me. I'll be back soon."

Angelica did as she was instructed. But after two hours, she started getting anxious and wondered if Reina would be true to her word and return. She'd been standing near the back door of the shop and was frightened by the sound of someone opening the door. She darted farther back into the dark and crouched down behind some trash barrels. A man in a white

T-shirt and black jeans came out of the shop and stood on the porch. He took out a pack of cigarettes that he carried rolled up in his short sleeve, then struck a match on the sole of his boot. As he looked at his phone, the smoke slowly swirled up to the porch light. Angelica's neck and shoulders tensed up—he might be there when Reina returned. She let out a sigh of relief when someone called him from inside; he cursed, flicked his cigarette away, and went back in. Soon, she heard footsteps coming from around the building.

Reina appeared and smiled at her. "Good news. I've got some things to help your feet, and I met with that guy and paid him, so we're all set. He'll drive us in his car. He said he bribes the border guards to let him take people through, so we don't even have to deal with the coyotes. He told me where to meet him in the morning and that he'd make sure we get to the border and across it safely."

"That sounds really good."

Angelica's limp had grown more painful now as they walked on through town and found a picnic table in a small park. She took off her boots and then watched as Reina removed her bloody socks, bathed her feet in water and hydrogen peroxide, applied a cream, then put on some bandages and a new pair of socks. She liked how gentle Reina was and how skillfully her hands worked.

Reina patted her leg. "There you go. You should be okay now, but don't lose the rest of this stuff. Keep it with you because you've got to doctor them each day. I bought you some socks so change them every day too. We can't have you getting sepsis."

"I'm so grateful, Reina."

Reina had also gotten some bread, apples, and water. Since the picnic table was secluded, they sat and ate and waited for the morning. They lay back on the table, side by side, as they looked up at the sky.

Angelica pointed and said, "Look! Wow, a falling star." They watched the brief arc descend in the northern sky. "It's so beautiful but so fleeting."

"Makes me think of life in a way. It *can* be beautiful. Why does it have to be so ugly sometimes?"

Angelica thought about what she said for a few moments, then her mind drifted to the days ahead. "So, what are you going to do when you get to Dallas?"

"I want to get back into nursing, working with kids again. And I only have a year left on my master's degree, so I hope to finish it too. I feel like I need to make up for all the years I lost by falling for Javier's trap."

Angelica thought of her own choices. "I should've left Antigua immediately after that gang threatened me at my shop—then Mateo and Paco would still be with me. And we'd be living in . . ." She covered her face with both arms.

"It sucks. No one gets through life without regrets. Everybody's haunted by something. Don't beat yourself up too much. It doesn't do any good. Believe me, I know."

"I can't help it. I *hate* myself so much for my mistake. It feels like I always will."

"You gotta remember, it was those men who killed them—not you."

"It's so hard." Angelica eventually moved her arms from her face and continued looking at the sky. "When I get to America, I want to open up a flower shop there."

"How'd you get into being a florist?"

"I love flowers. I love their beauty. And I enjoy making people happy—seeing their faces when I hand them their flowers."

Angelica dozed off at times as they lay silently the rest of the night. As it was getting light, Reina stood up, took Angelica by the hand, and pulled her up. "Come on, *amiga*. It shouldn't be that far."

They walked several blocks along the outskirts of town. As they passed an auto salvage yard, they heard barking and the dragging of a chain. From behind the junked cars, a large pit bull shot out, bounding toward them on a long chain. They took off running, and as Angelica glanced back, she saw that the dog flipped and landed on its back when it hit the end of the chain. After they stopped running, she bent over and grimaced as she rubbed her feet through her boots, but it didn't help.

Farther on, they turned down a dirt road that led out to an isolated house secluded in trees. Angelica's eyes instantly focused on a massive semi-truck with its long, enclosed trailer. There were no other vehicles in sight. The lime-green sleeper cab had dark windows and two towering chrome exhausts on the sides. The trailer was drab gray with the words *"Sinaloa Frutas"* in faded yellow on the side.

Angelica felt growing apprehension, "*That's* not it, is it?"

Reina looked angry and alarmed. "He said he'd drive us in his car. Maybe this is the wrong place."

When they got near the truck, a short man, head-shaven and wearing dark sunglasses, stepped around from behind it. One cheek was bulging out, the other had a scar, and both were stubble-covered. His shirt gaped open to mid-belly, revealing a muscular chest adorned with a cross on a gold chain. When he greeted them with a silent grin, Angelica saw his tobacco-stained horse teeth beneath his black moustache.

Reina asked him, "Where's Pablo? I gave him money to take us in his car."

"He said he had . . . what did he call it? . . . a family emergency. Don't worry, I'm going to take you."

Reina exclaimed adamantly, "No, sir. No, that was *not* the deal. I paid a lot of money for *him* to take us."

"Yes, but the deal has changed. I'll take you."

"Where's your car?"

"My stupid nephew borrowed it last night but didn't bring it back. He went to a party—you know boys. You can ride with me in my truck."

Angelica asked, "In the cab, right?" She had heard stories of immigrants being found in truck trailers in South Texas and that some of them had died from the heat and lack of water. But she also felt very uneasy about the truck cab having a bed.

The man spat a stream of brown juice into the dirt by her boot and wiped his moustache with the back of his hand. "Not exactly. You'll have to ride in the back, but trust me, it'll be fine."

"In the back of the cab or in the trailer?" Angelica felt her body tensing up all over.

"The trailer."

Angelica tugged on Reina's sleeve and pulled her a few steps away, where she whispered, "Let's get away from this guy right now. I don't trust this."

Reina looked worried. "Yes, I don't either, but I gave Pablo *all* my money and my diamond necklace."

Exasperated, Angelica shook her head, then turned to the man, crossing her arms. "The deal is off. We're not getting in that trailer."

Reina glowered at him. "Tell Pablo we're coming to find him, and he's going to give me my money back."

Upon hearing this, he said, "I don't think so," and whistled loudly. Two burly men in black uniforms stepped out from behind the trailer, looking sullen and holding rifles across their chests.

The man said, "Now, would you pretty ladies want to get in the trailer? You see, Pablo and I get paid by the head, as the ranchers say."

Reina spat on his face, and he flinched when it hit his sunglasses, then it slowly slid down his scarred cheek and dripped off his moustache. He wiped it off with the back of his hand, then snapped his fingers at the men and smirked. The men stuck their rifles in the women's backs and pushed them to the truck. When they opened the large heavy doors, they shoved them up into the trailer while groping their bottoms.

When Angelica's eyes adjusted to the darkness, she could gradually see that there, in the trailer, sitting on the floor all the way to the front, were men, women, and young children. They were all looking up at her and Reina. There was total silence, except for the cries of a baby. They all looked so sad, so worried, so forlorn as if the light was fading from their souls. Their faces reminded Angelica of some black and white photographs she'd seen in one of her schoolbooks of the faces of American migrants in the Dust Bowl on their way from Oklahoma to California. Now, as the heavy doors were shutting, she watched the light in the trailer slowly sweep across the faces, fading to black. When the doors slammed shut, she felt the trailer shake her, and she flinched at the clang of the sliding bolt. She took Reina's hand.

WISDOM

Brother Bob had a ritual of going to drink coffee every afternoon with Charley at his house. Charley's small house had exterior walls of one-by-twelve wood planks that, in places, had gaps between them so that the house was drafty. There was an evaporative cooler that hummed in the kitchen window on hot days, and a Dearborn open-flamed gas stove sat in the living room for winter days. The creaking wooden floors were covered in yellowed linoleum pock-marked with black burns from discarded matches. There was a corrugated tin shop out back where Charley repaired lawnmowers. Everyone in the community knew Charley—he had a reputation of being the best small engine man in the Panhandle, despite being blind.

Charley had told Bob that he was blinded many years before when he had gotten a farm pesticide in his eyes. Before he lost his eyesight, he'd been a ranch and farm hand. He wore small, round, dark green glasses with wire rims to cover up his damaged eyes. He was tall and lean and always wore the same thing: a black flat-topped cowboy hat, denim jeans, boots, and a long-sleeved gray khaki shirt stained with the white markings of dried sweat. He was never without his pipe in which he pressed Prince Albert tobacco that he got out of a red tin with an oval picture of the prince on it. He had smoked for fifty-four years and had held his pipe in the right corner of his mouth so long that there was a permanent U-shaped indention in his lower lip. He drank stout, black coffee every day at 3 p.m., even if it was hellfire hot outside.

He made the coffee in an old aluminum percolator with a hollow glass knob on the top, through which you could see the coffee splash up as it perked. The rhythmic bump of the coffee percolating up into the knob filled the small kitchen with a peaceful sound. Charley heated the coffee pot on a 1938 Frigidaire stove with porcelain knobs. The kitchen smelled of coffee, pipe smoke, and faintly of the fumes from the gas burners. Charley had never married, and no one in town had ever known him to have a date. He was, indeed, the town bachelor. He used to boast that he took a bath every Saturday night whether he needed it or not. Some folks in town wondered instead if it was actually every April.

Brother Bob knew Charley to be a down-to-earth, practical man. He had no tolerance for fools or nonsense, and he took a very dim view of the arrogant and those who put on airs. He was never outwardly unpleasant to anyone, but if he ran into someone in town that he disrespected, he said very little and instead would just puff on his pipe in silence. Although he never attended worship at the Methodist Church, he was a member, and he always sent in his monthly tithe. Bob knew he loved his dog, Buster, about as much as his pipe. Charley fixed him scrambled eggs every morning.

The snow made a crunching sound under his feet as Brother Bob walked through the streets to Charley's house. Through the window he could see Charley sitting at his kitchen table, smoking his pipe, and drinking coffee. A blast of cold wind followed him through the kitchen door before he got it shut.

Charley, having already recognized the sound of the steps on the porch, took three quick puffs from his pipe, grinned, and said, "Well, looky here at what the cat drug in. Take your coat off and come sit your ass down, Bob. You know, it's colder than a well digger's ass in Dalhart."

"Yes, or Texline."

Brother Bob poured himself a cup of coffee and sat at the table. He and Charley both faced the sink and the window above the stove.

Charley said, with obvious concern in his voice, "Is there any news about Joaquin's granddaughter?"

"No news on Angelica. Joaquin hasn't heard from her since last summer, and he has no idea what happened. He's told me he's so worried he can't sleep much. He's been trying to get a passport so he can go to Guatemala to look for her, but he's having a hard time because he doesn't have a birth certificate even though he was born here."

"Back when Joaquin was born, those old country doctors didn't worry much about birth certificates, especially for the Hispanic folks."

"When Joaquin calls the police down there in Guatemala, in that town, Antigua, they won't tell him anything. They say they never heard of her. After he told me that, I made about a dozen phone calls to them—thought they might listen to me since I'm a pastor. I finally got the police to go to the address that Joaquin had for her apartment to do a welfare check, and they later told me they went, but that it was vacant and was being repainted and carpeted for the next tenant."

"I don't blame him for being worried sick. Don't sound good at all, from what I hear about those countries down there, including Mexico. I sure hope that girl's okay."

"I keep reading and hearing that the cartel is really bad there. I'm not sure there's any law or order left."

"This ol' world has sure changed in my lifetime. It's not the same at all."

Both seemed lost in somber thought for a few moments before Charley said, "I've got an idea."

Brother Bob felt a tinge of hope. "About helping Joaquin and Angelica?"

"No, Bob, I'm sorry, I don't. I sure wished I did. I've never heard of anything like those cartels. Damnedest thing I ever heard of, people being so damn cruel. I was having another kind of idea, one not so serious."

"Okay, Charley, lay it on me."

"I've got that old nine-shot .22 pistol, and I've been saving up some beer bottles out there on the porch. Tomorrow afternoon, I want you to put about a dozen of those bottles up on top of the Church of Christ across the alley. We'll drink some beer and Wild Turkey, and then I'll shoot them off."

"What?"

"I'll shoot them off of the Church of Christ building. I understand they don't like alcohol."

"What? It's cold as hell, and there's ice all over that roof."

"Ain't you got a coat and some long-handled underwear?"

"Yes, but won't you—or we—get arrested?"

"Aw, hell no. Curtis is my friend. Nobody'll care."

Brother Bob couldn't believe what he was hearing, yet it was just like Charley to shock him out of his comfort zone. He fought with his fear. "So, you want the bottles way up there on the peak of the sanctuary?" he asked warily.

"On the peak. That's closer to God, I reckon."

"So, are you *sure* you want them way up there? How about on the low flat roof over the office part?" he asked in a timorous voice.

"On the peak near the cross. Last Sunday, I went outside to feed Buster, and I could hear them singing that hymn, 'Near the Cross,' so it seems kinda spiritual to put the beer bottles up there by the cross. Did you know they don't allow musical instruments in their services?"

"I know."

"They're serious that way but mighty good people, all in all."

"I don't know about your idea, Charley. I have acrophobia."

"Oh shit. And I thought you never tomcatted around. Can you get shots?"

"No, Charley. It's a phobia."

"What's a phobia?"

"It's a really bad fear. I have a fear of heights. I froze when I was a kid walking on that suspension bridge over the Royal Gorge in Colorado. My dad had to drag me off of it."

"Aw, hell. A feller has to face his fears, or they just get bigger."

"Then why haven't you ever had a wife?"

Charley took three long puffs on his pipe. "Well, it ain't fear. I hear wives can be a lot of trouble. But I had a gal across the river in Acuna one night when I was young."

"I've heard of Boys' Town there. Was her name 'Two Dollar'?"

"Okay, smart ass. No, it was 'Sofia.'"

"I think that means wisdom, doesn't it?"

"I'd just turned seventeen. She couldn't have been much older than me. She was the first girl to ever pull her britches off for me. I can still see her standing naked there in the lamplight in that tiny room. I'd never seen a naked woman before, except in pictures that my friend Bobby had hidden under a board in his barn. She was so beautiful it sort of took my breath away. She had a necklace with a crucifix, and she kept it on while we, well, you know. I didn't want to leave after. I told her right then I wanted to marry her, and I would have too, but she said she already had a husband, and she thought he wouldn't like her marrying me too much."

"You would have married her after *one* night?"

"Yes, sir. That was the best experience I've ever had in my life. I guess an experience like that for a young man gives him a glimpse of something deeper in life."

"But you never found anyone else you wanted after that?"

"Naw, not really. I got busy working, and I was broke most of the time. And I like my freedom."

"You said you felt something deeper? I don't think I've ever had an experience like that. Closest thing to it for me was one time at a revival when I was a boy. I got caught up in the moment and the music, but after a few hours, the feeling was gone." As he recalled that experience, Brother Bob felt the empty restlessness rising up, haunting him again. He shifted in his chair as he tried to push the feeling away. "Well, that's quite a story about your woman across the Rio Grande, Charley. I hope I find somebody someday, maybe somebody like Jen."

"Jen's a keeper, alright. A mighty fine woman."

"She sure is," Bob said with a sigh he hoped Charley didn't hear.

"So, about this phobia. I'm going to double-dog dare you so you can't refuse. You know, a feller can refuse a dare, but he can't refuse a double-dog dare. Besides, I'll give you a shot of Wild Turkey to give you a little inspiration."

"I don't know if I can handle that rot-gut stuff you drink, but alright, Charley. Alright. But I wouldn't do this for anybody but you."

The next day, Brother Bob arrived with a thirty-foot extension ladder he'd borrowed from the lumberyard. Charley had on insulated overalls and was sitting in his old, wooden-slatted, straight-back chair on the porch, puffing on his pipe in between sips of Wild Turkey. The bottle sat on the porch by his chair leg, and he held his old .22 pistol across his lap.

"I don't know about this, Charley. I'm afraid I'll slip on the ice on the roof and break my neck. Or if I don't, I'll get in trouble. I think I'd prefer breaking my neck to getting in trouble."

"Here, have a shot of courage, scaredy-cat. It'll warm you up. Besides, you're scared of a little height while ol' Joaquin's granddaughter is down yonder somewhere facing who-knows-what. Come on, Bob. Grow some balls."

"I know, but I just don't know about *this* crazy adventure," he said, now feeling quite small.

"Didn't you ever do wild things when you were a teenager?"

"Not really. Church every Sunday. Too scared and guilty to rebel. Didn't party even once, though my friends begged me. I wouldn't have sex with the girl I dated, even though she wanted to, and we were together a year."

"Damn, Bob, that's mighty sad. Seems to me like the good Lord was giving you blessings and trying to get you to loosen up and enjoy them, but you refused what he was trying to give you. Damn."

"I think so now. Back then, I was afraid of going to hell, like Billy Graham said. It's all kinda sad now that I look back on it."

"Sometimes you have to do the wrong thing to do the right thing. I reckon you can miss your life if you're religious in the wrong way, but hell, you're the preacher, what do I know? But I *do* know you can't find out the ways of the world and the wants of the women by hiding in your office with your books."

Charley puffed on his pipe in the long moments of silence as Brother Bob's shivered from the cold and the fears that tormented him: "Aw, Charley, damn you. I've gotten awful cold just standing here talking to you. Okay, give me a shot of that paint thinner you're drinking."

Brother Bob downed the shot with a grimace and a shudder, then took the ladder across the alley to the church. When he put the ladder up against the icy peak, it slipped sideways, but he stopped the slide before it fell to the ground. He shook his head and repositioned it. He walked back to the porch to get the dozen beer bottles Charley had collected in a five-gallon bucket.

"I got the ladder up. Now again, exactly, why am I doing this?'

"To have some fun. "

"Jesus, I'm going to get run out of town for sure—if I don't die."

Pale and stricken, Brother Bob ascended the ladder while fighting down the queasiness in his stomach and the rapid pounding of his heart. The ladder shook as he white-knuckled the rungs. Despite the cold, his body was already covered in sweat under his layers of clothes. The bucket of empty beer bottles swung out over the plunging depth below, making it difficult for him to keep his balance. Finally, he made it to the top, where the cold wind whistled about his ears and stung his face. Just as he reached up and was placing the first bottle next to the ice-covered cross, a bullet whizzed by his head and ricocheted from the metal cross.

Ping!!!! He was showered with ice fragments that went down his collar, and his left ear started ringing.

"Charley, you old rascal! You nearly shot me!"

Charley hollered back, "Damn it. I was checking my gun. My pistol went off before I wanted it to. You do counseling for that sort of problem, don't you? Could I get an appointment?"

"I'll schedule you the day after you croak and go on to glory."

"Did you get those bottles set up there yet?"

Just as he finished lining up the bottles, the ladder suddenly started slipping sideways. He felt his buttocks clench up, and he gasped as he grabbed the cross at the last second. With much straining and groaning, he slowly pulled it back upright. *Damn, that was close,* he thought as he breathed hard and fast for a few moments. *Dammit, Charley.*

"Are you alright?" he heard Charley yell.

"Hell no, I'm not alright."

He climbed down, but before he got to the porch, Charley fired off another shot, causing him to duck. This time the bullet struck the windshield of Charley's old 1953 Ford truck that had sat by his house for decades.

"Dammit, Charley! You're gonna kill me yet."

"What was that crash?"

"Charley, you hit your pickup."

"Shit."

"Well, if you would wait a dang minute, I'll guide you."

He stood behind Charley, leaned over, and put his hand on Charley's arm to help him aim. Out of habit, Charley closed his left eye and sighted down the barrel with his right. He laughed and said, "I guess old habits do die hard."

The first shot was wild, high, and to the right. "What'd I hit?"

"You hit the floodlight on the back of the church."

"Good. It shines in my bedroom window at night."

"How can you tell?"

"I can't. But I remember it. It used to keep me awake."

The next shot was very high and hit a small window at the top of the grain elevator a quarter-mile across town, causing a flock of startled pigeons to fly off the top of the elevator into the darkening sky.

"You hit the top of the elevator, and it scared off the pigeons."

"Did I hit a pigeon?"

"I don't think so. You hit one of the windows."

"Good. I don't like to kill innocent pigeons, even if they do make a lot of noise and shit on everything, like some politicians."

After several beers chased with Wild Turkey and two hundred rounds of .22 ammo, two of the twelve bottles on top of the Church of Christ were gone.

Charley said, "Well, let's quit."

"I'm happy to quit. I love this town and these people, and I don't want to get run off for helping an elderly delinquent shoot beer bottles off the top of the Church of Christ."

"A guy needs to live a little before he dies."

"What about the bottles that are still up there?"

"Leave them."

"But what will the people think when they see them?"

"Does it matter?"

"I don't like to upset people."

"Don't worry. They'll just think they're a sign to their preacher to get tougher on the backsliders."

"I know I worry about things that don't matter that much. Can't seem to help it."

"How about worrying about things that really matter? Look at folks like Joaquin and his granddaughter."

"Oh, I know."

"And remember, most folks aren't studying you like you think they are."

"Thanks, I think. It's just not so easy for me. Stuff gets stuck in my mind."

Brother Bob headed home, allowing himself to get lost in thought as he walked through the snow to the parsonage. He entered the quiet, dark house and sat down at the kitchen table, looking out the picture window at the bare elm trees and the rose bushes that never seemed to bloom. He crossed his arms on the table, then put his head down with his forehead on them. He was tearful and felt choked up. *I guess I don't get to go back in time.* Around 3 a.m., he went to lie down in his empty bed.

The next afternoon, Brother Bob was back at Charley's table, drinking coffee with him.

"Bob, you don't seem to be the big talker today that you normally are."

He looked out the window. "Oh, I know. Not feeling too perky today." It was too raw to try to tell Charley about the emptiness he had felt last night, and that had carried over through today.

After a very long silence and many puffs on his pipe, Charley said, "How's your sermon coming along for Sunday?"

"Not so good. I'm having trouble with it."

"What's the matter? Did your subscription run out to that place you buy those pre-packaged sermons? I can give you money to renew it if it did."

"Okay, ornery cuss, you know I don't use canned sermons. The problem is that the lectionary calls for a sermon on hell, and I don't believe in hell anymore."

"No kidding?"

"No kidding. I can't believe in it anymore. How can a loving God torture people?"

"I believe in hell."

"What? *You?*"

"Yep. Look at that unhappy fool, Gil. Everybody knows he's in hell."

"Yes. He's sure miserable, but he won't let anyone help him. I made some calls and found him a really good rehab, a famous one in California. It's expensive but he's sure got the money. Each time I even start to talk to him about it, he shakes his head and walks away."

Charley set his cup of coffee down hard, then said, "He's miserable, but he's also a damned mean cuss. It's one thing to be miserable, but you have to work at it to be mean."

"I don't know how Jen puts up with him."

"She's a good woman. No one knows this, but Jen paid for Mama's funeral when I couldn't pay it. She didn't want anyone to know, so Digger told me it was from an anonymous donor, but later, he let it slip out that it was her. I'll never forget what she did."

"Yes, she is. She volunteers with hospice too. She sits with people who don't have family, so they won't be alone when they die." After he said that, Bob looked over and saw that Charley's eyes had filled with tears behind his dark glasses.

After a few moments, Charley recalled, "You know that one time she climbed a barbed wire fence on Old Man Carter's place after she heard that he kept his German shepherd chained up and was kicking it. When he saw her come over the fence toward him, Old Man Carter started yelling and cussing at her about trespassing and calling her real ugly names, so she punched him in the face and took the dog home."

From Charley's broad grin, Brother Bob saw that retelling this story delighted him all over again.

"That old cuss was too startled and stunned to do anything. He just sat his nose-bleedin' ass down on the ground and watched her drive off with the dog. No one in this town had ever stood up to that old cuss. He was mean as a rattlesnake."

"Jen's good-hearted, but she has fire." Bob cringed at having said she had "fire."

"I heard she rescued a young coyote one time that'd been injured in one of those steel traps. Got him healed up, then let him loose in the wild again. Pissed off a lot of ranchers, though."

"I reckon Gil's one wild animal that she can't save, but I've never told her that." Then, without revealing his secret wish, he said, "She ought to set him free."

"Yes, sir. Wouldn't blame her."

Bob listened to the sound of the coffee percolating, and Charley smoked as they sat quietly, both lost in thought.

As Charley pressed new tobacco down into his pipe, he said, "Back to what we were saying earlier. You reckon hell is inside of us, and maybe heaven is too?"

Brother Bob was surprised at his question and perplexed. "What do you mean, *inside of us?*"

"The way I see it, we're given this life to enjoy. That blue sky out there and these ol' lonesome plains don't know nothing about all these ideas like hell that we cook up in our minds."

Brother Bob leaned forward to listen more intently as Charley continued. "As I see it, when we're kids, we just play a lot. It's sorta like the world is a magic place when we're kids."

"Yes, makes sense. I've read about the innocence of childhood."

Charley seemed mildly irked. "I don't know about those highfalutin words of yours. I just know kids play and usually seem mighty happy to be doing so. So, what happens to that? Why does that go away?"

Brother Bob frowned. "I don't know, Charley. It goes away, that's for sure."

"Yes, sir. I guess as we grow up, we can't see everything like a kid does. Maybe it's the hard times that change us."

"So, you think the hard times blind us to the awe and wonder that we feel as kids?"

Charley grinned wide. "Bob, you're asking the right person about blindness."

Brother Bob was slightly embarrassed. "I just mean, I'm wondering if the world is still the same magical place we felt it was in childhood, but we change somehow and can't see it."

"Aw, hell, Bob. This is making my head hurt. What do I know? You're the damn preacher, so you just let me know when you've got it all figured out."

"No, what you first said about hell made a lot of sense to me, Charley. It's making me think that *hell* is not being able to see that this life right here and now is *heaven.*"

"Well, we need to enjoy life now. I know that for sure. It goes by in a second. You studied all this stuff in that seminary, I guess."

"Yes, this makes me think of what one of my professors told us. In the Adam and Eve story, where it says that 'their eyes were opened and they knew they were naked,' the Hebrew word for 'naked' means 'a fortress without walls.' So, he said that they realized they were vulnerable. He said no wonder they got anxious and sewed little fig-leaf skirts to cover themselves."

Charley nodded. "Good thinkin' on their part. Or parts."

"Yes, but the professor asked us, 'How long do you think a little fig-leaf skirt would last in the hot Palestinian sun?'"

"I imagine about as long as it would in Pecos on a July afternoon. So, they saw the garden as a magic place until they got scared?"

"Yes."

Charley looked as if he had realized something. "Well, no wonder they got scared. Just look at the way it is . . . like ol' Joaquin being worried sick, Gil drinking hisself to death, and Jen being miserable. With all that folks suffer with, how *could* a person believe in heaven?"

"You got me there, Charley."

"Well, this old blind lawnmower mechanic sure don't know the answer."

Sensing he had overloaded Charley, Brother Bob started to get up to go, but he was still lost in his thoughts. "I just remembered that one of my other professors once said that 'Hell is not trusting that God loves us.'"

"Well, it's mighty hard to believe that God loves your goat-smelling ass when something horrible happens to you. Mama said, just before she died when she was almost a hundred, 'This ol' life requires an inner toughness.' But, you know, she said it with a smile. I reckon it takes a lot of faith sometimes just to keep going."

There was more silence. The pipe smoke drifted up to the bare sixty-watt bulb over the table. Brother Bob took another sip of coffee and then spit it out.

"Aw, dang it, Charley! There's another bug in the coffee."

"I guess I didn't see him. He's been percolated, so you can drink him or just pick him out of your cup."

Brother Bob felt disgusted as he tried to flick the bug out of his cup with his pocketknife. The bug wiggled tiny legs, trying to stay afloat.

After more silence, Brother Bob said, "People would understand if Jen left Gil, I think."

"Maybe. You know, I remember back before I lost my eyesight when they were just kids in high school. They used to park in the alley here by my house and steam up the truck windows. It'd rock and rock. The sap was sure enough rising in those two happy kids. Now, I reckon *that's* magic."

Brother Bob felt a hot surge of jealousy flood through him that he couldn't suppress. *This is so crazy. That was years ago, and she's not even mine.* Yet, the rush would not subside, and he couldn't get the image of Jen in the rocking pickup out of his mind. Frustrated, he got up, poured the rest of his coffee into the sink, and walked to the door.

Trying not to sound upset, he said, "Thanks for the talk and the bug coffee. I'm still not sure what to say in my sermon, but thanks."

"Aw, you'll figure it out."

"See you later, ornery."

When Brother Bob stepped off the porch, he glanced back through the window to see Charley taking another long draw off his pipe and appearing still deep in thought. He was amazed that this humble man who dropped out of eighth grade to go to work on farms and ranches could know so much about deeper things in life. He was also amazed that Charley's ideas had such an unsettling yet exciting effect on him in his own thinking.

DEMONS

Someone was yelling and then there was knocking at the door. Whoever it was sounded angry. They might be there to take her away, maybe. She was always being made to go where she didn't want to. But when Cheyenne peeked out through the blinds, she only saw Jen shivering in the north wind on the porch. She felt a little stupid—as often as her sister came, she should expect her by now. Though it never hurt to be careful.

With some loud grunts and groans, she moved the heavy couch that was blocking the door. When she yanked it open, there was Jen, dripping blood from one hand, holding a bag of groceries with the other, and looking none too happy.

"Oh no. Jen!" Cheyenne took the bag from her, and Jen quickly came in from the cold, a giant draft following her inside. Cheyenne slammed the door closed and locked it. "What happened?"

"It's not obvious?" Jen cupped a hand under the injured one, stopping the blood from dripping onto the floor. "When I knocked, I stabbed my palm with one of your nails again. Couldn't you please get *another* new front door and not drive nails through it?"

Cheyenne had driven dozens of large nails through the front door so that they protruded outward to menace any visitors. She lived alone, after all. And people were always taking her away. She just wanted to be left alone.

"It makes me feel safer. I'm sorry. Let me get you a paper towel."

Jen pressed the paper towel against the puncture on her palm. "I bought you chocolate chip mint ice cream, and I also got the dog treats that Buddy likes."

"That makes me and Buddy happy. I say, *Yum!* and Buddy says, *Woof.*"

Jen looked around the room. "So, how are you doing? You usually have a hard time after Christmas."

"This year wasn't as bad as the others—at least I didn't have to go to Big Spring again. But dang, it's so bleak and boring after the holidays."

"So, you're not doing so good, huh?"

"Maybe not. I've been having some real bad dreams about Angelica."

"Angelica?"

"Yes. I dreamed that red-eyed demons were chasing her down a road. Her eyes were big and scared, and she was running so fast she couldn't catch her breath. It was awful. I'm pretty sure they're the exact same demons that bother me. I felt, like, this deep, weird sadness for her in the dream because I know how she felt. I was there too, hiding in the bushes by the road, but I was too scared to help her. I couldn't move. I felt so guilty and ashamed for not helping her when I woke up. I've had the dream three nights in a row. I'm going to take extra medicine tonight because I don't want to keep having it."

"It's just a dream. Don't take too much. Remember, it makes you sleep too long."

"I know. I won't."

"I gotta go. Gotta get to the church to talk to Bob so we can decide on the hymns for Sunday's service. If you want to come join us Sunday, I'll pick you up."

"Naw, that's okay. You know how I don't like crowds much."

Jen gave her a very long hug and said, "I wish you weren't so scared. I love you great bunches."

The hug felt warm to Cheyenne.

Sometimes, Cheyenne could see the red-eyed demons with black hairy warts that lived in the crawlspace beneath the rough pine floor of her home. She could see them—but only in fleeting moments—in the cracks between the planks. When they appeared far down in the narrow darkness, she would shudder and suddenly feel cold. The hair on the back of her neck would stand affrighted, and she would sprint to her closet, fling herself down on the floor under a blanket, kick the door shut, and brace her feet against it.

She could hear them too—howling while thumping the underside of the floor with their heads. Sometimes, they hissed and rattled like snakes instead of howling. The instant she saw them—and they saw her—they howled furiously. She wondered why God never made any good demons, ones that were happy and that sang pretty songs instead of howling in such soul-piercing rage. Even Jesus, who she knew had calmly cast out demons in olden times, would turn and run fast away the instant he heard *these* demons howling.

After Jen left, Cheyenne thought that if she ate some ice cream, then it would help her quit worrying about the demons, but the two pints didn't help, and she kept getting more and more queasy. Her hands trembled, and before long, she felt that same old tingling sensation surge all through her body like electricity, just like it always did in moments like this. Her last therapist at the state hospital told her if she could just face her demons, then she would realize they were not real. Except, they were real, and nobody believed her.

By late the next night, the tormenting worries had exhausted her. She had no choice. She'd have to take the therapist's advice and confront them head-on and make them go somewhere else. But facing them made her heart race.

In preparation, she took off all her clothes—the demons would be less likely to grab them and pull her through the cracks. She began to crawl carefully along the floor, like a soldier, peering into the cracks by closing one eye and then the other, squinting into the darkness. As her long hair dragged across the floor, it stirred up tiny dust devils, miniatures of the ones she often saw whirling and dancing across the dry-plowed fields in the summer heat.

Suddenly, a demon appeared in the darkness through the crack. She saw its red, bulbous eye pressed hard up against the underside of the floor, peering up at her. The sight sent chills down her back. The demon angrily grunted and strained to shove its claws through the narrow gap. It managed to get two claws wedged partly through and began scratching vigorously on the floor, trying to pull itself out to get at her. Each time it lunged up and thumped against the floor, its red eye bulged out more. She shrieked and leaped to her feet. She began jumping up and down, stomping with both feet simultaneously, all the while screaming, "Get out! Get out! Get out!" When she paused to listen, the demon was still there, attacking the underside of the floor. It wasn't working. She raced to the closet and collapsed on the floor, moaning and rocking back and forth under the blanket.

After waiting what felt like a very long time, Cheyenne came out of the closet. She'd decided to try to scare the demons out of the crawlspace and then chase them outside—far out into the frigid, snowy plains. She hoped that if they didn't freeze to death, she would at least scare them so badly that they would scamper all the way to Big Spring or Odessa. Those towns had always looked like places God had forgotten, and so maybe the demons would be content to stay there and never come back.

She remembered she had a bunch of sparklers from last year's Fourth of July celebration—the extra big kind that she loved because they lasted forever. She reached for a box from the top of the closet, blew the dust off of the lid, got the dozen sparklers, and then lit them all at once in the open flame of the old Dearborn stove.

She scraped the hissing and popping sparklers against the wooden planks as she traced an outline of a charred cross on the floor. Small wisps of smoke had begun floating up from the old, dry wood. The delightful wisps were tiny angel soldiers rising up to help her, and they cheered her up, giving her some courage and hope. She let out little bursts of laughter, and it felt good to be giddy again. As the wisps of smoke spiraled toward the ceiling, she began singing her favorite old hymn she had learned in Sunday school. Her voice trembled at first but then grew more confident: "Standing on the promises of Christ my King, through eternal ages let his praises ring, glory in the highest I will shout and sing, standing on the promises of God." The upbeat tempo of the hymn and the happy memories of Sunday school inspired her, and she began to march triumphantly about the room, knees raised high with each step.

She felt like dancing, so she did, waving the sparklers around in big circles to make the demons leave. As the flames grew higher and the smoke more intense, Cheyenne stopped and looked down at the floor.

It still wasn't working. The fire had just made the demons madder. They were now calling up their reinforcements from the deepest darkness—there were now dozens of them, and the cacophony of howls was suddenly deafening. She tried to cover her ears, but the sparklers singed her eyebrows and burned her forehead, so she resumed waving them and dancing. The more frenzied the demons became, the more frenzied she danced about.

Buddy, her old, deaf border collie, had been asleep in the back part of the house, but now he was there with her, helping. Barking frantically, he ran in circles around Cheyenne. He began nipping at her heels, and she tripped over him and hit the floor hard facedown. Buddy was licking her face. She coughed uncontrollably. *When had it gotten so smoky?* But Buddy was there in the smoke next to her. She patted his head and told him, "I guess I've got to get you out of here. You're my only buddy, Buddy. I don't want you to burn up with these demons."

She struggled up unsteadily and stumbled toward the door with Buddy excitedly still nipping at her heels. When she opened the door, a blast of the frigid wind made her catch her breath. With Buddy just ahead of her, she ran out into the dark night and the pristine snow. The quarter moon reflected off the snow across the pastures, and the yucca stood like dark, silent ghosts. Cheyenne dropped down in the snow cross-legged and pulled Buddy close in to sit by her. He was panting hard, and drops of his drool froze quickly on her bare legs as he kept looking up at her worriedly. She shivered uncontrollably and felt light-headed.

After a few moments, she couldn't feel her bottom or the backs of her thighs. She slowly tilted over on her side and lay in the snow with her knees pulled up to her chest. Buddy moved to lay across her. As she felt herself falling into a darkness and the world fading away, she whispered, "Standing on the promises of Christ, my King."

———

Jen had not been able to sleep because she had a dream about James holding her, so she woke up with restlessness. She was also irritated by Gil's loud snoring, so she walked out into the night in her nightgown to feel the cold wind on her body for a couple of minutes. The frigid air felt especially good on her face and calmed her as she took a deep breath. When she turned and looked to the east, she saw the fire a mile away and knew that it was Cheyenne's place.

She rushed back into the house and grabbed the phone to call Danny at the Happy Volunteer Fire Department. "Danny, it's Jen. Come quick! I think Cheyenne's set the house on fire."

"I'll be damned. I'll get the boys, and we'll be out there as fast as we can."

"Go quickly. I'll try to get there, but I have to dig out the pickup. It's in a snow drift."

"We're coming, Jen. Don't worry."

"Danny, the flames must be really high—I can see them from here."

Jen ran into the bedroom and shook Gil, but he was out cold, and she couldn't rouse him. "Damn you! Damn it!" She quickly put on Gil's old Army coat and some work boots, then shot out of the house. She tried to run to the barn, but it was very difficult to get through the snow that had drifted between the house and barn. She was out of breath as she slid the heavy barn door aside and grabbed a grain scoop before making her way to the pickup. She shoveled furiously, but the drift had gotten as high as her head around the pickup. She flung a scoop full of snow so hard behind her that the force made her slip. She struggled up, threw many more scoopfuls of snow until she was too weak to continue. She flung the scoop aside, far from the truck—it was hopeless—and sat down in the snow, burying her face in her cold hands. She felt an old sorrow welling up from far down inside her—she had no words for it, only sobs that were making her rock back and forth now in the cold of the snow. Her cries drifted up to a silent but beautiful winter sky.

———

When he got the emergency alert from Danny on his cell phone about midnight, Brother Bob had just nodded off at his desk in his church study. The darkened room was illuminated only by a desk lamp that shone down on the blank pages of his writing tablet and on the many crumpled-up pages scattered on the floor around his desk—all a symbol of his struggle with a biblical passage he was supposed to use on Sunday.

The passage had always troubled him, and although he'd been working on it since Jen and the choir left earlier that evening, the effort to understand it had made him weary. He had translated it from the Hebrew himself, hoping that would give him some insights: "The Creator has made everything beautiful in its season; but has also implanted ignorance in the human mind, so humans cannot grasp the work that the Creator has done from beginning to end . . . there is nothing good for them but to be glad and enjoy themselves while they live . . . all is striving after the wind." *Why did they ever include that in the Bible?*

The cold air stung his face as he hurried down the steps to his car. He rushed to the old barn that served as the fire department's station and saw that Danny had already started the firetruck and the other volunteers were there. Brother Bob had told the town council more than once that it was time to replace the barn and the truck, a 1948 International that was now blowing a gray-black cloud into the cold night air. Rats were known to build nests of straw, paper, and rags in various places within it, including under the hood.

Danny greeted him, "It's Cheyenne's house. You ride with me in the rescue truck, and the other guys will follow in Old Bessie here."

Brother Bob jumped in the rescue truck, and Danny led the HVFD crew out to the edge of town, where they turned east on the farm-to-market. He didn't know how Danny stayed on the road because the snow had filled the ditches level-full so that it all looked like one snowy plain. Danny said, "I'll try to straddle where I think the center line is by how far I am from the fences on either side."

Bob was concerned, though, because the drifts were over the tops of the cedar posts and the barbed wire in places. As they drove on through the drifts, the fire engine was roaring behind them, blowing exhaust into the wind.

After what felt like an eternity peering down the snowy road, Brother Bob caught sight of the flames in the distance rising high into the night sky. "Oh God, I hope she got out of there."

Danny saw the flames too and sped up, cursing, "Damn, we've still got two miles to go."

Suddenly, they heard an explosion behind them. Brother Bob looked back to see flames erupting from the firetruck's engine compartment. It shuddered to a stop, and the men jumped out and started grabbing gear from the back. Danny stopped quickly, backed up, and he and Bob sprinted back to the firetruck.

Danny quickly assessed the scene and yelled at Bob, "I think her house must be a goner by now. You go see if she got out in time. I'll stay here and see if we can get this put out so we can follow. Go on now, Bob!"

Brother Bob drove away, tires spinning snow high into the air. As he drew close to the burning farmhouse, he saw two dark figures slumped together on the ground in the snow, illuminated by the flickering yellow light of the flames beyond. *Is that Cheyenne?* He drew closer, slid to a stop, then ran toward them with his heart pounding out of his chest as he yelled, "Cheyenne! Cheyenne!"

He was forced to stop short of Cheyenne because Buddy came at him, barking aggressively to protect her. Bob leaned down and held his arms out wide. "Buddy, it's me, Buddy!" The dog quickly stopped his barking, wagged his tail, and whined. Brother Bob was shaking as he kneeled in the snow, pulled Cheyenne upright, and put his arms around her. She still had a pulse, but it was very weak, and her naked body felt corpse-cold. "Don't you die, Cheyenne! Oh no, don't you die!"

He raced back to the truck and got a blanket, wrapped it around her, then scooped her up in his arms and carried her to the cab of the truck. He got in next to her, turned the heater on high, and began rubbing her arms and legs and patting her face. "Come on, Cheyenne. Come on, pretty girl," but she only moaned softly and moved her head to the side.

After several minutes, her eyes opened slightly. When she saw his face, she smiled and whispered, "Aw, sweet Brother Bob. Did you see any demons on fire running away?"

Before he could answer, he was startled by the sudden appearance of very bright lights fast approaching from behind him. *Is that the firetruck? No, the lights are way too high off the ground. What the hell is that?* As he held the blanket around Cheyenne, a very large red Case tractor with dual wheels pulled up next to the truck on the passenger side. Jen leaped down out of the high cab. He rolled down the window as she ran to the truck.

"Is she dead, Bob?"

"She's alive, but she's very cold and out of it."

He watched as Jen got in the truck, slid over close to Cheyenne, kissed the top of her head, and put her arms around her. Jen looked at her intensely with searching and sad eyes. She stroked Cheyenne's hair aside from her face, and Bob saw her singed eyebrows and the redness of the burns on her forehead. Cheyenne was drifting in and out, but as Jen's hand gently stroked her hair, she opened her eyes and smiled.

"Hey, Jen. Did you see any red-eyed demons running across the snow?"

It looked to Bob like Jen started to say, "No," but stopped herself. "Yes, I did, Cheyenne. I damn sure did. I saw a whole damn bunch of those ugly imps with their asses on fire, scared and screaming bloody murder, running like hell, going far way."

"Good. That's great, Jen. It worked." Jen looked quizzically at Brother Bob, and he shrugged, not knowing what that meant either.

Brother Bob saw that when Cheyenne heard the demons were gone, her whole body seemed to melt into Jen's embrace. She buried her face on Jen's shoulder and said, "I was so scared, Jen. I was so scared." She began to cry, softly at first, but then loudly, mournfully wailing.

The sound of her crying was so sorrowful, and the sight of Jen comforting her so touching that Brother Bob was stunned into silent awe. He thought back to the verse that had troubled him earlier, before he got the call from Danny, and fragments of the verse now came drifting through his mind: . . . *humans cannot grasp the work the Creator has done from beginning to end . . . everything made beautiful in its season . . . be glad and enjoy . . .all is striving after the wind.* Her cries made him uneasy, and he wanted to reach over and comfort her so that she would stop crying, but he pulled himself back—he just closed his eyes and listened.

A thought came to him: *Seems like an eternal sound, a sacred song, the cry of all the people and animals in the universe, past, present, and future.* Filled with an awe so powerfully moving, he took a deep breath, put his hand to his heart, and sat silently.

After several minutes, Cheyenne's crying slowly fell to silence, and this strangely powerful awareness in him began gradually fading. When he looked over at her, he felt he should be getting her to the hospital, so he started to tell them, but he held back again. *I guess some moments are so special they shouldn't be ruined with words.*

He waited.

A few minutes later, out of the corner of his eye, Brother Bob noticed that something had moved outside the truck—it was Buddy at his door on his hind legs jumping up and down to see in the window. *Well, hi, Buddy, come jump in and help us stay warm.* When he opened the door, Buddy scrambled across him into Cheyenne's arms. Her face immediately brightened, and she pulled him close in a tight hug with her head pressed against him. His innocent, joyous affection made her and Jen laugh. Brother Bob turned to look out into the cold night at the beautiful snow, the stars, and the dying flames of the old home, their brightness fading against the dark sky.

MISSION

By February, Joaquin still had not heard from Angelica. He continued with his daily ranch work, but he was beginning to lose hope.

Finally, late one evening, and to his great shock, he picked up the phone to the sound of her voice. There was anger in it and great fear. "*Abuelo*, the coyotes have got me and won't let me go."

"Angelica . . ." Joaquin began, but tears flooded down his face. He reached for his handkerchief and covered his face as he held the phone and fought back sobs.

"I'm in Ojinaga. These *pendejos* are demanding that you send them ten thousand dollars, but don't do it. Don't do it. He's holding a knife to my ribs right now to make me call you . . . Ow, ow dammit!"

Joaquin heard a struggle going on. Panicked, he yelled, "Angelica! What's going on?"

Joaquin heard the man hitting her and her cursing him. Rage and alarm flooded Joaquin's body, and his heart pounded faster and faster—he would have given his life to be there to protect her.

"Angelica! Angelica!"

Finally, she spoke again, breathing very rapidly. "This stinking *pendejo* punched me. I managed to cut his hand with his knife, but he's got the knife poking my ribs again."

When she caught her breath, she told him she had been there a few months with other women fleeing the cartels in Central America and

Mexico, and she was in some sort of warehouse. Joaquin could hear noises in the background: a man cursing, some slapping sounds, and a woman crying.

"*Abuelo*, they've beaten us and raped us."

Joaquin felt his stomach turn. *Mija, beaten and raped.* He covered the phone, leaned over, and threw up.

"Don't give these pigs any money. I don't want these pigs to have it. I'm ready to go on to heaven."

"Don't give up. Don't give up, *mija*. I'll bring the money, and we'll bring you home. Tell that man I'm bringing the money to Presidio, and we'll get it to them across the river somehow. We'll figure it out. Tell him to call me tomorrow. Now, listen to me, tell him, Angelica!"

"No, no. Don't pay these criminals anything. Just let me go on to heaven with my mama. If you pay them, they'll kill me anyway. What's the point?"

Joaquin's whole body was shaking now. He yelled, "I'm not going to let you die!"

When the call ended, Joaquin ran to his truck, tears streaming down his face. He had to get to James's house. He floored it, and the back wheels spun dust high in the air as he started down the road. Luckily, after a few miles, he encountered James driving out. They both braked, backed up, and rolled their windows down.

"Whoa, Joaquin. Mercy, *Viejo*! I know you ran pretty fast when Augustus was chasing you, but I didn't know that you'd drive as fast as a scalded imp—" James stopped abruptly, staring at him. "Good Lord, Joaquin. What's wrong?"

"Angelica's alive. She just called me. Those bastards are holding her in some building somewhere in Ojinaga. They're demanding ten thousand to let her go."

James's jaw clenched. He looked down the road for a long moment as if staring at something far off in the distance. He looked back at Joaquin with profound seriousness.

"Well then, Joaquin, let's go down there and have a little talk with those boys. Pack up and meet me at daybreak in town at the gas station."

"What about the ten thousand?"

"Oh, we're *not* giving those sewer rats a dime. Just sharpen up that big knife of yours and bring it with you. We might need it."

———

The instant Jen heard James's voice, she knew something was terribly wrong. "Jen," he was saying, "Joaquin and I are leaving tomorrow. We are going to Ojinaga to get Angelica. The coyotes are holding her there, and they're demanding ten thousand."

"What? So, where? That's Presidio on this side, right? And tomorrow?"

"Yes, at daybreak."

"I'll bring you the cash. I've got it in the safe, but I may have to wait 'til Gil passes out or goes to the barn so he doesn't know what I'm doing."

"No, no cash. I don't think we'll need the money. I sure don't plan on giving it to them. I plan on giving them a good ol' Panhandle hailstorm."

"Oh, James. Just in case, I'll get it to you in the morning. Where should I meet you?"

"Alright. Suit yourself. In town at the gas station."

Jen kept pacing the house until it got dark. Gil had already had a fifth of Old Crow through the day, but he was still alert and sitting in the living room in the dark listening to George Jones. She breathed a sigh of relief when, after a while, he got up to go out to the barn. She knew he would be there probably until morning.

She went to the closet of their bedroom, pushed Gil's clothes aside, and tried the combination to the gun safe. It wouldn't open at first. *Did Gil change the combination?* Her hands were shaking as she tried again, but this time, it opened. She moved aside the pistols, rifles, and shotgun to reach the money, which was in a metal box at the bottom and back of the safe. As she reached for the cash box, her shoulder knocked some photos off a shelf. She had forgotten she had put them there. One was of her father, mother, and her when she was a baby. She picked the photos up and flipped through them. There was another of her sitting on their father's lap, with baby Cheyenne nestled comfortably in her own. Jen paused only a moment to look at the picture. She put the photos back, took the cash out, put it in her gym bag, locked the safe, and turned to walk out of the closet. But then she gasped and dropped the bag.

There was Gil, red-faced and scowling, blocking the closet doorway. "What the hell are you doing? What's in the bag?"

"Just my workout clothes for tomorrow."

"I saw you locking the safe. Let me see the bag. I don't trust you."

"It's none of your business."

Gil grabbed the bag and opened it. "What are you doing? Going to run off with that shit-kicking goat roper you're so fond of?"

"No, although I should, seeing as how you treat me. It's for Angelica. She got kidnapped in Mexico, and it's ransom money. If the kidnappers don't get it, they'll kill her."

"I don't care. We're putting it back."

She jerked the bag out of his hands. "Jesus, Gil! Have you just lost your soul altogether? There was a time when you had a heart and would've helped out anybody, even strangers."

"We don't need another wetback coming across, so to hell with her. They're taking over the country as it is without our help."

"Dammit, Gil. I *hate* it when you use that ugly word. You've gotten so hateful I don't even know who you are anymore."

"You're one to talk. Seems like you can hardly stand the sight of me anymore."

"Everything is *not* about *you*! Shit. You make your own self a victim, unlike Angelica. She's the true victim. Now get out of my goddamn way."

He yelled, "I'm not letting you take my money."

"No, it's *our* money. Now move!" She pushed past him and grabbed her keys. Running outside, she got in her car and sped toward James's house.

When she arrived, she pounded on the door and heard James's boot steps. When he opened the door, he looked startled at her agitated state.

"Mercy, I've never seen you this mad. What's up?"

"I'm going with you tomorrow."

"Well, I can tell I won't be able to talk you out of it."

"I want to go. I'm sick of Gil. He tried to stop me from taking the money, and we argued."

"I imagine he may come over here tonight looking for you."

"No, he probably won't wake up 'til late tomorrow morning."

"Okay, tiger. Just in case he wakes up in the night, I'll let Jesus sleep on the porch. He'll bark if he shows up."

Jen couldn't sleep, so she got up at 4 a.m. to drink coffee, but she let James sleep a little longer. When he walked into the kitchen, she handed him a cup of coffee and a plate of biscuits and gravy, bacon, and eggs.

"Goodness sake, honey-pie. A feller could get mighty spoiled by this. Thank you."

"No big deal. I do it for Gil all the time."

"And he doesn't appreciate it, no doubt. Aren't you going to eat too?"

"No, just coffee. I'm still too mad about last night."

"What did he do this time?"

"He caught me taking the money from the safe, and he blocked me in the closet. We yelled at each other. He said just to let Angelica die because this country doesn't need any more wet . . . I can't say that word he used. It pisses me off."

James put down his fork and looked down at his plate. Jen knew that when he got really angry, he simply got quiet. They didn't talk for a few minutes.

"Well, I can see why you're mad. Makes me mad too. Joaquin's been like a father to me all my life, and that girl's his family, so she's family to me. I've never understood why some folks are so coldhearted. Just because someone's born on the other side of a damn river instead of on this side."

"Yeah, I know. Even some church-going folks can be coldhearted. Seems like they forget that thing they say—'What would Jesus do?'"

"Well, the Jesus out on the porch wouldn't take kindly to such folks. He can tell if someone's good-hearted or not. That's why he's fond of you."

"I thought he liked me just because I pay attention to him and pet him. I know that's why *you* like me," she sassed as she carried some dishes to the sink.

"Well, I have to say your petting is mighty appealing." James got serious again. "What happened to that good-hearted Gil we used to know so long ago?"

Jen looked at her wedding ring and sighed. "That Gil's gone. He's been gone a long time, and I don't think he's coming back."

James walked over to her, put his arms around her, and pulled her in close to his chest, then gave her a long, deep kiss. She felt some of the anger and tension in her body melt away. She felt him start to let go of her, but she pulled him close again and kissed him. He touched her on the tip of her nose playfully, then told her, "We should get ready to go meet Joaquin."

Jen stood in the dark chill of the morning and watched as James backed up the trailer to the corral to load Blaze. Blaze had his ears up and was looking intently at the trailer. The sight of the trailer made him spirited and agitated. "Calm down, boy. Save your fire for this little adventure," James said. Blaze snorted and kicked as he jumped up into the trailer, shaking his head up and down. James put the tailgate down and whistled for Jesus, who jumped up into the truck bed.

James and Jen didn't talk much as they drove the miles to town with the early morning light breaking behind them. Jen had her head against the window and was looking up at the fading stars in the west.

"What are you thinking about, good-lookin'?"

"I was remembering when I was little, and I'd sing that rhyme about wishing upon a star and how I'd wish for Mama to come back. I'd wonder if she was looking up at the same stars I was. I pretended she was, and it made me feel sort of close to her, somehow."

When they got to the Phillips 66 station, Jen saw that Joaquin was already there, standing by his pickup. Jen got out and said hello. She leaned against the truck by James as he was filling up and put her hand on his back. Just then, Brother Bob drove up in his old car, so she dropped her hand and moved over a step from James. She wasn't quite ready for Brother Bob to know, but she guessed that he already did.

Jen knew James couldn't resist the opportunity to poke at Brother Bob. "Well, Rev, what are you doing up so early? I thought you preachers slept in when it wasn't Sunday. I hear you guys only work one hour a week."

"Hey, Jen. James, you're such a kidder. No, I get up early. That's when I like to read and do my morning prayers. And this morning, I need to get to Amarillo to do hospital visits and take communion to the nursing home folks in Canyon."

"You're a good man, Bob."

Jen imagined Brother Bob's mind must be racing with thoughts of why she was with James so early in the morning and standing near him. She was coming to sense that Brother Bob was very fond of her—she had noticed how he looked into her eyes. But she didn't mind. His fondness felt warm to her because he was so easy to trust.

Brother Bob glanced toward the backseat of the pickup. "What are y'all up to this morning? Is that Joaquin?"

"That would be the old gentleman," James answered.

Bob turned to Jen and asked, "Well, where are you guys headed?"

She said, "To the river at Presidio to get Angelica. Joaquin finally heard from her yesterday."

"That's great!"

James replied, "Unfortunately, that's not the whole of it. Some bastards kidnapped her and won't let her cross the river. We're going down there to bring her back."

"Bastards? You mean the coyotes? You're going to Mexico to face the coyotes?"

Jen heard the rising alarm in his voice.

"Yep. Ojinaga," James said.

"But they're part of the cartels."

"Yep."

"Why don't you just notify the Mexican police?"

"Damn, you've got to get out of your office more often. Many of the Mexican cops on the border are paid by the cartel—they work with the gangs. If they refuse, the cartel will kill them or their families."

"So y'all are going down there to face those killers?"

Jen had been so upset with Gil that she had not yet thought much about what they might face at the river. Hearing Bob say "killers" in such an alarmed tone sent a shudder through her body, and she felt queasy.

"Yes, we are going to face those sonsabitches," James told him.

"You, Jen, and Joaquin?"

"Yes, sir."

"And your horse?"

"Blaze comes in handy sometimes. Besides, he likes to see the country."

"How are you going to rescue Angelica?"

Jen felt her body tense up at the question, and she bit her lip. James looked down the highway toward the south. "I'm still figuring on it. Real hard."

"Jesus, James, that's so dangerous." He looked at Jen as he said, "I'm sure worried about you guys. I'll be praying for your safety."

"Hold off on your praying and instead come with us," James dared him. "On second thought, come with us and then offer up some of those intermittent prayers. Isn't that what you call them?"

"I think you mean *intercessory*."

"I hear you're pretty good at them, except you can't make it rain worth a damn. Those cartel boys aren't too friendly, I hear. We might need you and your prayers tagging along. Come with us, Bob."

"What? Me? Go with you all the way to Mexico to face the cartel?"

"I say you ain't got a hair on your ass if you don't come with us. Besides, it might give you some colorful stories . . . spice up your sermons some. Get your ass in the truck. We're leaving as soon as I finish filling up, and we get some coffee for the road."

Jen knew Brother Bob well now, having spent so much time together planning the worship services. She knew he carried a small silver cross on his key chain and that when he got anxious, he fidgeted with it. He wasn't the impulsive type and certainly didn't like taking big risks, but she imagined he might like a break from the empty parsonage.

"Come go with us, Bob," Jen urged. "You've got four days before Sunday, and you just made hospital and nursing home visits last week."

Bob looked down the highway and then back at his friends. "Okay, y'all have twisted my arm off. I'll go. Wait, what about my car?"

"Go park your old beater at the parsonage, and we'll swing by to get you in a few minutes," James replied, with some apparent bemusement.

———

Brother Bob felt sheepishly excited when he came out of the parsonage to join them in the truck. He carried a small bag with some clothes and toiletries, and a black briefcase with the sermon he was working on. He was relieved but disappointed that he and Joaquin sat in the backseat and Jen was up front with James. Through the many long hours on the drive to Presidio, he kept sneaking glances at her. One time, he saw that Joaquin had noticed him staring at Jen, and he was relieved when Joaquin just nodded and said nothing. He thought Joaquin probably understood.

One after another, the big, heavy oilfield trucks zoomed by them aggressively on I-20 as James drove the pickup and trailer through Odessa. Brother Bob looked out on the vacant lots and fields of brittle brown weeds, rusted oil field equipment, run-down houses, and billboards. There was a billboard with a picture of a man with wild eyes and a bad toupee holding up a Bible and an aborted fetus. Another billboard portrayed a corseted, buxom young woman for a west Odessa nightclub called "*Adrenalina*." Farther on, there was a billboard ad for an attorney; the caption read: "Sic J. Robert, the junkyard dog of divorce attorneys, on your soon-to-be ex."

Brother Bob thought the rusted oilfield equipment seemed to stretch on all the way to the horizon and New Mexico. Fires from flares at the refinery whipped about wildly with the wind and poured smoke into the sky. When he commented on how much fire and smoke there was, Jen said, "Well, you know, this town makes me think of my marriage."

As they neared the city limit on the west side, the traffic came to a stop in both directions, with cars backed up each way. There were emergency vehicles and sheriff patrol cars up ahead with lights flashing. Traffic had apparently been stopped for a while because people were standing outside their vehicles. Brother Bob got out and walked up to a woman with a baby standing by her car.

"Do you know what happened up there? Is it a wreck?"

"I don't know for sure. That fat guy over yonder said it was a crazy person in the middle of the pavement trying to get run over or something."

"Wow. I'll go see if I can help."

He walked past several cars and got to the scene where several deputies had guns drawn on a woman lying flat on her back on the white line with her arms extended out. Her eyes were shut, and he could hear her singing a hymn he knew, "Standing on the Promises." A sheriff negotiator was talking to her from a few feet away, but she did not seem to be aware of him as she was immersed in her singing. As Brother Bob got closer, he gasped when he saw it was Cheyenne. *Good God! What's she doing way out here?* He started to run to her, but a surly deputy shoved him back.

"Get back, you! She might be dangerous."

"No, wait, officer. I know her—she wouldn't hurt anyone. She's from Happy. She's been sick a long time. I'm her pastor. Let me talk to her."

"Sick? What kind of sick?"

"She has manic-depression."

"What's that? Oh. So, you mean she's touched, that she ain't right?"

"I think that's one way of putting it."

"Let me ask my sergeant to see if he'll let you through."

"Please do. I'll be right back."

He sprinted back to the truck. "Jen, it's Cheyenne. She's in the middle of the highway," he said between rapid breaths.

"Cheyenne? Aw, no, Jesus. All the way out here?"

She bolted toward the scene with Brother Bob, James, and Joaquin right behind her.

The surly deputy raised his hand to stop them and said to Brother Bob, "The sergeant said you can talk with her and maybe get her to get up off the pavement at least. Wait, who are these people? You can't all go."

"They're family."

"Only two of you go. We still don't know if she's dangerous."

Brother Bob said, "I *told* you she's not dangerous. She's just sick."

The deputy glared at him. "Watch your attitude. I don't appreciate it."

Jen said, "I'll talk with her. I'm her sister. Let me go."

"You two go ahead then," the deputy said. "You other two stay back."

When they approached Cheyenne and kneeled beside her, Brother Bob saw that Cheyenne's blonde hair lay against the oil-stained asphalt, with the sunlight making the oil shimmer in iridescent colors. She had on an old

Army coat over a black T-shirt that did not cover her flat, white belly; the T-shirt had an image of a cross and the caption, "Romans 8: 38-39." She also had on some threadbare pink pants with blue and yellow butterflies on them. She wore running shoes with holes in them. When Jen touched her shoulder, she was startled and stopped singing. At first, she was afraid, but when she saw Jen, she calmed and even chuckled.

"Hey, big sister. Hey, Brother Bob."

"Oh, Cheyenne," Jen said. "What on earth are you doing all the way out here lying in the middle of this highway?"

"I'm praying and singing and waiting for Jesus."

Bob said, "I don't think Jesus is coming back right now."

"I guess not. But I was ready. The voices told me to come to Odessa and to lie here on this road in this spot because Jesus was coming to take me home, and then I would be free of the demons. The voices promised me."

"Are you sure you heard them right?" Bob asked. "I don't know if Jesus would *ever* come to Odessa even if he did come back. How did you get here?"

"I walked quite a ways out of Big Spring, out past the old airbase and the prisons. But then this guy in a truck hauling pipe picked me up and brought me to the truck stop between Midland and Odessa. When we got there, he wanted me to thank him properly, if you know what I mean, But I told him, 'No sir, buckaroo, I'm a good girl, and I belong to Jesus too, so nanny, nanny pooh stick your head in do-do.' He looked at me funny and let me out of his truck, so I walked the rest of the way."

Jen exclaimed, "Cheyenne, that's so dangerous! You can't be doing stuff like that."

"Oh, it was dark by then, so I knew I was totally safe. I hid in the ditches from the cars when they went by. One of them with a bunch of drunk guys in it saw me and slowed down and stopped, but I crawled in a culvert so they couldn't get me. They couldn't fit in the culvert, and I bit one of their hands as he grabbed at me, so they gave up. I have blisters on my feet, and I think some ants bit me on my butt when I was in the culvert. It itches."

"Wow, Cheyenne, it's ten miles from the truck stop to here," Brother Bob said.

Jen told her, "I can't believe you're here. I thought you were still in the state hospital because of what happened with the fire."

"I was, but they let me go yesterday. Something about reaching maximum benefit. They said I had to leave. I didn't want to. They treat me fine there, and we go to classes and the teachers are nice. And you can even smoke if you want to, outside. My doctor told me he didn't want me to go but that he had to discharge me because of the insurance. He was really upset. He's a really nice guy. I kind of had a crush on him and told him I wanted to marry him, but he said that he couldn't be with me because that would really hurt me because he was my doctor. I told him it would more than likely help me out." She laughed.

"Well, it's clear you weren't ready to be discharged. Why didn't you call me? I would have picked you up, and you could have stayed with me."

"I didn't want to bother you. You're always helping me. And I don't like Gil—to tell the truth, he kinda scares me."

"I know. Me too, sometimes. Wait, where's Buddy?" Jen looked around quickly. "He's still with Danny, right?"

"Yeah, no worry. He's still with Danny."

"Well, how about you get up, and if these deputies will let you go with us, we're going on a trip down to Presidio."

"I've never been there. That sounds fun. I could use some Mexican food."

"Great. Well, come on then, get up and let's go. I'll help you up."

Jen and Brother Bob talked with the deputy. The crisis negotiator had to do a risk assessment but said Cheyenne was okay to go as long as the family would take her. Jen had to sign a statement saying she would assume responsibility for her safety.

When they got to the truck, Jesus jumped out and ran to Cheyenne, wagging his tail.

She happily petted him. "Wow, aren't you a friendly guy? You're a lot like my Buddy. What's your name?"

Jen said, "It's Jesus."

Cheyenne said, "You don't look like I thought you would."

They all laughed, including Cheyenne. Brother Bob, feeling a little relieved, found himself laughing too. This was one adventure within their adventure that he hadn't counted on, and it had made him really anxious.

James told her, "Cheyenne, mercy, I'm sure glad you're okay."

"Thanks, James."

"What were you doing?"

"I was praying and singing."

"You know, a person should never lie down in the middle of I-20 in west Odessa to pray and sing. It's not generally a good idea. If you ever have to do that again, lie down in the ditch instead."

"I know, James. It seemed like the thing to do. The voices . . ." Cheyenne looked down at the ground, and Brother Bob felt sad for her and her terrible condition. "But I know better now, and I've got you guys. I think Jesus—not your Jesus here, the other one—sent you instead of him coming himself."

———

For Joaquin, the image of Cheyenne lying in the middle of that highway and being in such danger made his thoughts return to Angelica. He had noticed the very long tire marks from a braking eighteen-wheeler that led up to where Cheyenne was lying, and that curved off into the ditch just before they reached her. As they made their way on down I-20, he tried to push horrible thoughts and images about Angelica out of his mind, but it was futile. He had a small pocket Bible and tried to read Psalm 23 over and over, but it brought him no comfort. He bowed his head and closed his eyes while praying that Angelica would be safely freed and at home on his ranch with him.

At Pecos, James made the turn off the interstate to go south on the two-lane highway toward Balmorhea, Ft. Davis, Marfa, and Presidio. The mesquite-covered land soon turned to vast alkaline flats with mostly creosote bushes, one of the few plants that could thrive in such harsh soil with such sparse rain. When they topped a long hill, it looked to Joaquin as if the road went on to eternity, and he wrung his hands together in his lap.

Seeing the long, empty stretch of highway, he pointed and remarked to Brother Bob, "That seems like eternity. Such a long way. Hope we make it in time."

Brother Bob nodded.

After several miles, they could see the low mountains around Fort Davis far in the distance; they almost looked like grayish-blue clouds.

In Balmorhea, they stopped at a gas station, and Joaquin walked across the street to a café to get the others some food—he knew he would be unable to eat. When he walked into Rosa's Café, he saw a once-colorful pinata hanging high up over the counter. A large ornate antique brass NCR cash register sat on the counter next to a glass case that held various Mexican sweets and Chiclets. There was a small statue of Our Lady of Sorrows on each table. Through the kitchen door, he could see a woman with snow-white hair stooped over a large steaming pot at the stove, stirring and periodically tasting the contents. She appeared to be dressed for Mass. Despite his worry, he noticed the pleasing aromas of chiles, pork, posole, onions, garlic, and cilantro.

Rosa, a rather large middle-aged woman, greeted Joaquin with an interested smile as he stood restlessly at the cash register. She had a white orchid in her black hair, and she wore a bright pink top that offered a generous view of her bountiful bosom. Her dress was ruffled at the shoulders and across the low neck. Her skirt was full and flowing, much wider toward the hem, and brightly colored in layers of orange, pink, green, and blue. Her makeup was carefully done with deep red lipstick.

"Buenos días, Señor. ¿Como está? What would you like to order?"

"Buenos días."

She paused to study his face. "Somehow, you look familiar to me."

"Oh, I don't know how you could remember me. I haven't stopped in here for a few years."

"Yes, you look familiar. I don't forget faces, especially someone as handsome as you. You have very appealing eyes—so honest—and I love your graying hair. And you have so much dignity. Your weathered face and rough hands tell me you've survived some very difficult things in life."

"I guess most people have."

She leaned forward with her arms on the counter, showing more of her bosom. She winked and said, "I bet you've had a lot of women."

"When I was younger, I had my share," Joaquin said. "Now I'm old."

"An older man is the best kind. He knows what a woman wants."

"A wise man learns from each woman he is with."

"Now, what can I get you?"

"I want four burritos."

"My, you're a hungry one. *Rojo or verde*, mild or . . . hot?"

"Verde."

She wrote down his order and gave it to the waitress. She looked at him a long time with intensity, then seemed to let go of what she had been wishing for.

She sighed, "Ah, but we're not young anymore, are we?"

Joaquin nodded in agreement.

She motioned out the window across the street. "So, are you with those people out there with the horse trailer?"

"Yes, they are my good friends."

"There's a tall cowboy there."

"He's like a son to me."

"And I bet you're like a father to him. Where are you going?"

He answered quietly, "We're on our way to free my granddaughter from the coyotes in Ojinaga."

Rosa's countenance changed instantly. Gone were the friendliness, the seductive smiles, and the flirtatious glances. She spit on the floor forcefully, pounded the counter with her fist, and in a voice that made the other patrons stop and look at her, said to him, "Ay, those bastards! May God punish them in the sulfur fires of hell in eternal torment. They killed my nephew. He was fifteen."

Joaquin crossed himself. *"Lo siento."*

"I will pray for you and your friends every day. I will light a candle at each Mass for your granddaughter and pray for her five times a day. And may you kill some of those sonsabitches in my nephew's honor. Go visit them with God's own wrath."

Joaquin, moved by her anger, put his hand on her shoulder. *"Gracias."*

As he took the burritos from her and turned to go, she looked at him longingly and said, "Life is brutal but too short. We need to enjoy things. Come back to see me someday, in better times."

When they got on the road again, Joaquin looked out the window and thought about Rosa's angry words as they traveled on through the Davis Mountains on the winding road between the sparsely covered hills. There were cottonwoods and cedars lining the dry creek that the road followed through the mountains. The air was fresh and cool at the top of the pass. In Fort Davis, they passed the rows of small buildings, the reconstruction of the old fort. On the mountain to the northwest, Joaquin saw the white observatory shining in the sun.

South of town, they entered the vast grasslands surrounding Marfa. Off in the distance, there were Herefords grazing, and the sight of them reminded Joaquin of the many decades he had been working with cattle. He grew misty-eyed as he remembered the first time his father put him up on a horse. He remembered the first time he held Angelica when she was a few days old. As he surveyed the vastness of those grasslands, he felt they had their own unique beauty and hinted at something eternal. He thought, *These grasslands have been here thousands of years and will be here, just as silent, long after we're all gone.* It all made him feel rather small yet a little less anguished, somehow, because he knew he was part of something much larger. *Gracias a Dios.* Cheyenne was peacefully asleep next to him with her head resting on his shoulder, nodding gently with the bumps in the road. He closed his eyes and imagined that it was Angelica who was leaning on him.

RIVER

Brother Bob was awakened by the crunching sound the tires made on the gravel parking lot of the Palms Motel as James pulled the pickup and trailer off the road on the far east edge of Presidio. It was dusk when they arrived, and there was only one other car in the parking lot. The motel with its sand-colored stucco was one-story, and all of the rooms were in a long row with doors that opened onto the parking area. There was an open pasture on the east side, and beyond that, there was a house and barn with some pens.

As he walked to the office to check them in, Bob noticed that there was a pink and green neon sign in the shape of a palm tree near the door, but the neon outlining the trunk of the tree was burned out. Before he went into the office, he looked back at his friends who were lingering by the truck, stretching their limbs after the long drive. James had led Blaze out into the open pasture and was giving him some water out of a five-gallon bucket. Brother Bob heard James whistle and saw Jesus leap from the truck bed and begin running about, happily exploring the new territory.

Brother Bob found that the office door was locked. A piece of gray duct tape was stuck on the window with a scrawled message, "After 12 noon, ring bell." Brother Bob rang the doorbell, and after a long moment, a door opened at the back of the office to reveal a small attached living room, which was dark except for the flickering light cast by an old TV. A man emerged from the shadows and walked very slowly toward the office door. He was followed by a skinny old cat that was losing tufts of its gray hair; it walked unsteadily and coughed at times. The man was rotund and balding and appeared to be in his forties. His black-frame eyeglasses were crooked, and one lens was cracked. He had on a polyester shirt with images of saucer-shaped UFOs on it, khaki shorts hitched high, and he wore a cap that read, "They're here." He had a peel-off nametag that read, "Hello. I am—" after which he had written in thick, black marker, "Jimbo." Brother Bob imagined he had been to a UFO convention in Roswell.

Brother Bob said, "We need three rooms for tonight, possibly longer."

The man responded, speaking as slowly as he walked and in a dull, flat tone: "You mean, for all night?"

Brother Bob was puzzled. "Yes. Why wouldn't we want them for all night?"

The man looked at him for a moment while breathing through his open mouth, making a wheezing sound that competed with the muffled sounds of his wheezing cat and a game show on the TV behind him.

"Well, a lot of folks we get here just rent the rooms by the hour. Rich guys from Midland come down and bring girls from Ojinaga with them. But I don't pry into folks' private business."

Brother Bob felt himself blush. "Oh. Oh, I see. We're sure not here for that."

"Each to his own, I figure. Some of the local kids try to rent with fake IDs, but I don't let them. I don't need some girl's pissed-off father coming up here with his Springfield thirty-ought-six deer rifle aiming to send me on to glory for abetting the moral corruption of his teenage daughter."

"I don't blame you."

"That'll be $19.99 per room unless you want the amenities."

"The amenities?"

"Yes, the amenities are extra."

"What are the amenities?"

"The TV."

"The TV?"

"Yeah, it's extra if you want to use the TV."

"How much extra?'

"Three dollars."

"How many stations do you get down here? We're a long way from nowhere."

"One from San Antonio, one from El Paso, and one from Midland, but the one from Midland's pretty grainy. You can make out faces on it, though, if you squint. And the sound's okay. Sometimes, you can move the tin foil that's on the rabbit ear antennas and get it to be clearer. The TV in room seven is missing the channel knob, so I put a pair of Vice-Grips on it to turn it."

"I don't think we'll be needing the TVs."

In the corner of the small office, there were two orange plastic chairs and a small wooden table with an old electric percolator on it, sitting on a coffee-stained lace doily.

Brother Bob saw it and said, "Do you serve any kind of breakfast?"

"Just coffee, but it's mighty good. It's Folgers, not the cheap stuff. I used to fix the guests some eggs, but too many people were complaining of stomach problems, so I quit."

Brother Bob was relieved to get the keys and get away from the clerk.

———

Jen carried her duffel bag into her and Cheyenne's room. The orange shag carpet had been worn down so that there was a path of bare concrete from the door to the bathroom. There were two double beds with threadbare bedspreads, a chrome chair with holes in the vinyl seat and yellowed foam poking through, a small chrome table with a linoleum top, a wall heater, and a window unit that bumped and groaned loudly. There were two black velvet paintings over the bed. One was of a matador with a sword, fighting a wounded and profusely bleeding bull; the other was of a flamenco dancer with cleavage in a colorful dress, her arms and castanets flailing high. The lamp was in the shape of a saguaro cactus. Cheyenne lay down on one of the beds to rest. Jen was about to walk out to join the others who had gathered again at the pickup when her phone rang.

"Gil? What do you want?"

"I'm thinking about going to Kerrville to that rehab."

Jen was silent. She felt a sickening anguish well up within her. She was so tired of getting her hopes up so many times for so many years. She fought back hard against the hope that was stubbornly trying to take over her heart. But although she was trying to push hope down, she didn't want to win the battle against it, either. And what about James?

"You still there?" he said with some slurring of his words.

After a few moments, she responded. "You're really considering it? I've tried to get you to go for years. You're not playing a joke on me because you're mad at me over the money?"

"No. This time, I'm serious. I can't stand to lose you."

"You can't do it for me, Gil. You've got to do it for you, or it won't work. If you do it for me, you'll just resent me even more."

"I don't resent you."

"Sure feels like you do."

"I don't. It's just that I feel so hurt that you love your cowboy."

"He's not *my* cowboy. You don't understand. He's kind to me. You *used* to be kind to me, you know. Remember? Remember in high school? You made me feel like I mattered and that you loved me. That's how it is for girls—you made me fall in love with you by how you treated me."

"I remember. I'll make you fall in love with me again. I'll treat you right. You just wait and see."

"Gil, get sober for you. You have to do it for you."

"You'll see," he said as he hung up.

Jen felt queasiness in her stomach, so she sat down on the bed. She was quiet for a while. Cheyenne had been watching her.

"I guess that was Gil."

"Yes."

"When you talk to him, you always tense up all over."

"I know. Makes my neck and shoulders hurt."

"Are you leaving him?"

"Maybe. No, I don't think so. I don't know. It's just that I'm *so* tired."

"He doesn't treat you very nice. He doesn't treat you like how I see

James treat you. Or like how Brother Bob treated me when he found me in the snow after I scared off the demons."

"No, Gil's not like Brother Bob. Or James. He used to be. He said he would change. He said he's thinking about going to rehab, but I'm not going to hold my breath. Seems like he's doing it for the wrong reason."

"What it *seems* like is that you love James. You're happy when you're with him."

"I don't want to talk about that."

"I'll pray for Gil. Maybe the good Lord will help him. He can change hard hearts, like he did the Pharoah's."

"Well, the Lord will have to. I'm totally worn out from trying."

When Jen left the room to join the others, she looked around and saw that James had unhooked the trailer and was walking back from the house with the pens down the road.

She was puzzled. "Where's Blaze?"

"I talked to a woman there. She has horses, and I paid her to let me board Blaze there, at least for tonight. I didn't want to stake him out in this pasture. It turns out she used to live in Spur, down by Lubbock, so we actually know some of the same people who are on the roping circuit. I trust her. She's got cow dogs too, so I let Jesus stay there for a little visit. I reckon he also gets lonely."

Jen knew that he saw her looking troubled.

James asked, "What's wrong?" as they joined the others at the truck.

"Gil called."

Brother Bob said, "Is he okay?"

"He doesn't ever seem okay anymore. He said he might go to Kerrville to rehab."

No one said anything, then Brother Bob finally said, "Well, that's good. He would never go when I tried to get him to."

James said, "Maybe he'll pull himself out of the hole he's dug himself into."

There was a very long silence. Jen's thoughts turned to Angelica as they gazed at the buildings across the river. There were small flat-roof houses crammed together among various gas stations, shops, and markets, along with what looked like several large warehouses with no windows. In the midst of the town was a mission-style Catholic church with its palm trees, high roof, bell tower, and white cross.

James said, "Well, we're probably less than a half-mile from Angelica. Hopefully, she's still there." He glanced at Joaquin. "And safe. Once we find out where she is, then we can go and get her. I'm going to go across when it's darker and walk around, see what I can see, and talk with guys out on the street to see if they know where she is. I might also find a brothel above one of those bars and pay some of the girls to see what they know. Sportin' girls know a lot about a city."

Jen felt a little irritated and said, "I don't even want to hear how you know that."

"No, James," Joaquin said. "It's a bad idea for you to go across. A Texas cowboy walking around town at night will certainly get the attention of the police—or gangs. If the police stop you, they'll demand a bribe to let you come back across. If the cartel stops you, we'll most likely never see you again. I'm going to go across, but I can't cross at the bridge. I don't have a passport. Immigration might detain me for quite a while and possibly deport me."

Jen asked, "Joaquin, why would they do that? You were born near Happy and lived here all your life."

"I know, but they did that to my older brother because he had no proofs. He was two months old when our parents brought him across, and he lived here all his life. He worked cutting cedar trees for fence posts for forty years, and he raised children and grandchildren."

"And they still took him?" Jen asked.

"They did. He was never in trouble. But one day, his car broke down near Van Horn when he and his wife were going to her sister's funeral. The Border Patrol stopped and questioned him, and because he only had his driver's license, they arrested him and put him in a detention center. They kept him there for five months, and then they deported him."

Brother Bob said, "I heard about a girl who got pulled off her college campus. She'd been here since she was a year old when her parents brought her here. They deported her to Honduras after she spent a year in detention fighting her case. She didn't know anyone in Honduras."

Jen was upset by the stories. James turned the conversation back to Angelica. "*Viejo*, now what are you going to do when you cross over to Ojinaga? I'm kinda concerned."

"Don't worry. I know this area and how things are down here. We used to visit my grandparents across the river every Christmas, and my brother and I, and our cousins would play in the river. Back then, you didn't need papers, and everybody just went back and forth. About a quarter-mile upstream, there's some shallows this time of year because the snow up north isn't melting yet. I'll cross at the shallows and circle back into town. I think one of my cousins still owns a bar there. I lost touch with him a long time ago, but I'll see if I can find him. He might know something. I'll be back by daylight."

James said, "Do you want me to go with you?"

"No, I'll go alone."

"Put that knife in your boot, Joaquin," James warned. "And watch out for any rattlesnakes."

Jen and the others watched as Joaquin walked northwest in the dark, heading down to the river.

None of them could sleep that night—Jen lay awake listening to Cheyenne tossing and turning, and through the thin walls, she heard the guys sometimes moving about and pacing. Before dawn, the next morning, Jen, James, and Brother Bob sat on the tailgate of the truck without talking much. Cheyenne was still in her room. Just as daylight was breaking, they saw the lean, solitary figure of Joaquin walking up from below a rise out of the mist that rose over the river in the mornings. When he approached them, he didn't say anything and looked downcast.

Brother Bob said, "Joaquin, so did you find out anything?"

Joaquin was slow to answer. "I checked all the bars and finally found my cousin, Ernesto. He doesn't know anything. No one's talking. He said he'd heard the Zetas had some women kept in a building in town, but he didn't know where. He walked with me to look at different buildings, but we found nothing. He thinks some of the people who come to his bar know but won't talk. They're afraid the Zetas will torture them and leave their heads on the benches in the plaza."

They all fell silent and looked across the river again at the houses and buildings. Cheyenne walked up to join them.

"Ernesto said he'd heard that some Guatemalan girls are there."

"So, there's hope, right?" Brother Bob asked.

"I don't know. It's bad. The coyotes hold hostages for a certain amount of time, and after a while, if they think they're not going to collect a ransom, they kill them. He told me they use machetes or pour gasoline on them and set them on fire. There's a pit east of town that has dozens of women's bodies . . ." Joaquin's voice wavered and broke off. He turned pale as he sat down on the gravel, leaned against the truck tire, shut his eyes, and covered his face with his weathered hands.

James shook his head; Jen saw his fists were clenched. Brother Bob looked stunned and too choked up to speak. Cheyenne sat down next to Joaquin and put her arm around his shoulders without saying anything.

Joaquin took his hands from his face and looked up at them, his eyes red. "Ernesto told me to come back tonight about midnight—by that time, some of the people in the bar will be drunk enough to talk, but he told me not to get my hopes up. He said things usually end badly on that side of the river."

The rest of that day seemed to drag on for all of them. Although it was late winter, each afternoon was dry and hot, and the wind blew dirt across the parking lot. No one said much as they waited for midnight. Jen got tired of sitting in the room and went looking for James. She found him coming up the road from the pens, riding Blaze.

"Where are you two headed?" she asked.

"Down to the river, maybe ride along it up and down to get a good look across . . . get a good sense of those buildings and the layout of the town."

Jen's uneasiness was not fully diminished by his words. "James, I don't want you to go across. You know what Joaquin said. I couldn't stand it if you never came back."

"Just gonna ride down yonder and look across for a while. I'll be back."

She put her hand on his leg. "Promise?"

"A cowboy don't need to promise when he's given you his word, good-lookin'."

———

In the late afternoon, Brother Bob said he was going to walk into town and pick up food for everybody, and Cheyenne and Jen said they wanted to come along. "Good. I don't think it'll be all that far. Besides, Cheyenne, let's get you some Mexican food like you wanted," he said, making her smile. James was still out on Blaze, and Joaquin was sitting in the truck with the door open, looking at some thunderclouds forming several miles up the river. Brother Bob saw that he was looking at the clouds and said, "Those are towering clouds, so white way up high, then so dark lower down. Sure beautiful."

Joaquin nodded, then frowned. "Yes, Bob, but likely to bring a gully washer if they keep on building up."

Brother Bob was happy to get to be with Jen and Cheyenne by himself. They began walking down the dusty road, on into the town. In the distance were some tall palm trees and a white church. There were many large vacant lots among the scattered mobile homes and stucco houses with low walls in front. The open spaces were devoid of grass, just grayish gravel with a few scrub bushes, ocotillo, and prickly pear cactus here and there. Farther along, they passed a single-wide home that was faded pink with green trim surrounded by a low cinder block fence. There were toys in the yard, and a girl with sad eyes peeked out a window at them with the curtain pushed aside.

Bob was surprised when, in the middle of this low-income neighborhood, they came upon an expansive white-stucco two-story house with a Spanish tile roof. He was impressed with how elegant it was. "That must have cost a fortune," he said to Jen and Cheyenne.

As they got closer, they heard mariachi music coming from the house. Jen said, "Geez, that song sounds really sad. I wonder what it's about?"

Bob listened for a few moments to translate with the little Spanish he knew: "It's a song about a woman who cries day and night in grief."

There were two men in the brick-paver driveway washing a couple of restored cars: a black low-rider El Camino and a cherry-red Chevy Nova. Having a love of cars from that era, Bob was delighted to see them. He said knowingly, "Those are both from 1972, I'm pretty sure. So cool."

One man was spraying the cars with the nozzle-hose, and the other man was wiping them down, occasionally dipping a white rag in a blue bucket of soapy water. Suddenly, the one with the hose yelled, "Hey, Pablo!" and then sprayed the other man down, soaking him. Pablo responded by yelling, *"Ay, tu eres un cabrón, hermano!"* as he threw the wet towel at him. He missed, and it landed near Brother Bob, who picked it up and tossed it back toward them. The man with the hose turned to look at them, still grinning after hosing down his brother. He was short and bald with a scar on one cheek and horse-like teeth. Brother Bob gave him a friendly wave and a smile, but the man's grin quickly faded into a chilling stare.

Bob said, "Nice cars, man." Still, only silence and a glare.

When they got past the house, Jen said, "He gave me the creeps."

Cheyenne said, "I felt chill bumps go down my back."

"I have to say he wasn't the friendliest guy I've ever met," Brother Bob agreed, turning to look back at the house. He saw that there was a very large lot behind it, and parked there was a tractor-trailer rig with a lime green sleeper cab and trailer with *"Sinaloa Frutas"* painted on the side. He said to Jen and Cheyenne, who had also turned to look back, "Those guys must make a lot of money as truck drivers hauling fruit from Mexico. Maybe I should change professions so I can get cars like those."

Jen said, "We know that's not you. You don't care about money. Besides, you can't leave us. We'd miss you."

A few blocks down, Brother Bob noticed the Saint Francis Plaza, a small park enclosed by low sandy-colored stucco walls. He said, "I want to go check this out." They walked through the arch and saw that the worn, red-brick path led up to the far wall where a recessed alcove held a white statue of Saint Francis under its arch. Someone had laid some yellow roses at the base. There was a brightly painted mural on one of the other walls of the court-yard, and Brother Bob moved closer to study it. There were conquistadors in their armor on their white horses, carrying the flag of Spain and a flag of the

Cross. Following them was a group of friars in their brown hooded robes, leading a pair of oxen pulling a cart with solid wooden wheels. Beneath the scene were the words, *Crux Christi pro toto mundo, 1660.*

"Bob, what does that mean?" Jen asked.

"It's Latin, 'The Cross of Christ for the whole world.' I guess the Franciscan monks established a mission here in 1660."

Jen said, "That's hard to even imagine. I wonder, how'd they make it across the ocean to Central America or Mexico, then all the way up here to this desert place?"

Brother Bob thought of his own struggles with doubt. "I don't know how they had that much faith to overcome all the hardships. They must have been very scared at times, and I'm sure many died."

Before long, they found an old woman who sold tamales from the trunk of her car in a liquor store parking lot. Bob said, "Here we go. How about let's get the authentic thing?" The woman's face and hands were wrinkled and leathery, and she was stooped over, dressed all in black. When she saw them, she grinned, revealing one solitary white tooth that protruded out from the center of her upper jaw. Brother Bob thought that she must brush that tooth often, given how white it was, and he figured she must be proud of it.

The old woman greeted them as they walked up. *"Buenos días."* She looked intently at them for a moment. "You don't live here, do you?"

Brother Bob said, "No, ma'am, we're just visiting. Can we get some of your tamales?"

"Are you visiting family?"

"Something like that. We have a friend across the river we hope to rescue."

The old woman suddenly stopped smiling. Instead of getting the tamales, she just looked at their faces for a very long time, studying them without saying anything. She was silent for so long and stared at them so intensely that Brother Bob found himself growing uncomfortable.

"Ma'am, about those tamales . . ."

She cut him off with a wave of her hand as her face brightened with a dawning recognition. "I recognize you. You were in my dreams last night. I saw all three of you." She looked at Cheyenne. "I dreamed that you have had many sorrows and that you were lying on your back in the middle of a black road, praying."

Brother Bob was stunned by what the old woman had dreamed. He had never experienced something quite like this. Cheyenne smiled, hugged her, and said, "You must be a prophet like Amos and Jeremiah."

The old woman turned to Brother Bob and Jen and said, "I saw you both. You were naked in a beautiful meadow with flowers and sunlight and a clear lake with snow-capped mountains all around. You didn't know or care that you were naked. You were talking and laughing, and everything was peaceful, beautiful, and wonderful. But then the sky grew dark, and the sun was blotted out with black, rolling clouds. You got scared. A fierce, freezing gust of wind shook you, and all the flowers wilted over and died. The meadow turned black. A ferocious storm crashed upon you with deafening thunder, and you saw the dark clouds towering high up all the way to the heavens. Lightning was in the clouds and all around you, and it began to pour rivers of freezing rain. You ran and hid underneath a rock outcropping, shivering as you held each other and looked out. You were both terrified.

"Then there was a tremendous crash. The sky split open in a flash from horizon to horizon, and a monstrous beast emerged from the black clouds. The beast had a bloody gaping mouth, long curling tongue, thousands of sharp teeth, long twisted horns, and wild blood-red eyes. Its roar shook the earth, and its sulfurous breath made you recoil and cover your faces. You were horrified. The beast snarled, 'I am the *mysterium tremendum!*'

"Then there was an explosion of light. The monstrous beast and the thick black clouds were all gone. Slowly, the sun, sky, field, flowers, and mountains returned just as they had been before—unchanged. They were all just as beautiful and glorious. But you two were no longer happy or at peace. You were changed."

Brother Bob was perplexed and disturbed by the woman's story. Jen shifted nervously by his side. They waited for her to continue or to explain the dream, but she said nothing. She turned her back and reached into a cooler to get the tamales.

Jen said, "Excuse me, is that it? Is that all? Is that how it ended?"

The old woman turned around and grinned broadly, flashing her tooth, "Oh yes, *bonita.*"

Brother Bob cleared his throat—it felt dry and tight. "Ma'am, what does that dream mean?"

She stopped grinning, looked into his eyes, and said somberly, "We can't see the beauty of this world once we see the beast. But when the beast disappears, it's the same beautiful world as it was before."

The old woman didn't seem disturbed by her dream one bit and began humming a lively tune as she put the tamales in a paper bag. When it became clear that she was not going to say anything more, Brother Bob felt frustrated and disturbed. He paid her for the tamales and thanked her, then they began walking back to the motel. The wind, coming from the thunderstorm upriver, was picking up and felt almost cold on their backs as it swirled dust down the road before them.

Cheyenne said, "The beast in her dream was red-eyed, so I know it's the same as mine, just a lot bigger."

"Well, her dream troubles me a lot, and I don't understand it," Jen said. "Bob, esteemed Reverend, you're the scholar with theological knowledge and a master's degree from SMU. What does it mean?"

"Jen, I don't have a clue, but it feels like something bad has happened—or is going to."

When they got to the motel, James was just riding up from the river. He tied Blaze to the truck bumper and joined them at the picnic table that sat at the end of the parking lot.

Jen asked, "So, what do you think about what you saw over there?"

James looked worried. "That's a lot of buildings. I sure wish we knew which one."

Joaquin was standing alone and silent away from them, leaning against the truck, resting one elbow on the hood. He was looking over at Ojinaga. Blaze was also staring across the river with his head held high and his ears up.

THIRST

Charley sat lost in thought, smoking his pipe at his kitchen table and listening to the wind and the sound of the coffee percolating on the stove. He was quite worried about Brother Bob and the others. It was a dangerous endeavor, going down to Presidio to get Angelica, but he understood that there was no true choice but to do it. Charley thought, *I reckon it's the standing up to intolerable things that matters. If you don't, you can't look yourself in the mirror in the morning.*

Charley heard a knock at the screen door. That was odd—anyone who knew him just walked right in at coffee time without knocking.

Charley hollered, "Come on in."

"Charley, it's me, Gil."

Charley paused for a moment and took a long puff on his pipe. Gil had not been to his house since high school, although Charley had sometimes seen him at the post office.

"Well, ol' Gil. Good to see you. Come on in and sit your ass down. Before you do, grab a couple of cups and pour us some coffee. I'm too lazy today to get up."

Charley heard what he took to be Gil blowing dust out of the cups, then he listened to the sweet sound of the steaming coffee being poured.

Gil put Charley's cup by him on the table. "Here you go, Charley— right by your hand." He then sat down, quietly took a flask from his pocket, and poured some amber into his own cup. Charley's keen ears heard it and understood, but he said nothing.

"What are you up to these days, Gil? How's the farming?"

"The winter wheat is blowing out due to the drought, so I'm not going to make a crop this year. I'm just going to graze it out and sell the cattle in April. I'll get by, though. We'll be alright."

"Dryland farming is like gambling. Did you hear the one about the farmer who won five million in the lottery? They asked him what he was going to do, and he said, 'I guess I'll keep farming a couple of years until I use it all up.'"

Charley laughed and slapped his own knee, but Gil didn't laugh. Charley could feel the heaviness that hung over Gil and knew his effort to make him laugh had fallen flat.

Gil said, "I've seen worse times in farming. They say it's not as bad as the thirties or the fifties. Daddy used to talk about those days."

"Yessum. I remember the fifties. A whole lot of farmers sold out, or the bank closed on them. Those were rough times. But folks got smart about how to plow the fields with lister ridges so they didn't blow as much dust. How did your dad survive those times?"

"He was stubborn and tough."

"I guess everybody needs some of that. But you know he was tough on you too."

"Why do you say that?"

"One time when you were just a little feller, I'd say about five or six, I was working at the feed store, and you and your dad were there loading sacks of cow feed. I think it was cattle cubes because it was winter. The sacks were too heavy for you, but you were doin' your best, struggling hard, and your dad kept cussin' you. You dropped one and it hit the corner of the tailgate and busted open and spilled on the ground. Your dad jumped off the loading dock, yanked you out of the pickup bed, threw you down, and started kicking you, cussin' up a blue streak and calling you names.

"Me and ol' Clyde Collins grabbed him right real quick and dragged him off you. Clyde was a big ol' boy, about three hundred pounds, I suspect, so he just sat on him. We had to hold him down for quite a while because he kept cussin' and spittin' at us, and he bit Clyde on his ass. Clyde just laughed. Madder than an old yeller tomcat that got whipped in an alley fight, your dad was. Aw, he finally cooled off."

"I don't remember that. You pulled him off of me?"

"Yessum. I can still see your face. You were really scared, and your lip was busted. I helped you up into the pickup seat and tried to wipe your face with my handkerchief, but you turned your face away from me. I know your dad was in D-Day and went all the way to Berlin 'n' all, but a man shouldn't ever treat a boy like that."

"He never talked about the war. I know he had nightmares for years. I'd wake up and hear him screaming in his sleep."

"Someone told me your dad was a tank commander in Patton's Army. They said one time, near Bastogne, I think they said, your dad was manning the machine gun and standing up in the tank turret with his friend beside him. They were watching a line of German prisoners marching past them. Suddenly, a sniper shot and killed his friend. As your dad was grabbing him to keep him from falling out of the turret, the sniper shot again and hit your dad in his shoulder."

"He never told me any of that. I wish he had. I just knew he had trouble lifting his right arm up very high when we were hauling hay."

"You know those World War II guys weren't much for talking—they mainly kept it all to themselves. Oh, some would talk a little if they had a few beers at the VFW. I heard your dad recovered from his wound and wanted to go back and fight again, but it went all the way up to Ike, and Ike wouldn't let him. Your dad went anyway and rejoined his platoon. He went on to help liberate one of the concentration camps."

"I can't believe he never told me all that. Or Mother. Of course, he sure didn't talk to her much either."

"I know the soldiers who liberated those camps had to cover their mouths and noses in order to stand it. I guess all that stuff would change a feller forever. No excuse, though, to beat a little boy. It's a choice to be mean, no matter what you've been through." Charley took a sip of his coffee. "Did your mother ever try to protect you from his anger?"

"A few times, but she was scared of him too. The teachers called the sheriff a time or two, but I told them nothing happened. I'd just told them

I fell off the haystack when I was feeding the cows and hit the trough . . . stuff like that. I knew it'd be a lot worse if I told them. And they couldn't really do anything about it. Kids got bad whippings back then."

"Gil, it was more than just a whipping you got."

Charley got out his Prince Albert can and slowly refilled the bowl of his pipe, pinch by pinch. As he did, some of the flecks of tobacco fell, scattering onto his sweat-stained khaki shirt. He then puffed on the pipe with six quick puffs as he drew the flame of the match down into the bowl. After a few puffs, the tobacco was burning on its own, and he felt satisfied. They sat in silence, just listening to the wind for a while.

"Gil, I hear you've been having some rough times these days."

Charley knew his comment was stepping far over the bounds of typical conversation between men in Happy, but he also knew that Gil had not come there just to drink coffee. There was a long pause, and Charley heard Gil set his cup down on the table.

"Yeah, Charley, I don't want to admit it, but I guess I have been. My drinking is driving J . . . J . . . Jen away."

"Well, damn, Gil. That's a mighty fine woman. You'd be a sack of dry corn husks if you lost her."

"Feels like I already have. She says she doesn't know me anymore."

"That's too bad. You probably don't know this, but I remember you and her sitting on the tailgate of your pickup down the alley here when you were in high school."

"You saw us back then?"

"Yes, that was before I lost my sight. You two steamed up the windows of your truck pretty good."

"Aw damn, Charley. We thought we were hidden by the dark."

"There was a streetlight on down the alley, but I reckon you two were too—let's just say *involved*—to notice."

"We had some great times, and I really loved her. I still do. Looks like the Old Crow has got me by the short hairs. She says I get mean to her."

Charley frowned. "Well, sir, do you want to quit?"

"Drinking or life?"

"Either or both."

"Oh, I'm not ready to go on to glory yet, I don't think. Truth is though, sometimes I am."

"I guess we've all thought about that at times, especially in the roughest times. We're all goners, Gil—might as well hang around and see what we can make of this. It's gone in the blink of an eye anyway. It'll be over before you know it, so why not try to do some good and enjoy it all?"

"I've got to stop drinking, though, or I'll lose her for sure."

"I understand that to get out of a hole, the first thing to do is to put your damn shovel down and stop digging. Then step up on the first rung of the ladder."

"I've heard that."

"Well, sir, there you go. You're a good man, Gil. You've just gone and fallen in the outhouse basement. Can happen to any of us, you know. I remember how folks used to talk about you around town when you were younger. They'd say, 'You can always count on ol' Gil Jenkins to help you out if you're in a fix.' When James's dad got killed by that horse, I know it was you that delivered that big truckload of hay out to his ranch for his cattle while everybody was at the funeral. He didn't know who it was, and you didn't tell anyone."

"How'd you know that was me?"

"I saw you passing down the road in your dad's farm truck as I was walking to the funeral. You had the bales stacked seven high."

"I didn't want anyone to know it was me."

"That was you back then—doing good and not wanting anyone to know. I didn't tell anyone it was you. I knew you were that way. I bet James doesn't know it was you to this day."

"I don't like to think about James now."

"That's what I've heard. A woman like Jen won't leave the man she fell in love with unless it's really, really bad. It must be real bad for her. And for you too. Jen still loves you, but you can mess it up if you want to, though."

"Reckon what should I do?"

"Up to you, Gil. You're free to choose. But I'll tell you this: whichever path you choose, you're the one that has to live with it."

Gil got up and put his coffee cup in the sink. Charley listened to his footsteps make their way over to the screen door.

"Thanks, Charley."

"You bet, Gil. You take care of yourself, you hear? I'll be praying for you."

"Yes, sir."

———

Gil sat in his truck for several minutes after talking to Charley. He looked down the alley and thought of those times with Jen when they were young. He started crying, something he hadn't done in a long, long time. He took the silver flask out of his pocket and threw it out the window into some weeds in the alley. He backed out, drove down the worn bricks of Main Street past the post office, and turned south to head down Highway 87 toward Kerrville.

Later, as Gil drove through Big Spring, he saw the state hospital buildings on his right. He was familiar with the hospital because he'd gone there with Jen to visit Cheyenne sometimes. Jen had told him about its history. The red-brick two-story hospital buildings had been built in 1939. Back then, it was very much an asylum because there were no decent medications, and some patients lived there their whole lives. There was even a cemetery in back for the ones who had died while there and who had no family. He remembered Cheyenne used to like to sit under the big elm trees in the cemetery. He was thinking about Cheyenne and those visits they made there when his cell phone rang.

Jen said, "Hi, Gil."

"I'm surprised you called. Where are you? I've been worried."

"We're still in Presidio. I'm with Joaquin, Brother Bob, James, and Cheyenne."

"Cheyenne?"

"Yes, she was lying in the middle of the highway, and we picked her up and brought her with us."

"In the middle of the highway? So, what happens now?"

"We're waiting to find out where Angelica is across the river. Joaquin has a cousin over there, and he's going back tonight to talk to him some more."

"I'm sorry for what I said about Angelica the other night. I was wasted."

"Yes, well, yesterday you said you're thinking about going to that rehab at Kerrville."

"I'm passing through Big Spring right now, and I'm on my way. I'm going to stop drinking, so you'll start to love me again."

"Oh, Gil. I don't know. I do love you, but we've been through too much all these years."

"We sure have. And I've put you through too much. I'm so sorry."

"Gil, I can't get my hopes up. You've tried many times before to stop."

"This is different, honey." Gil felt a knot in his stomach and his hope sinking. "Don't give up on me. Please, don't give up on me."

Gil watched the sunset over the Hill Country as he neared Kerrville. The rehabilitation center was only about ten more miles outside of town, down a dirt road in a remote area. He was starting to feel the effects of not having had any alcohol for a few hours. His body had grown tense, his heart was racing, and his hands were shaking, yet he kept driving. He soon broke out in a sweat and felt sick to his stomach, then he started seeing animals crossing the road that he knew were not real. *Oh, great. Now I have the DT special—hallucinations. Damn.* He kept squinting and blinking and shaking his head in an effort to see the road as the hallucinations were making it very difficult, but he persisted. He rolled down his window to get some fresh, cold air—it felt good on his sweat-covered head.

He was only about two miles from the gate to the facility when he heard a thud as the truck bounced hard once over something. He stopped on the deserted road. *Did I run over something? Or am I hallucinating that too?* By this time, it was dark, so he got his flashlight out of the console and walked around behind his pickup. There in the road was the lifeless form of a small dog. He ran and kneeled next to it. He heard a voice deep within him, a voice that did not feel like his own, crying *Oh, no. Oh, no. Oh, no. Please, God, no!* He shined his flashlight on the poor dog to see him better, then he felt a shock run through his body—the dog looked just like his Jack.

For a while, Gil could not move, and he felt like he was being pressed down into the earth by an unseen, powerful force, yet he kept gently petting the dog. He was finally able to get the strength to get up and walk unsteadily to his pickup. He got a shovel and dug a grave in the ditch by the barbed-wire fence. He carefully laid the dog down in the hole and then sat down by it for a long while, staring at the lifeless body. He said over and over, "I'm so sorry," and eventually fell silent and put his face in his hands.

After he filled in the grave, he got in his pickup and drove on the two miles to the facility gate, where he parked and shut off his truck. It was late, no one was around, and the buildings were a half mile from the gate. He sat there for hours. Many, many times through the night, he reached up to turn the key in the ignition and drive on to the facility. But each time, something caused his hand to fall away.

At daybreak, a car approached from behind him. Since it was still early, he figured it was some of the staff workers at the facility going in for their day shift. The car slowed down and pulled up next to him; they were all looking at him sitting in his pickup. One of them, a pretty, smiling redhead, got out and walked over to tap on his window. Gil rolled the window down.

"Are you okay?"

"Yeah, I'm okay."

"I gotta say you don't look so okay." Her voice was warm and friendly. "Are you wanting to come to rehab?"

Gil looked at her intensely for a long time without saying anything.

"What's your name?"

"Gil."

"Where are you from?"

"Happy."

"Happy? That's up in the Panhandle, isn't it? I had a friend who played high school basketball at Nazareth, and she said they used to play Happy. Funny name for a town. What's their slogan, 'Town without a Frown?'"

"We used to play Nazareth when I played football, but that was a long time ago now."

She put her hand on his shoulder. "Well, Gil from Happy, come join us. Come with us. We'll help you. I promise."

Again, Gil did not say anything but kept looking into her friendly eyes as she patiently waited. Her hand on his shoulder made him feel like crying.

"No, no, sweet young lady. I don't need help. I didn't come here to go to rehab. I just got lost. That's all. I just got lost. And I fell asleep here."

"We're just the right place for lost people. In fact, we specialize in that. Let us help you."

Gil smiled at her. He gently took her hand from his shoulder and rolled up the window. He started his truck and pulled forward toward the gate to turn around and head back toward Big Spring. In his rearview mirror, he watched the pretty girl standing in the road and looking at him as he drove away. The image of her got smaller and smaller until she was entirely out of his sight.

LIGHTS

Angelica saw the lights in the darkness across the river. She was sitting under a mesquite tree, rubbing her legs and breasts, which had been bruised and cut by the coyotes' fists and machetes. Her forehead was still bleeding from being cut. She could see the silhouettes in the moonlight of the two coyotes who squatted a few yards away, drinking liquor. One was very obese, and the other was skinny. Sometimes, the red glow of their cigarettes briefly lit up their faces, and the sight made her shudder and sick at her stomach. She looked again across the river at the lights.

Two vastly different worlds separated by such a narrow band of water. *Tierra de promesa y tierra dolorosa.* She could see safety and freedom just a few yards away, yet it was an infinite distance. As she looked at the lights, she began to hear singing in a small church across the river. It was the voices of children who sang, "Jesus loves the little children, all the children of the world. He will take you by the hand, lead you to a better land—Jesus loves all the little children of the world."

One of the coyotes, the fat one, started staring at Angelica again. Light from his cigarette revealed his yellow grin. His look made her feel cold and sick inside. He kept taking long drinks from a bottle, swaying and laughing loudly with his friend. After a few more drinks, they began to sing *"La Cucaracha."*

Angelica spit on the ground and thought, *You are uglier than cockroaches!* He looked at her again and, still grinning, flicked his cigarette at her while he blew smoke out of his nostrils. He stood to walk toward her but stumbled and fell face down in the dirt. He did not move for a few moments, and so she thought she would be spared for a while longer, but then he roused himself and began to crawl toward her. The skinny coyote, leaning with his back against a boulder and a bottle in his hand, was now passed out from drinking.

As the fat coyote crawled closer, she saw that his eyelids were half-closed, his mouth hung open, and he was drooling and belching. A gust of wind carried his odor to her, and she shuddered. He crawled very close, put his forehead against hers, and breathed heavily. His breath smelled of garlic, liquor, and smoke. In a very deep voice and with slurred words, he said, "*Pinche, mi amor. Pinche, mi puta. Pinche, mi ángel. Pinche, pinche, pinche.*" Angelica turned her head away and looked again at the lights. She remembered the children's singing from the church, ". . . take you by the hand, lead you to a better land."

The coyote shoved her back flat on the ground and took out a knife to cut the ropes that bound her ankles together so he could spread her legs apart. He lay on top of her, and his heavy belly pressed her into the ground so that she could not breathe. His fat, bearded face with the thick lips and yellow teeth loomed over her, and he continued to drool, belch, and grunt. He pulled up her shirt and began to slobber and suck on her nipples.

He could not get an erection, so he cut the rope that bound her hands, grabbed her left hand, forced it around his penis, and began to move her hand up and down. "*Por favor, mi puta. Por favor, mi ángel.*" She knew if she screamed or fought back, he would only choke her until she passed out, as he had done many times before. He closed his eyes and kept moving her hand up and down, slowly then faster, saying, "*Sí, sí, sí, me gusta, mi amor!*"

Just as he was beginning to get hard, she quickly grabbed one testicle in her right hand and squeezed it with all her strength while she gritted her teeth. She felt it burst like a grape inside his sack. He screamed and collapsed on her, unconscious from the pain. She struggled to shove him off of her to the side, pushing him with her hands while kicking with her legs. With one final shove, his massive body rolled limp beside her, and his head flopped about. She saw that his eyes were rolled back, and his tongue hung out the side of his mouth in the dirt. Angelica jumped up and started to run in a flash to the river, but she suddenly stopped, turned around, and ran back to the fat coyote, where she spit on him and kicked him in the face.

Angelica ran fast to the river and did not slow down as she dived in. She began to swim, but her wet clothes started pulling her under. She held her breath underwater as she pulled off her clothes, kicking them away from her. She swam on toward the lights. She was cold and could not feel her arms and legs, but she sensed that they were still moving. Bullets began to hit the water near her, and she heard a man yelling. The skinny coyote had come to and was shooting at her. More bullets hit around her in the sand as she hurriedly crawled up on the bank and into some bushes, where she collapsed, gasping rapidly for air. Two or three more gunshots rang out but then they stopped as she lay hidden and still in the dark of the bushes.

She lay there for a long time out of fear that if she crawled out, the skinny coyote would shoot her. She eventually peeked out of the bushes to look across the river. When she saw no movement there, she crawled from her hiding spot and up the bank toward the village and the church where she had heard the singing. The church was silent now. She was too weak and injured to stand up or walk, so she crawled on very slowly, dragging herself along with her arms. She finally reached the church, moaning and grunting as she crawled up the steps. She dragged herself down the aisle toward the altar and, as she did, left a trail of blood and water on the white stone floor.

When she got to the altar, the room began to spin around—the crucifix above the altar passed her vision three times. Each time, she saw Jesus's anguished face, his scars, and the red blood dripping from his wounded hands and side. "*Señor, ayúdame. Señor, ayúdame,*" she whispered. Then all went dark like a veil being pulled over her eyes.

———

Father Rodrigo entered the sanctuary to close up for the night. As he was about to turn out the lights, he noticed the blood and water on the floor and then the dark form lying still on the floor before the altar. He cautiously approached.

It was a woman's body—naked, wet, badly bruised, and bleeding. He kneeled by her and saw the many cuts on her legs, bottom, and breasts. When he gently turned her over, he saw that the word "*Basura*" had been carved into her forehead. He gasped, crossed himself, and whispered, "*Dios! Dios! Pobrecita. Kyrie eleison.*" He saw that she was wearing a silver necklace, a crucifix, but it was broken and had lost the Savior. Her body was ice cold to the touch, and he couldn't detect any breathing. He thought she was dead, but as he was getting up to call the police, she moaned.

"*Ayúdame, por favor, Padre. Yo soy Angelica.*"

SANCTUARY

Just before midnight, Joaquin had reached the edge of the river and was ready to cross over to see if Ernesto had found out where Angelica was. As he looked across the river, it was just as he feared earlier—the storm upriver had caused the water to rise, and he could no longer see the rocks of the shallows. *I've got to get across no matter how deep it is, even if I have to swim.* He slowly stepped down the bank into the river and found that it came up to his waist. The current was stronger than expected, but he was able to stand. He carefully made his way about halfway across, but then his phone vibrated, and he pulled it from his shirt pocket.

"Hello, this is Father Rodrigo Castillo with the Immaculate Heart Church in Casa Piedra. I am calling for a *Señor* Joaquin Benavides."

Surprised and puzzled, he answered, "This is Joaquin."

"I got your number from your granddaughter, Angelica. She is here at the church with me."

"What? She's with you?" he asked, his voice rising.

"Yes, sir. When I went into the sanctuary tonight, just a little bit ago, I found her lying at the altar. She's bloody and badly injured, but it looks like she may survive. But I don't know what to do because she won't let me take her to the hospital. She's afraid that some of the people at the hospital may have relatives in the cartel and that the cartel will find out and send men to kill her while she's there. She asked me to call you." The priest explained that his church was in a small village on a rise next to the river, about four miles east of Presidio.

"We'll get there as soon as possible," Joaquin told him. He turned hurriedly to go back to the motel, but the current made him slip on the slick rocks, and he splashed face down under the water. His cowboy hat was carried away with the current. He struggled up, but when he stood, he felt a stabbing pain in his lower leg. He fought the current until he made it to the riverbank, where he sat down and took off his boot. The knife tucked inside the boot had gashed his leg. The blood was coming quickly, but he thought he could staunch it. He wrapped his bandana around the cut tightly, put on his boot, got up, and ran on as fast as he could.

When he got back to the motel, he saw that they were all standing around the truck, and they looked alarmed as he approached, breathless and river-soaked.

"She's been found!" he yelled. "She's about four miles away, on this side—at a church. A priest is with her."

"Let's go," James told them. "Now!" They all rushed to get in the truck.

"Which way, Joaquin?"

"Past those pens, east, along the river."

James drove them down the primitive, gravel road by the river the four miles southeast toward Casa Piedra. The truck was noisy as it bounced over the rough road, but luckily, the Border Patrol, if they were nearby, did not hear them. Joaquin gripped the dash the whole way as he leaned forward, focused down the road, impatient to see the church. They rounded a curve and came to the church, which stood only about fifty yards from the river. Through the darkness, they could see light coming through the stained glass windows and the open sanctuary door.

When they hurried into the sanctuary, they saw Angelica sitting on the floor near the altar, wrapped in a blanket with the priest beside her. Her hair was wet, and she was still shivering as she took sips from a mug the priest was holding up to her lips. Her face was so cut and bruised that Joaquin didn't recognize her at first. One eye was swollen shut, and her lips were split open. He was stunned when he saw the word "*Basura*" cut into her forehead. Brother Bob asked what that meant, but Joaquin could not bring himself to speak. James leaned toward Bob and whispered, "It means she's trash.'"

Joaquin heard James, and after a few moments, he said, his voice break-ing, "It means she's a child of God, dammit. She's a child of God."

The blanket fell open about her naked body. Joaquin could see the silver crucifix necklace lying on the damp skin of her chest. He saw the multitude of deep cuts and bruises on her breasts, belly, and legs, all the way down to her ankles, and he had to look away for a moment. Cheyenne moved to cover her with the blanket, and his gaze returned to his granddaughter. Jen and Cheyenne—who had never met Angelica—sat down on either side of her, each with an arm around her shoulders. Joaquin could see how moved they were by her condition, and he felt tears welling up in his own eyes. Jen kissed Angelica's cheek lightly and stroked her hair, and Cheyenne held her hand. Angelica did not resist their gentle touches.

Joaquin kneeled in front of Angelica, placed one of her hands in both of his and slowly patted her hand.

She smiled with cut and bruised lips and said, "*Mi abuelo. Mi abuelo.* You came."

Joaquin said, "*Mija*, I thought you'd been killed."

With the help of the mug of coffee, the blanket, and the warmth of the sisters' arms around her shoulders, Angelica had finally stopped shivering. With some painful pauses, she told the story of what happened to her in Antigua. Cheyenne had closed her eyes and was whispering to herself.

Joaquin said to her, "You were so brave and strong to escape that cell in Antigua."

"You damn sure were, Angelica," James added. "But how did you get from Guatemala to the river?"

Although she was weak, she told them the story of walking at night and sleeping on the ground, of meeting Reina and Reina helping her, and of being deceived and loaded into the trailer at gunpoint.

Joaquin felt himself getting angrier as he listened.

James asked, "How far did you have to ride in that damn closed-in trailer?"

"It seemed like we sat in that darkness forever, but someone said they thought it was four days and nights. We didn't have food or much water, and it was so hot it was hard to breathe. An old man and a baby died."

Jen asked, "But at least you had your friend Reina with you, right?"

Angelica stopped talking and closed her eyes. After a few moments, she whispered, "For the first two days. But she died too. She had asthma. And in that hot trailer, she ran out of her inhaler. I kept screaming and banging on the trailer walls each time the truck stopped—some of the others did too—but we couldn't make the drivers open the doors."

Joaquin shook his head and squeezed her hand.

Brother Bob said, "That's so awful. So, did they haul you all the way to Ojinaga?"

Jen said, "Wait, Bob, let her rest a minute. Let her drink some more coffee."

"I'm okay. I want to tell you the rest. When we got to Ojinaga, they opened the doors and kicked us out on the edge of town, then just drove away. Some men helped me bury Reina in a field by the road. When I got into town, everyone told me I had to hire a coyote to cross me over. They said that the Zetas controlled the border and that no one crossed without their permission. Some had tried but had ended up as carcasses floating down the river. Some people I met gave me the name of a coyote and told me I could find him in a bar called 'La Rata.' They told me his name was 'Scorpion' and that he was very obese. They promised me he would help me—he'd helped one of their cousins.

"I found him in that bar. His partner was a tall, skinny man, and his name was 'Flaco.' Scorpion had a yellow grin, like a rat, and the skinny one had eyes that gave me the chills, and he had a skull wrapped in a snake tattooed on his neck. Scorpion said that he'd charge me to get me across the river. When I told him that I didn't have any money but that I had a silver ring a girl had given me, he pulled it off my finger and looked at it and laughed. He told me it was worthless, but he put it in his pocket. I knew it was hopeless. When I turned to leave, they grabbed me, dragged me outside, and forced me into a van. I was screaming, but no one in the bar did anything. There were two *federales* in the plaza who watched the whole thing—they just looked away and kept smoking. Flaco put a black hood over me and punched me in the mouth because I was screaming and calling them names.

"They drove for a while and then locked me in the warehouse. There were nineteen other girls there. But over the few months, three died from the beatings—they'd beat and rape us even if we did everything they asked. Other men would come to the warehouse and pay the coyotes so that they could rape us too. The girls said some of those men were police and one was a judge and another a preacher. The coyotes forced all of the girls to try to get money from their families. Sometimes, even when the money would come, the coyotes would just kill them anyway. They had what they wanted."

She stopped for a minute to rest as her voice was growing weak. Joaquin felt her hands shaking as he held them. The sisters held her tighter.

"Scorpion kept beating me to force me to call my grandfather and get the money, but I refused because I had decided it was better to die. I didn't want those pigs getting any money, and I didn't want to live anymore in a world like this. I'd come to feel that God had abandoned me and this world. I couldn't believe there is a loving God."

The priest crossed himself, kissed the crucifix he had about his neck, and, with closed eyes, began to pray in a whisper.

James said, "But then you called Joaquin anyway."

"Yes, because Scorpion eventually told me he had connections with a gang in Lubbock and that he would have them kill my grandfather. He told me he'd found out that my grandfather lived near Happy, so I knew he wasn't lying."

Brother Bob said, "A couple weeks ago, Digger said two tattooed strangers showed up at the funeral home asking where Joaquin lived. Digger didn't like the looks of them, so he told them that Joaquin had died and that he'd buried him a while back. When they asked to see the grave, he took them to the cemetery and showed them a new grave that didn't have the marker yet and told them it was Joaquin's."

"Digger told me," Joaquin said.

James asked, "So, did the coyotes finally cross you over and dump you here on this side of the river even though they didn't get the money?"

"No. After the phone call, I told them that my grandfather was coming with the money. A girl had told me about a little village east of Presidio and that there was a church there and a priest that helped migrants. So, I told Scorpion that my grandfather was going to bring the money to that village and that he'd bring it to the middle of the river where they could take me and hand me over and get the money."

James said, "But you only knew that Joaquin said he was coming to get you. You didn't know where he would be or when he was going to be here."

"That's right, I didn't know. I knew my grandfather *wouldn't* be there because he didn't know where I was. I just thought if I could get out of the warehouse and get them to take me to the river, then I might have a chance to get free and get to that priest. And if not, I'd drown myself in the river so that they couldn't get the pleasure of killing me. Or maybe drown them with me. I was sick of their arrogant smirking."

Jen asked, "So, how did you get free?"

"We were just across the river here. Scorpion got drunk and started to rape me again. I crushed one of his *huevos* with my hand, and he passed out. I shoved him and his fat belly off of me and started to run for the river. Flaco didn't get me because he was passed out from drinking. That's when I swam across. Flaco woke up and shot at me as I swam, but he missed."

With deep sadness in his eyes, Joaquin could see now that the crucifix lying against her chest was broken, missing the Savior. Angelica closed her eyes, leaned forward, and put her arms around Joaquin, who held her for a long time. No one spoke as they sat on the floor in front of the altar with the statue of the bleeding, anguished Jesus hanging high above them.

JUDGMENT

Joaquin could see that Angelica was slowly losing her strength and starting to drift off. He said, "Angelica, we have to get you to a hospital."

Angelica opened her eyes wide and said, "No, the girls said the cartel was on this side of the river too. They may have people who work at the hospital."

Joaquin said, "*Mija,* we have to take you there. We'll protect you."

"I can't go there."

"I have an answer," Father Rodrigo said. "There's a doctor in town who helps refugees. I know her. She works from her house and isn't with the hospital. I'll call her and tell her you're coming to her. She works alone."

"Father, I'm scared."

He said, "Yes, but I know her. She's a good person. I've sent refugees to her before, and she helped them."

Angelica whispered, "The girls told me about you, so I am going to trust you."

He turned to James. "The first street after the Saint Francis Plaza, turn right and go a block. There's a small yellow house on your right. There's no sign out front, though."

Brother Bob said, "We saw that plaza this afternoon. I know the way."

Cheyenne wrapped the blanket tighter around Angelica before Joaquin picked her up and carried her out to the pickup as the others followed. She put her arms around his neck and laid her head on his shoulder. As he carried her, she felt very light, and the memory came to him again of the first time he had held her as an infant. Though he was being very gentle with her, Angelica moaned in pain as Joaquin lifted her up onto the truck seat. He slid in beside her and put his arm around her, and she rested her head on his chest. The others got in, and James said, "Let's get going."

James drove them back down the rough road. Joaquin kept glancing out the window into the dark, worried about the Border Patrol finding them. To Joaquin's surprise, James stopped at the pens where Blaze was boarded. He got out and said, "Y'all go on and get her to the clinic."

Jen said, "James, what are you doing?"

"I'm going to go see a man about a horse."

"James, I know what you're thinking," Joaquin said. "Don't go alone. Wait, and I'll go with you."

"No sir, you don't run as fast as you used to. Remember Augustus and the fence? Y'all go on now. I'll be back later."

Jen said, "No, James, don't go after those guys. It won't do any good. I've got a bad feeling."

He said, "It'll be alright, Jen," and he turned to Brother Bob. "Since you know the way, get Angelica to that lady doctor."

Brother Bob moved to the driver's seat. Joaquin looked down the road toward town where the doctor would be, then gently kissed the top of Angelica's head, and for the first time in months, he felt hope rising within him.

———

James saddled Blaze, laid his rope on the saddle horn, and led him out of the pens. Then, he mounted up and rode east down the road along the water. When they got to the church, James studied the bank on the other side of the river. He could see some trees on the left, then another group of trees on the right, farther upriver. As he scanned the space between the trees, he caught sight of a faint light on the riverbank. He studied it closely—it was a campfire, and he saw a form briefly pass in front of it.

James turned Blaze down the slope toward the river, keeping the horse moving slowly. He could see the moonlight on the river, and he could now hear the water running. Joaquin had told him the storm had raised the river. He rode upriver about fifty yards so he would be beyond the grove of trees on the right—that way, he wouldn't come out of the water on the other side directly in front of the coyotes' camp. He turned Blaze toward the water. Blaze did not want to take to it at first and briefly balked at the water's edge. The current was swift, and James was amazed that Angelica had been able to swim across. James gave Blaze a slight kick, and he lunged into the water and began to swim. James slid off the saddle, held onto the horn, and swam alongside. To the best of James's knowledge, they weren't noticed—Blaze's black coat blended seamlessly with the water.

Blaze bounded out of the water on the other bank, and James remounted. Blaze shook his head and mane, and water flew high, its spray reflecting in the moonlight. He turned to the left and rode in the tree cover along the river until he made it to a place where he could see the men, but they couldn't see him. The skinny one was standing up and drinking from a bottle, talking to himself and laughing. The fat one was sitting down on a large rock, holding his groin and cursing. A black van was parked a few yards up the hill above the camp; one of the doors was open, and the radio was playing music with a pounding bass rhythm. James quietly eased Blaze up to within about twenty yards of the camp. The men did not see him.

The skinny one was singing along with the music when Blaze and James burst out of the grove of trees. He turned toward the noise about the time that Blaze's chest hit him and knocked him rolling for several yards. The fat one tried to get up to get his gun, but he fell down and grabbed his groin again, writhing on the ground. James reigned Blaze in and turned to make another run at the skinny one, who was now standing with a machete. Blaze shot toward him, and as they went by, James flailed him with his rope, knocking him down. But as he was falling, he swung the machete and cut Blaze's left haunch. Before James could get Blaze stopped and turned again to make another run, the man ran screaming at them with the machete raised high. Just as he swung at Blaze again, Blaze kicked with both hind legs. His hooves caught the man in the chest; he flew backward and lay still and silent on the riverbank.

The other man had gotten up and grabbed his rifle, but he was large and slow, and James sped toward him and roped him before he could shoot. His arms and rifle were pinned next to his body by the rope. James quickly cinched the rope to the saddle horn, turned Blaze toward the river, and kicked his heels into his flank. Blaze made a powerful lunge forward, which jerked the rope tight and slammed the large man against the ground. Blaze bolted for the river, dragging the cursing man through the rocks and cactus. They got to the water's edge, and this time, Blaze did not hesitate but plunged in—he seemed to understand the seriousness of the task. As they swam, pulling the coyote through the water, James could hear the man's gurgling, coughing, and cursing. He again dismounted and swam alongside Blaze, who was now laboring to pull the heavy man through the water. James and Blaze dragged the man up on the rocky shore. The back of the shirt was gone, as was the skin on his back. James stood over the man and looked down. The man moaned and began to curse James anew.

"*Pinche tu madre, vaquero.*"

"Well now. You seem kind of grumpy. I hear you're missing one of your *cojones.*"

"*Pinche tu madre y tus hijas! Cabrón! Cabrón! Jota!*"

"It looks like raping and torturing and killing refugees isn't working out very well for you. Have you thought of getting into another line of work?"

James was startled when Joaquin appeared out of the dark, just as James was tying the coyote's wrists tight together. James looked up and saw the truck parked by the church.

"Did y'all get Angelica to the doctor?"

"Yes. She was starting to take care of her when I left. The others stayed with her. I had to come back. Is this the one?"

"Yep, the fat one she talked about. The skinny one couldn't join us. He had chest pains."

The coyote kicked at James, so he tied his ankles together. Joaquin leaned over the man and looked hard into his eyes for a long time as if he were trying to understand what made a man become nothing but evil. He pulled his long knife out of his boot and held it closely to the man's face. The scalpel-sharp blade flashed in the moonlight.

"You tortured and raped my granddaughter. You've hurt so many women. Well, you cruel bastard, your raping days are about to be over."

The coyote's anger turned to fear. Joaquin cut open the man's wet jeans and reached under his massive belly. All the decades of castrating young bulls had given Joaquin great skills. He worked quickly but with smooth efficiency with the big knife. He cut out the one testicle that wasn't crushed. As he did, the man screamed curses and spat at Joaquin. Joaquin seemed unaffected and remained calm. Joaquin held the testicle very close to the coyote's face and said, "Not very big *huevos* for such a big body."

Joaquin threw the testicle on the riverbank. He kneeled on top of the man so that his knees were pinning his shoulders to the ground. The man's eyes were very wide now, and he was shaking. Joaquin slowly moved the knife closer to his face and then began to cut on the man's forehead. The man was crying now. After Joaquin finished cutting on his forehead, he told the coyote, "I've put a little message on your forehead, like you did to my granddaughter. This way, when the Border Patrol finds you, you'll have a lot to explain."

When Joaquin stood up, James could read what Joaquin had carved on his forehead: "Zeta."

James sat the man up and shifted the rifle around inside the rope, so it was pinned in the center of the man's back and couldn't be reached by him. He figured that possession of an assault rifle would cause the man worse trouble with Border Patrol. James and Joaquin then dragged him over to a large live oak tree, sat him with his back to it, then bound him to it with another rope from the truck. When they finished, James told Joaquin, "Most likely, Border Patrol'll be by here in the morning."

James walked down to the river with Joaquin so he could wash off his knife. As Joaquin slid it back into his boot, James noticed a cowboy hat stuck in some weeds by the bank nearby. He pointed and said, "Looks like somebody lost a good hat. The *pendejo* didn't have one." Without saying anything, Joaquin waded in to retrieve it, shook it, put it on, and looked at James while water was dripping from the brim.

James said, "*Viejo*, you know your hat's all wet."

"When I fell down upriver, it went for a swim. Like your coyote."

"It's in better shape than he is."

James watched the taillights of the truck receding down the road as Joaquin drove on back toward the motel, and he and Blaze followed behind. James leaned over and patted Blaze on the neck, saying, "You're my hero, Blaze." The moonlight still shone on the river, and the night was silent except for the rushing sound of the river and the cursing James could hear fading behind him.

RETURN

After Brother Bob turned down the street just past the Saint Francis Plaza, Jen pointed and said, "There's the yellow house. Looks old, but that must be it."

Joaquin carried Angelica, still wrapped in the blanket, in his arms and stood next to Jen on the porch. When Jen knocked, the doctor opened the door and greeted them without smiling. She focused intently on Angelica for a moment, then said firmly, "Bring her to the back room."

She led them briskly down a hall and into the small room she used as her clinic. Jen looked about and saw it had once been a kitchen, and that supplies were scattered in disarray on a countertop and in open cabinets. In the corner was a metal trash can full of bloody bandages. Joaquin carefully placed Angelica on the exam table, turned, and said, "Thank you for helping my granddaughter, Doctor." He put his hands on Angelica's upper arms and looked into her eyes. "She'll take care of you, and I'll be back in a little while." Joaquin turned and hurried out.

Jen was impressed with the doctor's kindness and concern as she examined Angelica with great care. She appeared to be in her seventies or older—her white hair shone under the exam lights as she worked—yet she was lean and wiry, had bright, intense eyes, and seemed full of energy despite looking tired. She frequently asked Angelica if she was hurting her as she cleaned and bandaged her wounds. With professional seriousness but obvious concern, she told Jen, "She'll need lab work for infections and other issues when you get home, but I'm going to go ahead and give her a shot and some medications. Her right foot has some infection for sure."

When she finished bandaging Angelica's forehead, she said, "She may need stitches here, but I don't want to put her through that tonight, plus she might not need them. Also, when you get back, they should do some scans of her face—I don't have the equipment. She might have a slight fracture of her cheek bones and this orbital area. Her arms or legs aren't fractured as far as I can tell." The doctor then gestured to show Jen, saying, "But I don't know about these ribs here." When she finished her work, the doctor stood back, looked into Angelica's eyes, nodded, and lightly touched her face. "You're going to be okay, Angelica."

The doctor gave them a ride back to the motel in her old SUV. Jen lingered by the doctor's window for a moment as Brother Bob and Cheyenne helped Angelica to the room, with their arms about her waist, supporting her on each side.

"So, you always work totally alone?" Jen asked the doctor.

"Yes, I work in secret. The cartel would kill me if they found out I helped their victims."

"And you only work with refugees?"

"Yes. I decided that this is what I'm supposed to do here at the end of my life."

"But they can't pay you, right?"

"No, I never accept money from them, even if they could pay."

Jen couldn't hold back her curiosity. "Why do you do it?"

The doctor paused, reached into her pocketbook, and pulled out a black and white photograph, tattered on the edges and cracked diagonally across. Jen saw that it was of a teen girl in a plain dress with the Statue of Liberty in the background.

"This was my mother in May of 1941, on Ellis Island. One day the previous October in Poland, she was walking home from school and saw that men in black uniforms with red swastika armbands had surrounded her family's home. Just as she started to run to her family, a neighbor who had been watching grabbed her, dragged her into her house, and wouldn't let her go, even though she was kicking and biting her. As she looked out her neighbor's window, she watched the SS march her parents and little brother and sister out. She learned later that they had been put on a train to Auschwitz."

"Oh my," Jen said. She saw the sadness in the doctor's face as she told the story.

The doctor then pulled a necklace out from her shirt to show Jen; it was a small bronze Star of David. "My grandmother gave this to my mother the day before the SS took her away. You see, although it's a different time now and a different place and different people, it's the *same* human cruelty. The same *ancient* cruelty. If that neighbor had not helped my mother, she would have been gassed with her family at Auschwitz. And I wouldn't exist. So, that's why . . . that's why I help people like Angelica."

Jen was deeply moved. She asked, "Can I touch your Star of David?" As her fingers traced the worn star, she felt a profound sadness for the woman who had worn it before she was detained and killed.

After a few moments, Jen said, "Wait a minute, Doctor. Please don't go yet. I have something for you."

Jen went into the motel, got down on her knees, reached far under the bed, and got the gym bag out with the ten thousand. She returned and gave it to her. "Take this. It'll help you buy supplies for a while or just give it to others like Angelica to help them get safely away from here."

The doctor peeked in the bag and then gave Jen a weary but knowing smile. "May God bless you."

"Already has, Doctor."

The next morning broke with overcast gray skies and a cool east wind. Angelica had slept in Jen and Cheyenne's room—Jen had stayed up during the night watching her and tending to her between frequent trips to the door to look out and see if James and Joaquin had returned. When she saw the truck headlights and Joaquin drive up without James, she raced out of the room to the truck, sickened by the thought that James was not coming back. She grabbed the truck door with both hands and gasped for breath.

Joaquin quickly said, "Everything's okay, Jen. He's not far behind. He'll come along in a few minutes and be putting Blaze up in the pens."

At that news, her body relaxed. After she got back in the room, she began taking care of Angelica again. But a few minutes later, she went to the door and peeked out to look down the road. There, on down the road past the pens, she saw the dark figure of James and Blaze slowly making their way back.

Although the doctor had given Angelica some meds for the pain and sleep, she still had a fitful night. During the long hours, Jen often looked at the bandage on her forehead and shook her head in disbelief at the evil of the cartel. Angelica moaned in her sleep through much of the night, sometimes punching and kicking at the air while growling, gritting her teeth, and breathing rapidly, sometimes yelling, "No! No!" Jen sat by her through the night, repeatedly saying in a soft, kind voice, "You're okay. You're safe. The bad things are over with."

By five in the morning, sweat had drenched the long T-shirt Jen had given her, and her hair was wet. Angelica finally stopped fighting in her dreams, opened her eyes, and hugged Jen tightly. She began to cry, moaning so mournfully that tears rolled down Jen's face. Angelica kept whispering, "*Dios, ayúdame! Dios, ayúdame, por favor!*"

As Jen held Angelica and felt her bruised body shaking, she thought back to her own sorrows. She remembered the pain in her chest that early morning long ago when she sleepily awakened to the image of her father's sad face and the news that her mother had gone away. And she remembered waiting by the mailbox in her prom dress, looking up the empty road. She saw the forlorn eyes of the German shepherd that Old Man Carter had been beating and the sad, scared eyes of all the other animals she had saved. The distant memory of the exhilarating thrill of those first dates with young, handsome Gil faded into the image of Gil's angry face now, with the scowl engraved on it like words on a gray granite gravestone. She imagined Cheyenne and Buddy sitting in the snow by the house going up in flames. She thought of the flashes of lonely sadness in Brother Bob's eyes when he briefly allowed his public mask to fall.

In this night's darkness, holding Angelica, she not only felt Angelica's sorrows as her own, but it seemed like she was feeling the sorrows of every person and animal who had ever suffered.

———

As the gray sky grew lighter, Joaquin and Brother Bob were hitching the trailer up and loading up the pickup. James was out in the pasture walking Blaze. James inspected the cut on Blaze and saw that it was about twelve inches long but not deep. James was relieved. He put some antibiotic salve on it, and Blaze jumped forward and kicked. "Stings, don't it, Blaze? Sorry. But you'll be alright. If it doesn't heal soon, we'll let the vet patch you up. You fixed that skinny bastard's wagon, though, didn't you?"

Jen walked up as James was stroking Blaze's forehead. "Is he going to be okay?" she asked. "Oh my, that cut looks really bad."

"Not as bad as it looks—just long, not too deep. He'll be okay."

Jen and James stood close to each other, and her presence soothed the lingering tension he felt from last night's violence. There was no sound except for the breeze and for Blaze, now munching hay. Jen put her arms around James's waist and pulled him close and put her face against his chest. He put his arms around her and rested his chin on the top of her head. For a few moments, she was quiet, but he could feel the wetness of her tears soaking through his shirt.

She said, "That poor, poor girl. How can people be so cruel?"

"I don't know, Jen. I don't reckon we'll ever know. I don't think the smartest people on earth can answer that. All we know is that out there in the brush, there are rattlesnakes and scorpions. That's not the way we want it, but that's sure the way it is."

"When I realized you were going across the river, I thought you were never coming back. I felt that if you didn't come back, then I'd never be able to stand it."

"Oh, you know, you're a pretty tough gal, and you'd be okay. Besides, it's mighty hard to knock a good cowboy down."

She looked up at him apprehensively. "What did you do to those men?"

"Let's just say that there are two coyotes who won't be hurting women anymore. Joaquin got to have a constructive conversation with the fat one that will help him reach high notes when he sings in the shower. Blaze let the skinny one know that he didn't much appreciate him cutting him with his machete."

Jen grimaced. "Oh, Jesus, James! Such ugliness."

"Damn sure is. Terrible ugliness. But it'll be alright, Jen—for Angelica and all of us."

James and Jen joined Brother Bob and Joaquin, who were talking by the trailer.

Brother Bob asked, "How are we going to get Angelica past that Border Patrol checkpoint on the highway to Marfa?"

"We could take the backroads through the ranches and circle wide around it," Joaquin replied. "But they also patrol those ranch roads sometimes with planes or that blimp they keep near Marfa. We've got the trailer and the horse, so it might not look suspicious driving through the ranches, but we might still get stopped and checked."

Jen asked, "What happens if Border Patrol takes her?"

It was exactly what worried James as the next thing they had to face.

Brother Bob said, "I'm afraid nothing good. I've been keeping up with the news about the refugees. From what I've heard, it looks like they'd say she entered illegally, then she'd be turned over to ICE, who would probably lock her up in a detention facility. There, she could apply for asylum. She might get a bond so she can live here while she works on getting asylum, but the chances of getting one may not be good."

"How not good?" James asked. He wanted to know exactly what they were getting into.

"Trouble is," Brother Bob replied, "the process can take months or even a year, maybe more . . . I hear many refugees never get a bond. So, she might remain locked up for a long time. She should eventually get to tell her story to an immigration judge in order to get asylum, but she has to convince him she's in danger in Guatemala. I think she'd have to show documents to prove that."

James asked, "Documents? What documents?"

"Police records."

Jen shook her head. "But the police are part of the gangs there! She can't get documents! That's impossible."

"That's exactly right," Brother Bob agreed. "So, there's a good chance she'll stay locked up as her case goes through the courts, then be denied asylum and sent back to Guatemala."

James said, "To be murdered by the men she escaped from." It just made no sense to him. All this red tape nonsense over a girl who just needed a safe place to go.

"Yes."

Everyone was silent, but James felt his anger building into a hot fire. "That's the biggest load of bullshit I've ever heard. Damn, some of these politicians with their propaganda—and the fools who believe them. We just rescued her from the cruelest bastards I've ever heard of. For Christ's sake, I thought this was America."

Joaquin said solemnly, "Seems like it used to be."

"Well, you know, like some people believe," Brother Bob said dryly, "all the people who cross over are criminals. And Jesus said, 'Hate your neighbor' and 'Don't dare let the little children come to me' . . . "

Jen said, "I know that's what *some* Americans believe, but how can they? That's not who Jesus was."

"Of course, it's not who he was, " Brother Bob responded with anger evident in his voice.

James kicked the pickup tire with the toe of his boot. "I'd just as soon be in hell with my back broke than to let that girl get sent back. The government and those so-called Christians can just kiss my ass. If we let them send her back to be murdered, then we're a sorry, worthless bunch of people. She's got more courage and faith than any of them. None of them would even make a wart on her ass." James spit on the ground. "We're by god not letting the government take her so they can pen her up for a year and then send her back to be killed."

Jen said, "Well, how will we get her back home?"

James replied, "There's a feed store in town, and I'm going to go get several bales of hay. We can stack them all in the front of the trailer and leave a space in the center of them for her to hide in and then shut the mid-gate. We'll put Blaze in the back. At the checkpoint, they'd have to take Blaze out and unload the hay to find her."

Brother Bob said, "What about Joaquin? He doesn't have any proof of citizenship."

"Joaquin, maybe we can fit you into the trailer too," Jen said.

"No, I'm an American. I shouldn't have to hide in a haystack from my own government. I'll ride in the truck. If they get focused on me, then they might be less likely to search the hay for Angelica."

Jen said, "But they really might take you. Like they did your brother."

"I know. If they take me, that might satisfy them and make them think they've done their job. I want to do this for Angelica, especially if it makes her less likely to get caught. Even if they do deport me, I'll come back."

James drove into town to the feed store, and when he returned, he had several alfalfa bales he'd tossed into the trailer. He turned to Brother Bob and said, "Preacher, come help me stack these like we need them."

They stacked the hay very tightly in the front half of the trailer. From the windows on the front and front sides, all that could be seen was the green of the hay. They made a small space in the middle of the bales for Angelica. Joaquin hugged Angelica and explained that she was going to need to hide in the hay to get past the checkpoint. She nodded, but James thought she looked really scared. Jen put a blanket in the space with a bottle of water and kissed her cheek. James was touched by Jen's tenderness toward Angelica, and it made him adore Jen even more. He hadn't told her such things directly—it wasn't his style—but he tried to show it, and he hoped she knew it. James carefully stacked the hay around Angelica, closing up the space. She looked really scared as the last bale was being put in place.

James said, "You're alright now, Angelica. We won't let you down." James shut the middle trailer gate on the hay and then loaded Blaze in the back.

As they were about to get in the pickup, Jen asked James, "How far is it to the checkpoint?"

"About twenty miles."

"Let me drive."

"Why do you want to drive?"

"I have an idea."

Jen drove them north down the two-lane highway. The sun was starting to break through the overcast sky. After a while, far off in the distance, they could see the white Border Patrol vehicles with the diagonal green stripe on the door sitting near the columns and flat roof of the checkpoint that stretched across the road. Jen slowed down some. She reached inside her shirt and undid the front snap of her bra, slipped it off, and threw it in the back seat, where it landed on Brother Bob's glasses, then fell in his lap. His mouth dropped open as he looked down at the bra. James laughed.

Jen said, "Hold onto that, Bob."

"What?"

"Just hold that in your lap when we get there."

"Hmm. You playing a joke to lighten things up since we're all worried sick about what's going to happen up there when we get stopped?"

"No, Bob, I'm serious."

"I don't understand, but I will hold it."

Jen said to her sister, "Cheyenne, are you hearing any voices now?"

"No. I held Angelica's hands this morning, and we prayed together for blessings to happen to us all, and they went away. Least for now. I'm not seeing any demons either."

"Good. So, when we get to the checkpoint, just act like you're responding to voices. Can you do that?"

"Are you kidding? Believe me, if anyone knows voices, it's *me*."

James was looking at Jen trying hard to figure out what she was up to, then she surprised him by unbuttoning her shirt the rest of the way to her navel. She left it gaped open some. He knew then that it was so the officer would be able to see her full curves. He said to her, "Jen, you're a mighty smart gal."

There were five cars in front of them, so they had to wait for a while. They watched as imposing, unsmiling agents in dull green uniforms with black belts and black boots interrogated each driver and the passengers. While one officer talked with the people in the vehicle, another held a mirror attached to a long metal rod and moved it along underneath and around the vehicle. Still, another agent circled each vehicle with a German shepherd sniffing for drugs. James glanced back at the truck bed and saw that Jesus was watching all the activity intently, especially the German shepherd. They pulled forward as there was only one car ahead of them now. The officer finished with the car ahead and waved for Jen to pull forward. He was writing down their license plate number as he walked up to Jen's window. He appeared stern and somewhat bored. While still looking down and not yet looking at Jen, he began his standard speech, "This is United States Border Patrol. Let me see your driver's license. Where are you coming from, and where are you going?"

"To Happy, Texas, sir."

James leaned partly across Jen and said, "We're from Happy, up in the Panhandle by Amarillo. I have a ranch there. We've been down to Presidio. I was looking at cattle to buy."

He glanced back at the trailer. "I don't see any cattle."

"I didn't buy any. The old codger wanted way too much for them, then I learned from guys in town that he'd had anthrax in his pastures years ago, so I sure couldn't chance it."

The officer seemed satisfied with the answers. James noticed that he had been stealing glances at Jen's breasts and seemed bothered. The officer moved to the back window, where he saw Brother Bob with the bra on his lap.

"Let me see your license. What are you doing with that bra on your lap?"

"It's mine, sir."

James interrupted, "Oh, that's Brother Bob. He's our preacher."

"Your preacher?"

"Yes, sir."

"What's with that bra?"

Brother Bob said, "Oh, sir, it's a fetish of mine."

James was shocked to hear what Bob had come up with and fought back an impulse to laugh.

"That's all. A fetish. I'm in therapy, trying to give it up. It's not going well. I may give up therapy instead."

James couldn't resist. "On Sundays, he wears it under his clergy robe, but you can't see it, so it don't hurt anything."

The officer shook his head in apparent disgust and was growing more visibly irritated, but then he noticed Cheyenne talking to herself and holding her hands up toward the sky. He asked, "What's wrong with her?"

Jen said, "She's my sister. She's hearing voices. She was lying in the middle of I-20 in Odessa, and so we picked her up to go with us on the way down here. They let her out of Big Spring too soon. The state hospital there."

"In the middle of I-20?"

"Yes, she was waiting for Jesus to come."

Cheyenne said, "But he didn't, doggone it. It's not the first time he let me down."

"When did you pick her up?"

"A few days ago. You can call the sheriff's office in Odessa. They'll tell you."

"I'll be back in a minute."

The officer went into the building, and James saw him making a phone call. He came back and continued his questioning. He did not seem quite as suspicious until he saw Joaquin.

"Who's the old Mexican asleep in the back seat with the crazy ones?"

James said, "That, sir, is the finest old *American* cowboy you could ever have the honor to meet. That is *Don* Joaquin Benavides."

"Wake him up, please."

James reached back and poked him on the knee, and Joaquin took his hat from his face and sat up. The officer went to the other side of the pickup to Joaquin's window.

"Are you a citizen?"

"Yes, sir."

"Where were you born?"

"In the Panhandle, on a ranch near Happy. My parents were born in Mexico, but I was born here."

"Sir, let me see your passport."

"I don't have one. I didn't know I needed a passport just to travel in the U.S."

"Do you have your birth certificate with you?"

"I didn't know I had to carry one with me, but I don't have one anyway. I was born on April fourteenth, Palm Sunday, 1935, at home during a really bad dust storm. The old country doctor didn't believe in filling out birth certificates for any child who wasn't white."

"You don't have a birth certificate?" The officer paused. "Let me see your driver's license."

Joaquin gave him his license. The officer frowned as he studied it for a long time. It was everything James could do to keep his mouth shut as he grew increasingly angry at the questioning.

"I may need to detain you."

"For what? For being a good citizen, never in trouble, and hard-working for over seventy years?"

"So we can check your story."

Joaquin stood firm. "What is this, Nazi Germany? Are we supposed to say, 'Heil, Mr. President'?"

James felt his body tensing up as he listened and watched the officer in his side mirror. He could tell the officer was about to lose his temper, and he wished Joaquin would back down some, but he knew it was not like him.

The officer said, "Now you're pissing me off. I'm just doing my job trying to protect the citizens of this country. You're being disrespectful."

"Well, sir, I *am* a citizen, and you are disrespecting me with your attitude and threat."

James thought, *Come on, Joaquin. Just be quiet.*

"You're a mouthy old cuss."

"Sir, I have dignity and worth just like you. Your Bible says so, I believe. We're all the same—brothers and sisters."

The officer glared at Joaquin for a full minute. He reached for the handcuffs on his belt but then seemed to change his mind as he glanced back toward Jen. He walked back to her window and asked, "Ma'am, what's in the trailer?"

Jen said, "Some alfalfa and the horse. Go ahead and look, officer."

James leaned across Jen again and said, "Yes, why don't you go take a look in the trailer? Just be careful when you lead the horse out. That's Blaze. He don't like strangers too much unless you give him a carrot when he first meets you. But I bet you boys don't keep any carrots in your hut there."

The officer looked at James as if he wanted to kill him, turned, and walked back to the trailer. Another agent had completed the mirror sweep under the truck and trailer. When the third agent walked the German shepherd past the trailer gate, Blaze kicked the gate hard. James watched in the mirror as the bang startled both the agent and the dog, making them jump backward. He smiled inwardly: *Attaboy! You tell 'em, Blaze!*

What James didn't like was how the officer stood and looked at the hay for a very long time. He motioned to a fellow agent, and they talked as they walked around the trailer, peeking inside every now and then. James was glad he'd stacked the hay in tightly, wall to wall and floor to ceiling, but then the officer turned to his assistant and said, "Go get the infrared camera." Upon hearing that, James clenched both fists as they rested on his legs. Jen put her hand over one of his fists, squeezed it very tightly, and didn't let go. He heard Brother Bob whisper in the back seat, "Oh no. We're toast now."

The agent soon returned from the building with the camera, but James heard the officer say, "It's down. Go get another battery." The assistant went inside, then returned with an apprehensive look.

"We don't have any batteries left. Sullivan forgot to pick some up from supply. Do you want me to go to Marfa to get more?"

The officer paused for a moment, then said, "No, that'll take too long. Let's let it go. It's hot, and I don't want to move that horse and unstack all that hay." James saw him glare at the truck as he said loudly, "These people are a messed-up bunch—a preacher with a bra fetish is a first for me." He turned back to the other agent. "But their story is true about that crazy woman there lying in the middle of I-20—Ector County dispatch confirmed it when I called."

The officer walked farther back and opened a side window to get a good look at Blaze and the back of the trailer. Blaze poked his head out. James watched as the officer reached out to pet him, and Blaze nipped his forearm. The officer dropped his clipboard and grabbed his injured arm, then marched back to Jen's window.

"Who owns that damn biting horse?"

James said, "I do. But like I told you, he don't like strangers much. On the other hand, since you boys wear green uniforms, maybe he thought you were hay. I'm sure sorry, sir. How bad did he get you?" The officer showed him his torn sleeve and bleeding arm. "That's pretty bad, but you're lucky. The last feller got it worse. I hope y'all don't have to detain him for assaulting you. He's how I make a living."

"Just get the hell out of here, you crazy sonsabitches! Get on out of here!"

As they pulled away from the checkpoint, James watched the other agents gather around the bitten officer. He was gesturing wildly with his good arm and pointing toward the pickup and trailer. James watched them until they slowly faded out of sight.

Jen turned her head quickly to look at Brother Bob and said, "Bob, when we stop, you *have* to give me my bra back."

Brother Bob said, "Jen, I was thinking I might just keep it. It does have sentimental value now. After all, it sort of saved us."

For the next few miles, James could not stop smiling, and when he glanced around at the others, he saw that they couldn't either.

WATER

Once they had gotten some distance from the checkpoint, Joaquin felt it was safe enough to stop. He had Jen drive the trailer down a remote dirt road on a very large ranch, where they pulled in behind an old, weathered cattle shed so that they couldn't be seen from the highway. James unloaded Blaze, then Joaquin and Brother Bob started unstacking the hay.

When Joaquin finally moved the bale that allowed him to peer into the small space Angelica was hidden in, he saw her young, bruised face through the opening. She appeared a little wild-eyed at first until she saw that it was him and not the Border Patrol moving the hay bales. She was pressing her broken crucifix up to her lips, but her fearful expression quickly turned to a weak smile of relief.

When Joaquin got her free from the space, she hugged him tightly. As he held her, he brushed pieces of the hay from her dark, shining hair. "*Todo está bien, mija. Todo está bien.*" One of her eyes was still swollen shut but not quite as badly as last night. Her face was still a rainbow of blue, yellowish-brown, and purple bruises.

They decided to drive on until dark and camp for the night at the spring-fed lake at Balmorhea. It was a peaceful, pretty site with the dark of the mountains off in the distance. The expansive sky with the moon and its dome of infinite stars reflected on the smooth water, and the cottony wisps from the tall cottonwood trees around the lake floated on the night breezes. The pristine air carried the fragrance of some tall sycamores, and Joaquin found himself finally truly breathing again. Some coyotes howled off in the distance as he watched the dark form of an owl in graceful flight about the lake. Scattered above the shining water were the luminous, fleeting flashes of the fireflies.

Joaquin and Angelica sat on a blanket away from the pickup near some cottonwood trees. Joaquin had built a campfire of mesquite wood in front of them.

"I like the smell of the burning wood," Angelica told him.

"Yes," Joaquin said softly, taking her hand in his. "Look how the smoke drifts up toward the stars."

They listened to the pops and crackling of the fire for a while. Being with her made Joaquin think of her mother. He thought he would tell her about her mother—he hoped the stories would soothe her.

"*Mija*, you remind me so much of your mother."

"I don't know all that much about her. Father would never talk about her."

"You know she grew up in Mexico with her mother, right?"

"I knew that part."

"I remember the day she graduated high school in Mexico. I was at her graduation. After she walked the stage, she hugged me, so happy and excited."

"You went to her graduation?"

"Yes, I saw her from time to time when I could as she grew up, even though her mother and I weren't together. It was at graduation that she told me she'd decided to go to Guatemala to teach in a school for children whose parents had been disappeared by the gangs."

"She wanted to help kids?"

"That's right. Did you know how your parents met?"

"He wouldn't tell me a thing. Anytime I asked anything, he just walked away."

"While working there, she fell in love with your father, who also taught there. They got married, and she was soon pregnant."

"I know she died when she was delivering me."

Joaquin felt the old familiar heaviness in his chest. "Yes. Due to a hemorrhage. We learned later that the doctor had been morphine drunk when he did the C-section."

Angelica looked sad. "So, if he hadn't been drunk, I might have had my mama?"

"I think that's true."

"The only picture I ever saw was of her in her wedding dress. I carried it in my pocket all my life, but I lost it with my clothes when I was trying not to drown in the river."

"I have some pictures we can look at when we get home."

"I'd like that a lot."

Joaquin and Angelica talked late into the night. He saw that she was weary, yet she still listened with rapt attention to the stories he told her about the mother she never got to know, and she told him she did not want him to stop.

"What was my mother like?"

"Well, she looked a lot like you. She was pretty too and had your long dark hair and your very dark eyes. And she had a good heart. She was very loving."

"Did she want me?"

"She called me when she found out she was pregnant. She was so excited she said she thought she was going to pee her pants. I'd never heard her so happy. She said she couldn't wait to see you. She knew you were a girl, and she gave you your name. Your first name was her middle name—she was Ana Angelica. She told me she already loved you before you were born."

"When she died, what did that do to you?"

Joaquin felt sad and wistful. "Well, you know, it's been over twenty years now. I think of her every day. It still hurts. I know it always will. I've just learned to live with it and go on. When I went to Guatemala for the funeral, it was the first time, of course, that I saw you and held you. You were four days old and so very tiny, but you had your beautiful black hair, and you had this, like, fire in your eyes as you looked at me so intensely. At that moment, I knew that even though your mother was gone, she had given us this precious gift—and so, in a way, she was still with us. When I'm sad, I think of that moment."

He watched the sparks drifting up from the campfire into the beyond. A mourning dove was making its lonesome sound.

"Did she believe in God?"

"Yes, she went to Mass each week, prayed the rosary, and taught catechism to the children in the orphanage. When she decided that she should go to Guatemala and teach, she said that's what God wanted her to do."

"I believed in God until the gang and the coyotes tortured me. I cried to God a thousand times to save me. I was so abandoned and alone. How can there be a loving God who allows such things to happen?"

"I don't know, *mija*. Maybe God doesn't allow it. Maybe it just is. I like to think God cries when we cry."

"Do you believe in heaven?"

Joaquin thought for a while. Two mallard ducks were gliding along the water. The moonlight was making their colors iridescent, the deepest green and cobalt blue. They were leaving silent and disappearing ripples in the water in the shape of a "V" as they swam gracefully together across the lake.

"Heaven? Not like most people do. You see those two ducks and the ripples they're leaving in the water? You see how the ripples are there and then they fade back into the water as they spread out? I think we're like that, like those little waves. We pass back into the water. But I think, even though we die and are no more, it's all still so beautiful because we are part of the water, and so we always will be. We always have been. I think that whatever happens to us, in the end, we'll be alright, as James says. That's how I see heaven."

"So, we're the waves, and we all someday disappear, but we are also the water?"

"Maybe so. That's what I like to believe."

Angelica moved closer to her grandfather's side. He wrapped a blanket around her shoulders and put his arm around her. The flickering campfire light shone on her injured face. She looked so vulnerable, yet he saw that her intense eyes reflected a defiant, determined spirit. *Strong as blue-tempered steel,* he thought.

———

As Joaquin and Angelica talked, Brother Bob was with James, Jen, and Cheyenne at the truck. They were talking about everything Angelica had gone through.

Brother Bob's thoughts turned to the checkpoint. "That was *something*, us getting through that checkpoint. Lord have mercy."

Jen said, "Cheyenne, you were wonderful. You made that agent really believe you."

"Well, I *have* had a few years' practice at it, you know."

Brother Bob said, "You know it's funny now, but I was scared to death. I've never been that scared in my life, except maybe when I almost fell on that thirty-foot ladder putting beer bottles on the Church of Christ for Charley to shoot off. But now I'm worried about what my church people will think if they hear this story, me lying about why I was holding a bra."

"Well, if you were scared, you didn't show it," Jen said. "You're a good actor. I think when the congregation hears this story, they'll love it and find it as funny as we do."

James commented, "Preacher, it might even move you up a notch in their estimation, seeing as how you were trying to help save that poor girl."

Bob said, "Makes me think of what Charley told me one time: 'Sometimes you've got to do the wrong thing to do the right thing.'"

James said, "Yes, sir. And if people don't see that, I reckon they can go sit in the mud with the pigs."

James went to the pickup toolbox, rummaged around, and brought out a bottle of tequila, then walked toward the water. He called back to his companions, "Come on, Jen. Let's go down to the lake."

"Very good idea after the events of this day. I'll get the blankets."

James said, "Come on, Preacher. Come go with us. You too, Cheyenne."

Jen got the blankets, and they all walked down to the water's edge. The four of them lay on the blankets and looked up at the sky. Because the area was so remote, the sky was filled with innumerable bright stars, and the Milky Way shone in various hues across the vast sky. Brother Bob looked up in awe and said he had never seen so many stars. James offered the bottle to Cheyenne first, but she declined, saying, "It makes me too crazy." The others took shots from the bottle. Bob felt its mellow warmth as his body relaxed. Sometimes they talked, and other times, they were content simply to look up at the sky, feel the breeze, and listen to the wind rustle the cottonwood leaves.

After a while, James asked, "Bob, what made you want to become a preacher?"

His question made Bob feel uneasy for some reason. "Oh, I think I just wanted to help people. Some pastors I knew and respected inspired me to think about higher ground, so to speak, about the deeper mystery of this life. Something like that, that's why."

Jen said, "But, Bob, if it's your calling . . . well, you know, once in a while, you seem kind of unhappy. You get this look in your eyes like you're sad or something."

"You can tell? Shoot, I try not to show it. How long have you seen that?"

"I saw that look just a few months after you came to Happy."

He felt hesitant to say too much, but he trusted his companions, and the liquor helped. "Truth is my beliefs have changed from what I grew up with. I'm not sure what I believe anymore. Just doubts, you know."

Jen said, "So? Who doesn't have doubts?"

"I know, Jen, but it feels like life is speaking to me, and I can't quite make out what it's trying to tell me. Like what life's really about is different from what I thought. Maybe faith is too."

James said, "Bob, I don't reckon any of us go through life just farting rainbows and butterflies. How can a person not have doubts sometimes?"

"Or regrets," Jen added. "So, Bob, I guess you're not special. Neither are your doubts. Turns out you're one of *us*."

James added, "Yep. Ain't none of us ten feet tall and invisible to bullets."

They lay on the blankets without talking, listening to the bullfrogs and the crickets that had started up in the cool of the night. Brother Bob looked up at the sky—the owl had perched in one of the tall sycamore trees and was keeping a keen watch over the lake. After a while, Jen began humming a hymn that she had been teaching their church choir for the past few weeks. Brother Bob had asked her to have the choir learn it because it was his favorite. He knew it was by Charles Wesley, brother of

John Wesley, Methodism's founder. The lyrics were based on the biblical story of Jacob set to a lovely old Scottish tune. Brother Bob recalled the story as he sat looking at the water: Jacob had sent his family on across a river and was alone. During the night, God came to him in the form of a man, a stranger. Jacob fought fiercely and wrestled with the stranger all night long in the darkness.

As Jen started softly singing Jacob's song, Cheyenne joined her:

Come, O thou Traveler unknown, Whom still I hold but cannot see;
My company before is gone, And I am left alone with thee;
With thee all night I mean to stay, And wrestle till the break of day.

Yield to me now, for I am weak; But confident in self-despair;
Speak to my heart in blessing speak; Be conquered by my instant prayer;
Speak, or thou never hence shall move, And tell me if they name be Love.

Brother Bob was speechless, in awe of the sisters' beautiful harmony as it drifted up into the silence of the starry sky. The story of a man wrestling with life struck him deeply as his own truth. He looked up to see the owl had resumed its graceful, silent flight again over the lake.

He was shaken out of his deep thoughts when Jen suddenly jumped up and said, "Come on, y'all! Let's go skinny dipping."

He watched in disbelief as she took off her boots, jeans, and shirt, then in shock as she took off her bra and slid her thong down to her ankles, kicking it free. He held his breath and stared incredulously, taking in the image of her in the moonlight, naked. James jumped up and also took off all his clothes, but then he put his boots and hat back on.

Jen collapsed with laughter. "You're going to wear your boots and hat to go swimming?"

"Yes, ma'am. I prefer to live with my hat and boots on."

"Dang, I guess you *are* a real cowboy." Jen turned to Cheyenne. "Come on, sister, hop up and join us."

"No, I'll pass. I'm too scared of the water. I'll just watch you."

Brother Bob could not take his eyes off Jen's lovely nakedness. His heart pounded rapidly, and he felt blood rushing to his groin. He was without words, enrapt in the mystery of her beautiful being.

James said, "Get up, Preacher. Come join us."

"Oh no, I can't. I can't do that. Y'all go on, have fun."

Jen smiled and said, "Come on, Bob, honey, live a little. "

"Oh, no, but thanks. I *really* can't. My parishioners will kill me. Go without me."

Jen and James looked at each other knowingly, then each grabbed one of his arms and pulled him up. He started to protest more, but deep down, he really did want to be in the water with Jen. He complained and acted reluctant as he took off his clothes. Jen looked at him with some interest. "Oh my, Bob—you look good."

James teased him. "Do the ladies in town know what you've been hiding all these years? And you know, if you don't use that thing, your cods will turn blue, shrivel up, and fall plumb off."

Brother Bob suddenly felt very shy and reached for his shirt to cover himself, but Jen laughed and yanked it away. "Lighten up—don't be modest. You need to enjoy your life before it's over."

"And it gets over 'fore you know it, Bob," James added.

To boost his courage, Brother Bob took a long swig from the bottle, and then they splashed into the water, flailing and laughing. The water was cold but felt good on his naked body. The sky and the moon were magnificent. They swam, laughed, splashed each other, and talked. After a while, Brother Bob began to shiver. Jen must have seen he was cold because she moved closer to him. "Come here, poor baby. Come close, and I'll warm you up." She drew him close to her body, face to face, wrapped her arms around him, and held him tightly.

Brother Bob did not know if heaven really existed, but he had always hoped so. He sometimes felt like a fraud when he preached about heaven at funerals. His doubts were like a dull headache that came and went but that never really went away, and it made each moment less happy than it could have been. But in this moment—with the laughter, the sky, the water, and the delicious warmth and feeling of Jen's body against his—in this moment, he was overwhelmed with a thought: *This is it—this is heaven. It's the experience of this life's glorious mystery. The eternal is now.*

Still shivering, he looked into Jen's eyes and whispered, "I now know what the doctrine of the Incarnation means."

Jen rolled her eyes and looked at him curiously. "Huh? You come up with the strangest thoughts at the strangest times. I don't even know what you mean with all your theology. Most folks just call this 'life,' and this life is pretty wonderful, even though sometimes it hurts like hell."

Later that night, as Brother Bob was about to drift off to sleep in his sleeping bag under the stars, he remembered some of the lines of the final verse of the hymn that Jen and Cheyenne had sung earlier about Jacob wrestling with God:

> . . . *I hear thy whisper in my heart;*
> *The morning breaks, the shadows flee; Pure universal love thou art.*
> *To me, to all, thy mercies move; Thy nature and thy name is Love.*

Just as his eyes were closing, he saw the mallards in their graceful movement across the water, the ripples spreading out behind.

RAINBOW

Angelica felt very happy and was softly humming as she, Jen and Cheyenne, and members of Jen's choir were finishing twisting red, white, and blue crepe paper and streaming it along the edges of James's flatbed trailer, which they were using for their float in the Fourth of July parade. On the trailer, they had placed three wooden crosses Joaquin had made, with the middle one standing taller than the other two. Along the edge of the trailer, between patriotic banners, they had placed a sign they had made which read, "Welcome to First United Methodist Church—where grace and mercy abound, and everyone is welcome." Angelica really liked the choir and enjoyed singing with them on Sundays. She felt she belonged, and this morning, they were all talking excitedly about the parade. They had started their work before daybreak. Angelica noticed the sunrise and told the others to look. They saw the light coming through the clouds and a double rainbow that stretched across the expanse of the sky.

By this time, Angelica's bruises and cuts were healed. She was pleased that even the scar on her forehead was nearly gone now. The day they got to Happy, Jen had taken Angelica to an old doctor in Canyon who examined her. "Those cuts on her forehead are going to heal up okay," he told Angelica. He did a full workup with labs and CT scans and gave her medications to help with infection, pain, and the nightmares. When Angelica told him some of what she had been through, he looked visibly angry and upset. When Jen tried to pay him, he shook his head and pushed her hand away. He took Angelica's hand and said, "You're a fighter." Just a few weeks later, Angelica got a card from a San Antonio agency that helps refugees. She learned that the old doctor had given them a large donation in her honor.

Angelica was aware that most everyone in the community knew her story, and she was grateful that they welcomed her as one of them with such genuine warmth and kindness. The Bible study groups in the churches prayed for her to find healing of body and spirit and also prayed for all those like her who were trying to escape evil. The Lions Club remodeled and furnished a small house for her. Different women in the community bought her new clothes, and Berniece at the Beauty Box gave her a year's gift certificate for hair and makeup. The youth groups of the churches joined together and held car washes and bake sales, raising several hundred dollars, so she would have money to live on as she settled in. Many others in the community made donations—some of them quite large—to the fund Brother Bob set up for her at the bank, and most did so anonymously.

She still had many sad and troubling moments, but on this parade morning, Angelica was the happiest she had been since leaving Antigua.

Jen had told Angelica and the others that their float was to go last, so when they finished decorating, they stepped off to the side so they could watch the other participants go by. Angelica looked down the street and saw that the sidewalks along the storefronts of Main Street were filled with people of all ages. She could feel their excitement. She jumped, then laughed and quickly covered her ears when the wail of the siren from the new firetruck signaled the start of the parade. It was followed by the high school marching band. Jen leaned close to her and said, "That song is called 'America the Beautiful.'" Behind the band, cheerleaders were smiling and laughing as they waved their pom poms and threw candy to the children who were jumping about with excitement.

Next came men and women in white cowboy hats, starched white shirts, boots, and jeans, riding beautiful horses. Angelica clapped and waved when she saw that they were led by Joaquin and James. Joaquin was riding a big, buckskin horse while he held the staff of a large American flag. James was holding the Texas flag as he rode Blaze, who was spirited and prancing as they moved down the street. The sun shone brightly on the flags, waving in the breeze. The floats of various organizations and businesses came into view, one after another, all with smiling people aboard: the John Deere implement company, the Farmer's Coop, the Lions Club, and the Masonic Lodge.

———

Just as Jen, Cheyenne, and Angelica were about to take up their place in the parade and had gotten in James's truck, Gil's Denali slowly appeared from behind the Baptist Church, followed by a white SUV with a green diagonal stripe on the door. As they neared, Gil pulled aside, stuck his arm out the window, and pointed at them. The Border Patrol SUV sped up and pulled in front of them, stopping them from joining the parade. Jen glared at Gil, who then turned around and drove back down the farm-to-market road to the west. Jen was frozen in fear—all this work to rescue her new friend, and Gil may have just made it all for nothing.

An officer walked up to Jen's window. "I'm an agent of the U.S. Border Patrol," he told her. "I'm looking for a woman named 'Angelica.'"

Jen asked, "Why, sir?"

"I need to talk with her."

"But please tell me, why?"

"I have orders from my supervisors. I was informed by someone that she is here illegally."

"Who told you . . . never mind. I know."

"I'm not at liberty to release that information."

The women stared at the officer and one another in disbelief. Jen felt her heart sinking into an abyss of despair.

"Is one of you Angelica?"

"I'm Angelica."

The officer fixed his gaze on Angelica, and Jen took her hand.

"Ma'am, I need you to get out of the vehicle. Please."

Angelica let go of Jen's hand. She got out and walked around to where the officer was. As he reached for his handcuffs, he said to her calmly, "I just need you to turn around with your back to me and stand with your hands on the vehicle and your legs apart."

Jen couldn't stand it. As Angelica was turning around, she jumped out of the truck and stood between the officer and Angelica. "What are you doing? She doesn't have any weapons. Don't touch her. She's been traumatized. Please, don't touch her."

The officer stopped and looked at Jen. He seemed unsure of himself for a moment, then told Angelica she could turn back around. Jen stepped aside.

"I really need you to come with me, Angelica. Let's go."

As he led her to his SUV, Jen pleaded, "Please, officer. Please, no. You have no idea what she's been through. They tortured her and almost killed her several times."

"I have to do my job," he said, and Jen could see that he didn't, in fact, look happy about what he was doing. He said, almost apologetically, "After we got the phone call, I was ordered to come pick her up and detain her. It's the policy."

The officer placed her in the back seat of his vehicle. Jen yanked her phone from her pocket and called James, but he didn't answer. She then called Brother Bob—he had told her he was going to sit on the church steps to watch the parade—and she prayed that he had his phone on him.

"Bob, help, help. The Border Patrol showed up—they're taking Angelica."

"Oh God, no."

"We're at the Baptist Church. He's pulling out now. Big white SUV—looks like he's turning down County Line Road and going to the highway."

"I'm still at the church. I'll try to catch him before he gets to the highway."

———

Brother Bob jumped off the steps and sprinted the five blocks north until he came to the edge of County Line Road. He stooped over with his hands on his knees, trying to catch his breath, while he watched the road to the west. Soon, he saw the white SUV drawing closer, and it didn't appear it was going to slow down. Brother Bob hurried to the middle of the pavement while he waved his arms frantically at the approaching vehicle. It was still not slowing down, so he flung himself down and lay across the white line, blocking the path. Just at the last second, the agent swerved the vehicle, ran off into the ditch, and stopped.

The officer jumped out and stomped toward Brother Bob. "You damn fool sonofabitch. What the hell's wrong with you? I almost ran over you!"

Brother Bob got up from the hot blacktop and faced the officer. He stared at Bob with dawning recognition. "Bob?"

"Yep, that's me. You look familiar too . . . wait, aren't you Tommy? I haven't seen you since high school. Nobody ever knew what became of you after graduation night. So, you're with the Border Patrol?'

"Yeah, just for two years now. But Bob, what the hell are you doing, jumping in front of me like that?"

"You've got Angelica. I had to stop you."

"What? You know Angelica?"

"Oh, yes, I sure do."

"I have orders to take her to detention. She's here illegally. Someone here reported her."

"I think I know who that was. Tommy, I know you have your orders. But don't take her. Let's go to my church office."

"You're a preacher?"

"Yes."

"Well, I'm not surprised. You'd never get drunk with us or chase girls. We thought you were a boring stuffed shirt."

"I know. I was."

As Brother Bob was getting into the vehicle, he noticed that Angelica looked at him in a way she'd never looked at him before, and she smiled. For a moment, he felt like a bit of a hero. And maybe he could be. Tommy drove them to the church and parked in the shade of the old elm tree with the gnarled roots. They all three went up the steep steps and entered the sanctuary.

Tommy said to Angelica, "You go sit down on one of these benches in the church there while I talk to Bob. And now, don't you run off—I really don't want to have to shoot you."

"I won't run," Angelica said solemnly. "I'm tired of running."

Tommy and Brother Bob sat in his office with the shelves of books. A slowly oscillating fan hummed in one corner and occasionally rustled the edges of the papers on the desk. Brother Bob told Tommy Angelica's entire story. Tommy listened intently and carefully. At first, he seemed skeptical and defensive, but as he learned more of what had happened to her, he seemed less tense and guarded. When Bob finished telling him Angelica's story, Tommy stood up without saying anything and walked over to the small window that looked out on the tree. He stood there without speaking as he looked out. Brother Bob fidgeted in his seat. He was unsure what impact, if any, Angelica's story might have on him and on her fate. The longer Tommy did not respond, the more uncomfortable Brother Bob got.

Finally, Tommy spoke. "I had a sister, Diana," he said. "You never knew about her because she didn't make it to high school with us, and my family didn't talk about her. She was two years younger than me. We lived on a farm along a creek. One May evening, a bad thunderstorm rolled in from the southwest, the kind that has those towering white thunderheads that seem to reach to the moon. It roared so loud it seemed like it was going to blow the roof off of the house. Us kids were scared. Lightning cracked all around, splitting the trunk of an old tree out by the cow barn. That tree was like the one that you have here, just outside this window. After a big rain like that, the creek down in the pasture would run full for a day or two. It'd get raging full, with floating branches, cow pies . . . It carried along all sorts of debris."

"I know that kind of creek," Brother Bob said softly.

"Yes, well . . . the next morning, Diana and I went down to play by the creek. Mama told us to be careful and not get in. We threw rocks and sticks in the water, teased the turtles, and chased each other around, you know, like kids do. There was a narrow part you could jump across if you got a good running start. I jumped across and dared her to jump after me. She was scared, but then she gathered up her courage. She made a hard run and jumped, but she didn't quite land with both feet on the other side and started slipping down the muddy bank. I ran to grab her outstretched hand, but I was too late, and the water took her. I saw her floating down the creek, her arms reaching for me. She was yelling my name. A week later, they found her in a creek east of Canyon, half-buried in the mud."

"Oh, Tommy. I'm so sorry. I never knew that."

"She looked kind of like your Angelica."

Brother Bob watched as Tommy drove away slowly from the church and turned to go north on Highway 87, past the "Town without a Frown" sign. He sat on the church steps, with Angelica by his side, as he called Jen to tell her the news.

HARVEST

Angelica was excited because each fall, the people of Happy had a harvest festival that was held in the community building behind the Methodist church, and this evening was going to be her first time there. People had told her that most everyone attended, and it included a potluck dinner and a dance afterward.

All afternoon, she had been preparing her favorite Guatemalan dishes to share, and as she carried them into the hall, she proudly showed them to the other people and told them what she had made. Her recipes had been handed down through generations in Guatemala, just like the women of Happy who used recipes handed down from great-grandmothers who lived in the Panhandle before fences and roads. Angelica talked happily with the others and sampled the various dishes they had brought, marveling at how tantalizing the aromas and flavors were. She was still amazed at how many people came up to greet her with a smile and a hug.

Once she got her dishes placed on the long tables, she walked about the room, looking at the craft booths that lined the walls of the long hall. Local artists and crafters had tables of wooden crosses, painted birdhouses, and handmade jewelry boxes. She felt quite sad for a moment as she thought back to the jewelry box Mateo had made for her, but the image of his proud smile helped ease her pain some, so she moved on to look at the other tables. There were several paintings, many of Longhorns, blue-bonnets, windmills, and old farmhouses. Other booths sold homemade jams, pickles, fudge, cookies, and bread. She walked out on the porch and saw that there were games under the trees and face-paintings for children. The festivities made her a little lonely. She thought, *I wish Mateo was here with me.*

Angelica waved to Brother Bob as he was coming up the steps. He joined her on the porch.

"Hey, it's good to see you!" he said. "How are you doin' this evening?"

"I'm pretty good, Brother Bob. I enjoyed making some dishes, and it's such a pretty day."

"It's my favorite time of year. I love fall nights in the Panhandle. The air's so crisp, and I like the sound of the breeze rustling leaves down the sidewalks." He pointed to the east. "Later, the harvest moon should come up over there."

"What's a harvest moon?"

"This time of year, when farmers are harvesting grain sorghum, the moon is larger than usual when it first rises. Seems to take up the horizon. It's a beautiful color too."

"That sounds lovely."

"Do you like to dance?"

Angelica frowned. "Mateo and I used to dance sometimes in my apartment. Paco, my little dog, would bark at us and make us laugh. I haven't danced since then."

"Well, it's okay if you don't want to, but I think you'll find the guys here will be gentlemen. They'll be happy to teach you how to dance Texas dances."

"I'll try to be brave."

"Angelica, you're one of the bravest people I ever met."

Later, at the dance, Angelica found Brother Bob and told him, "You were right—these men are gentlemen."

Several of the young cowboys had asked her to dance, each taking off his hat first and asking, "Ma'am, may I have the honor of having this dance with you?" This small gesture touched her deeply because it said so much. Although she still had some lingering pain in her feet, she did her best to dance gracefully, and she saw that many in the crowd smiled at her in an admiring way. She had some trouble learning the two-step at first, but the cowboy teaching her was patient, and she often laughed as she struggled over the steps. When she left the dance floor to catch her breath, she sat with Brother Bob and Charley.

Angelica knew Charley was blind and understood when Brother Bob told him, "Charley, Angelica's just sat down with us here."

"I *know* that," Charley said, indignant but smiling. "I could tell by her perfume that a mighty fine young woman joined us." He turned his wrinkled face toward Angelica. "Hello, Angelica. It's good to see you," he said, reaching out his hand.

She took his hand and said, "Thank you. It's good to see you, Charley."

Brother Bob said, "When you were dancing, the lights of the hall were shining on your hair and your colorful dress. You made a lovely sight."

"I can see it now," Charley said. "I see you dancing, Angelica, and it makes this old blind man very happy. This town is blessed to have you here."

"Well, I hoped I look prettier than my dancing does!"

Charley said in a kind tone, "Aw, a pretty girl can make a couple missteps without anyone payin' no mind."

Angelica admired Jen as she danced with different men and laughed and talked with her friends. She seemed *so* happy. Jen had told Angelica earlier that she was waiting for James to arrive. He was working late on a ranch way up by Channing. Angelica noticed that the other people were watching Jen too, and at times, they whispered to each other with knowing looks. Brother Bob leaned over and told Angelica, "I haven't ever seen Jen this happy."

James didn't arrive at the dance until almost eleven. Angelica watched as he walked across the dance floor to where Jen was talking with friends, spun her around, took her by the hand, and led her out on the floor. A pang went through Angelica as she remembered the feeling of Mateo's arms around her when they danced.

———

Jen and James danced several songs together, including two-steps, waltzes, and the Cotton-Eyed Joe. Jen felt light and free, though she could feel the people watching her and James. She noticed that some looked at them admiringly, except for one of them, Cindy, his ex, who had shot at him. Jen kissed the scar on his earlobe and whispered, "I see *somebody* here's jealous of me being with you."

He teased her, "I saw her glaring. Does she have her .22 with her? I might oughta get a better head start this time. But how could she not be jealous? Look who you're with."

She slapped him playfully. "Don't get a big head, cowboy. I know I'm the best thing that ever happened to you."

Jen sensed that most of the townsfolk were happy for them. Brother Bob had told her he heard that the Church of Christ preacher had started preaching against adultery more often now, but he told Jen that no one he talked with ever criticized them or looked down on them. In fact, he told Jen that one of their church members—an old, tough, conservative rancher—pulled him aside one day after church and told him if he ever heard anyone from the church "judging those two people," that Brother Bob should come tell him, and he would get them straightened out. He'd then told Brother Bob, "Now, dammit, you know what the Good Book says, 'Judge not that you be not judged.' That Jen Jenkins has had hard times in her life, and James is a good man."

Jen asked the band to play "Amarillo by Morning." James pulled her close to his chest, and she nestled her head under his chin as they glided around the floor. She couldn't stop smiling, so she turned her face more to his chest. When the song ended, they walked hand in hand out of the hall and across the alley to the Methodist church and stood under the old elm by the steps. The lights were on in the church, and so the stained-glass windows looked beautiful and cast some light out into the darkness. They were alone. They held each other, and Jen gazed up at the rust-colored harvest moon. The slight wind felt cold on her face, but she didn't mind.

But as she stood there, enrapt, a part of her felt uneasy. When she heard the sound of a footstep on gravel, she turned to see Gil, a few yards behind them in the dark, with a bottle in one hand and a revolver in the other. Something about his pose made her think he'd been standing there watching them for some time. He took a few steps closer into some light, and she saw that his eyes were bloodshot red, but his face showed no emotion. It looked as if he were dead inside.

He said nothing, but pointed the pistol at James, then at Jen, and then at James again. He just stood there, silently pointing the pistol.

Jen cried, "Gil, please don't. Please don't. I'll come with you."

James had let go of her and gently tucked her behind him. "Gil, man," he said gently, "killing us won't solve your problems. It won't make you happy. But if you have to shoot one of us, shoot me and let her go."

Unfazed, Gil still said nothing, still with a flat expression on his face. They waited an eternity. Jen felt sick and was trembling. He lowered the gun, spun the cylinder, pointed it at his own temple, cocked it, and pulled the trigger. Click. Jen screamed. Ecclesiastes came running out to see what was going on. Gil pointed the gun at the dog. Click. Then he aimed it at one of the stained-glass windows and pulled the trigger. Boom! The window shattered, and some of the falling glass hit Ecclesiastes, who yelped and darted down the sidewalk. Gil looked at James and Jen one last time, stuck the gun inside his belt, turned, and slowly walked into the darkness and silence of the night.

Deputy Curtis, Brother Bob, Joaquin, and a bunch of other people came running up from the dance hall. As he hurriedly looked about, Curtis asked, "What happened? Anybody hurt?"

With her heart still pounding, Jen managed to say, "No. Nobody's hurt. It's Gil. He walked off toward the post office."

"I'll go look for him. Y'all better call it a night and go on home."

James said, "Jen, you better come stay out at the ranch with me. Gil may come home to kill you."

"I know. I think he will."

James and Jen drove out to his ranch house. They sat at the kitchen table, drinking coffee as neither one could sleep. James had Jesus lay on the front porch to stand guard in case Gil showed up. Right around three, Jen's phone rang. It was Gil. His voice was low, flat, and void of feeling.

"Goodbye, J . . . Jen."

Jen felt a wave of cold dread fill her whole body with an intensity she had never felt before. "Gil, no, Gil, no. Where are you?"

"It don't matter."

"Gil, please tell me where you are. We can get you some help. Please!"

"Nothin' can help the fact that you used to love me and don't anymore. You told me you couldn't trust me to change. You were right. I can't."

"I *still* love you, but you make it so difficult. You're so unhappy."

"Not for long. Maybe I'll see you on the other side if there is one."

Jen held her breath. There was an incredible boom, then silence. Then, more silence, except she could hear the muffled sound of the wind blowing, and then the call dropped. No words would form in her mind—all she could do was feel her dry mouth, racing heart, pounding head, and the terror that was racing through her body like wildfire.

Finally, she was able to muster up the words. "James, I think he did it," she said, cradling her temples with her fingers. "I think he shot himself. He wouldn't tell me where he is. Oh God, oh God, oh no."

"Lord have mercy. I'll call Curtis."

Before James could call, Jen's phone rang again, and it was Curtis.

"Jen, I found him. Gil's on top of the grain elevator with his feet dangling off. He just fired his gun at some pigeons and then pitched the gun off the elevator. I've got my spotlight on him. I can't find a way to get up there. I've been hollering at him to come down, but he won't answer. Can you come and talk with him?"

———

When James arrived at the grain elevator with Jen, Brother Bob and Danny were already there. The deputy still had the spotlight aimed at the top of the elevator. James looked up. There, about a hundred feet up, was Gil with his legs dangling off.

Jen yelled, "Gil! Gil! Come down. We can talk. Come down!"

Gil still said nothing and just continued to swing his dangling legs.

James said, "How do we get up there?"

Danny said, "I know this old elevator. Used to come here with my dad. There's a mechanical cage inside that goes to the top."

James and the others ran into the space that lay underneath the massive concrete grain elevator. In the dusty dark, they found that the metal, one-person cage was still at the top where Gil had left it when he had gotten out. James stood in front of the cables that suspended it and looked up. Danny ran to the dust-covered operator box on the wall and pushed a red button; the cables jerked and began to move, and the cage slowly descended. It clanged on its way down, hitting the sides of the frame that held it, and it bounced when it hit the floor in front of them. Brother Bob rushed to open the door and was stepping in when James grabbed him by his coat collar and jerked him back out.

"Dammit, James! What are you doing? I should go."

"No, Bob. It's a one-man ride up, and he might shove you off. This town can't afford to lose the one fine preacher it's got."

Jen said, "No, James, no. I'll go. Let me go." She moved toward the cage, but James put his arm across her to stop her.

"No way. He, sure enough, might take you off with him." James stepped into the cage, and Danny pushed the button. Just as the creaking cage jerked to start its long ascent, James's eyes met Jen's. She was biting her lip and had her hand over her heart as she looked at him. He yelled, "It'll be all right, Jen." Behind her, he saw Brother Bob running to a metal ladder attached to the far wall, but there was no time left to argue.

James got to the top and opened the cage door. He saw Gil's form silhouetted against the bright, rust-colored moon. Gil was sitting on the very edge, his shoulders slumped. James walked over and sat down beside him and let his legs dangle off the side also. Gil did not look at him. Neither spoke at first.

"Gil, that's a mighty pretty moon."

More silence, then, "Hello, goat roper."

"Gil, I reckon you didn't come up here just to enjoy the view and to sit in pigeon shit."

Gil turned and looked at him. James had never seen anyone look so sad and so lost. "I'm a broken man, James."

"I know."

"I'm done. I'm just done with this life. I'm going to see what's on the other side. I'm going to see my dog, Jack. I loved Jack."

"Jen loves you."

"She doesn't love me anymore. Her heart's with you."

"She still loves you. That's what you don't understand. It's just you've been awful mean to her."

"I know I have been."

"But you've been meaner to yourself most of all."

There was more silence.

"Come on, Gil. Let's get down from here."

Still more silence.

James said, "You and I both know this life's mighty tough. One time, Bob told me, 'No bad thing *has* to have the last word about our lives.' So come on now, and let's go back down. Don't give up. Jen will drive you to the hospital. The whole town will help you. We all know you're a good man, but you just fell off in a ditch. We've all done that before."

"No, James, I'm done. There's no hope for me. I'm done with this life. I don't want it anymore."

Gil started to jump. James lurched forward and grabbed one of his wrists, but Gil still slid over the edge. He was swinging in the air over the dark chasm below, held only by James's hand around his wrist. He started kicking his legs wildly and flailing his free arm, trying to shake James's grip. James felt Gil's wrist gradually slipping through his hand. He gritted his teeth, and sweat broke out on his forehead as he gripped his wrist as hard as he could. Gil's furious kicking and swinging of his legs in the air was pulling James closer to the edge. James yelled, "Dammit, Gil, quit kicking. Stop it. I'm losing you."

He felt himself about to slide off the edge. But Gil wouldn't stop. *I can't let go. I can't let him go. Oh, Jen. Oh, Jen. My lovely Jen.* Cold air started rushing past his face, and he felt himself merging with the long, long, silent fall into the deep, silent darkness.

———

Brother Bob had looked up and seen that the ladder went far up into the narrowing darkness. He grabbed the first rungs and hurriedly began to climb.

He stepped off the ladder out onto the roof, his whole body trembling, aflame with fear. He ran around the little building that sat on top of the grain elevator, but he slipped down in the pigeon droppings and scraped his hands and face. He jumped up and sprinted on. When he came round to the other side where the men were, he saw only the empty ledge and the harvest moon beyond. As he stared in sickening shock at that vacant ledge and moon beyond, the cold wind was wailing low as it was blowing through the broken windows behind him. He dropped to his knees, shut his eyes, clenched his fists, and started beating his legs, crying, "No, no, no, no. No, God, no!"

FREEDOM

Jen looked out on the prairie with its short native grass, prickly pear, and yucca that surrounded the small cemetery. Its level plain stretched to the west horizon and blue sky, broken only by a few shallow draws with dry creek beds. To the east, the prairie extended to the edge of Happy with its church steeples, the water tower, grain elevator, the shining tin roof of the Lions Club, and the bright blue of Berniece's Beauty Box. There, on the north side of town, she could almost make out the "Town without a Frown" sign.

Jen sat alone in a gray metal folding chair underneath the funeral tent that Digger had set up beside the grave. She had chosen her simplest dress for the occasion, though it was of a fine cloth. The black fabric stood in contrast to the whiteness of the tent. She fixed her eyes on the mound of dark earth adjacent to the open pit of the grave. The mound had been covered with a rectangle of artificial grass as if to disguise the reality of death.

It was quiet except for the sound of the wind softly whipping the canvas, but soon a mockingbird—perched on top of a headstone on a nearby grave—began singing. The headstone was that of James's father. The engraving read, "W. T. Armstrong, 1930-1978." Beneath his name, his silver roping championship belt buckle had been inlaid in the smooth gray granite. A gust of wind suddenly ruffled the mockingbird's feathers, almost blowing him off the stone, but he caught his balance and continued to sing, undeterred and with apparent joy. The wind was chilly, but the sky was a radiant blue with some luminous white clouds, and the sunshine felt good on Jen's face.

Jen had not gone to the community luncheon at the Lions Club building, which had been prepared by the Methodist women. She had tried to go, but when she walked around the corner and saw that people were lined up at the door and far down the street waiting to get in, it was all too much. The sight of all those people made her feel she was falling into a dark abyss, and the sadness in her chest made it difficult to breathe, much less talk. So now she sat alone at the grave, waiting for the others to arrive, with her hands in her lap holding Sunbeam, now well-worn with the years.

As she sat there, staring at the mound of dirt and the carpet of artificial grass over it, she felt herself growing more and more angered and repulsed by that sight and by the attempt at illusion. She rose from where she sat, dragged the green plastic grass off of the mound, and threw it aside with a final kick. "There! Dammit!"

When she saw the fresh dirt, relief flooded her. She dropped to her knees, scooped dirt into her hands, felt its warmth, and took in its fragrance, and then she let it slowly sift through her fingers. Somehow, the sight, smell, and feel of the good Panhandle soil comforted her—her spirit was part of that warm earth and at one with the eternity of the Panhandle plains. She looked at the grave, then up at the blue sky, saw the sunlight on the white clouds, and finally shifted her gaze to the open prairie. She felt the wind on her face. She could almost breathe now.

After a while, she could no longer bear to face the grave. She stood up and turned around to look toward the town to the east. The elegant white hearse shone brightly in the sunlight in front of the Methodist Church steps and the old elm, its branches now bare. Deputy Curtis's patrol pickup was parked in front of the hearse just down the street. People were starting to line up to walk behind the hearse the quarter mile to the cemetery, and the line was already extending from the church several blocks east to the grain elevator. Jen could see that just about everyone from the community was there, along with many people from around the Panhandle.

When Jen saw the lights of Curtis's patrol pickup come on, and the hearse slowly start to move forward, she trembled. She thought, *Well, I guess this is it.* Jen watched the shining white hearse with all the people walking behind slowly coming toward her. As the procession got closer, it came to a shallow draw that was on the east side of the cemetery. The patrol pickup briefly disappeared from Jen's sight as it entered the draw, but after a moment, the patrol lights slowly came into view, then the truck itself. Next, Jen saw a cowboy hat and then the lean figure of a cowboy gradually emerge from the draw. The cowboy was walking in front of the hearse, leading a riderless black horse. As they got closer, she saw that it was old Joaquin leading Blaze.

Deputy Curtis led the procession on toward the cemetery's wrought iron gate, but when he got to the gate, he pulled his truck to the side so the procession could pass. He got out and stood facing the procession in solemn attention, and he took off his gray Stetson and placed it over his heart as the hearse neared him. When Jen saw this simple gesture of respect, she caught her breath and put her hand to her heart—such deep feelings welled up within her.

Through her tears, Jen watched as Joaquin, Blaze, the hearse, and the people slowly made their way into the cemetery and approached the grave. Although there were hundreds of people there, including many young children, everyone was silent. There was only the sound of the windblown canvas of the tent and the mockingbird. Digger stopped the hearse a few yards from the grave. Led by Digger and Brother Bob, six cowboys in boots, jeans, and black shirts slowly carried James's casket to the grave, where they set it on the stanchion.

Digger looked stern and unsmiling; gone was his ebullient manner. The people gathered around the tent, still and silent. Cheyenne and Angelica sat down on either side of Jen; Angelica put her arm around Jen's shoulders, and Cheyenne reached to hold Jen's hand. Danny led Charley to the chairs. Charley was wearing his black cowboy hat and had his unlit pipe in his mouth with one hand on the bowl of it, holding it in place. Several other of Jen's friends, including elderly people who made their way unsteadily and warily in their walkers from their cars nearby, sat in the folding chairs under the tent as well.

Just before Brother Bob started to speak, Joaquin led Blaze up to the grave so that he and Blaze were standing just behind the casket. Jen gazed at the beautiful dark mahogany casket, which was unadorned with any flowers, and then she looked beyond the casket at Joaquin standing by Blaze's head, holding the reins. Blaze had his head and ears up and was looking intently at the casket, the tent, and the people. His black coat was sleek and shimmering in the sun. James's rope hung across the saddle horn.

Brother Bob stood by the end of the casket, holding his Bible. With tearful eyes and without speaking, Brother Bob looked for a long moment at Jen, Cheyenne, Angelica, Charley, and all the people, then turned and nodded at Joaquin. Joaquin turned and took James' rope from the saddle and placed it on the casket. The silence was then broken by many of the people softly crying.

Brother Bob tried to speak, but then his voice faltered, and he stopped. He turned his face to the side, away from the people, and looked out across the many headstones of all shapes and ages and the vast prairie beyond. Jen knew he was gathering his strength. Soon, he turned back and looked intently at her, Angelica, Cheyenne, and all the people, then began again with a wavering voice:

"James was our friend. Our hearts are broken, and our sadness unbounded. We don't know *exactly* what happened on top of the grain elevator that night with James and Gil. Yet, on the other hand, I suspect all of us do know because we know who James was. We know that James *could* have let go of Gil's arm, but then again, we know that he *could not.* The man who would have let go would not have been the man James saw when he looked in the mirror. Or the man we knew and loved.

"James's not letting go was about character and faith. And faith is about who you are deep down. When we think of who James was, we see that faith is not about religion—at least, not necessarily. Religion is talking about faith in our efforts to understand it. But faith's not about whether you believe in God. *Belief* is about where your mind is. *Faith* is about where your heart is."

He paused, looked at Angelica, and nodded, then looked back at all the others. "We all know Angelica's story. So, we know Angelica's heart. In her story, we see that faith is about courage and grit, keeping going when all is truly lost."

He looked at Jen. "And we all know Jen's story. So, we know Jen's heart. In Jen's story, we see that faith is about not letting life's hardships turn your heart to stone.

"And we knew James's heart. He was a man you could count on, day or night. Scorching sun, blowing dust, or howling blizzard—didn't matter. You could count on James to ride up to help you, and he always showed up with a grin. He never quit on anyone. The cartel coyotes learned the hard way he didn't quit on Angelica. And he didn't quit on Joaquin, or Jen, or me, or any of you. And now we know, he didn't quit on Gil.

"When I came here fresh out of seminary, I thought I had the faith and that I was supposed to teach *you* about it. Turns out I was mistaken. I had it backward—in walking beside you down the roads we've traveled, you showed *me* what faith really is.

"As I came to know your struggles—and as I wrestled with my own— you showed me that faith is about trust and letting go. James helped me see that faith is about joining in life's dance with joy and gratitude. It's about being open to this life, with its highest joys and deepest sorrows, and yes, even with its profound, incomprehensible evil.

"In moments like this, when we are broken by the pain of saying goodbye to James, we may briefly see that we are part of a deep Mystery whose name we do not know—the Mystery that set our hearts to beating and will, one day, quiet them again. In this moment, we catch a glimpse of a higher ground.

"There's an old hymn about 'leaning on the everlasting arms.' From those eternal arms we came, in those arms, we live, and to those arms, we will return someday. So, we can say eternity is *already* here. It is *now*, not someday, and it is *here*, not out yonder. When we're able to look with new eyes, we experience eternity. You might see it when you look into a loved one's eyes and therein see yourself, the mystery of their being and your own. Right now, we can see it in this blue sky and white clouds, and feel it in this Panhandle wind, and hear it in the mockingbird's song. Look at Blaze. We see it in Blaze's shimmering black coat and his flashing eyes. Look at James's rope on his casket. The rope makes us think of the good, good gift that James was—and will always be—to us. We see eternity in the gift. Eternity is the awareness of a Grace that gave us each other and gave us this magic garden to enjoy. It's the Grace that gave us James. Yes, it is, *amazing* Grace.

"So, you won't be surprised that, even though he's gone on before us across the river, James is waving his hat and grinning, inviting us to join in the dance. To dance life's dance with grateful joy and to trust in the loving Mystery from whom we came, in whom we live, and to whom we belong forever. This means as James said to Jen a few minutes before he died, 'It'll be all right.'

"Now, with broken but grateful hearts, and in the name of the Father, Son, and Holy Spirt, we say goodbye to our James and give him back to the everlasting arms of the divine Love that gave him to us."

After leading the people in the Lord's Prayer, Brother Bob walked to the front row of chairs and put his arms around Jen. When Brother Bob had said, "Dance life's dance with grateful joy," the image of James on Blaze, rope in gloved hand, waiting his turn at the steer roping the first night they made love came to her mind, and so now her body was shaking with waves of sorrow. With her cheek pressed to his, she whispered, "Oh, Bob. My James is gone." When she told him this, she felt his tears flood down against her cheek and heard his muffled cries.

He held her tighter and whispered with a broken voice, "He loved you so much." He slowly raised up, began wiping his eyes, and kissed her forehead.

Cheyenne was praying with head bowed, but when he took Cheyenne's hands, she opened her eyes and said, "Hey, sweet Bob. The Lord gave you some good words."

He moved over in front of Angelica who stood up and hugged him and kissed his cheek. She said, "I know he was your hero too." When Brother Bob took Charley's hand to shake it, Charley placed his other hand on Bob's shoulder and held it there.

Some of the people gradually began to talk with each other quietly, but many remained silent out of sadness and respect. Jen watched as the people began the walk back to town, and the cemetery was eventually empty except for Brother Bob, Cheyenne, Joaquin, Angelica, and Blaze. Jen told the others, "We have one more thing that James wanted us to do. We need to go to his ranch."

Before they started the walk back to town, Jen walked over to stand by the casket. She put her hand on James's rope and felt its roughness, and then she ran her hand over the casket and felt the smoothness of the mahogany. She thought, *Just like James. Just like life itself.* She stood there for several minutes while the others waited beyond the tent. Finally, Jen leaned down and kissed the casket and then let her hand slowly slide down free from it as she turned around to walk away.

Once they were back in town, Joaquin loaded Blaze in the trailer, and they all got in the pickup and began the drive out to James's ranch. As Joaquin drove them down the dusty roads, Jen thought about the previous afternoon when she and Brother Bob had taken Gil's ashes to his parents' old home place.

When they drove up, Jen noticed the house and how it had changed since she and Gil were in high school. For almost a hundred years, the house had valiantly survived the rolling dust, the merciless heat, the bitter cold blasts of the north wind, and the deluges of the summer storms. Now, the empty house, with its weathered gray wood and broken-out windows, was leaning precariously. Yet, it was still standing in these last days as a silent sentinel, watching out over the vast, lonesome prairie, while steadfastly guarding, as secrets, all of the stories of struggle and hope that it had witnessed. To Jen, the house seemed a poignant symbol of time, and people, and dreams passing away.

Jen and Brother Bob walked the place until they found the old pine tree where Jack was buried. There, in the pine needles and dirt, was the top of an old wooden cross Gil had made. Jen scraped away the needles and dirt so that the full cross could be seen. She and Brother Bob could not make out the words that had been scratched into the wood with a boy's pocketknife so many years ago. Brother Bob took his handkerchief and rubbed and blew the dirt from the scratches in the cross. Finally, they were able to read, "My friend Jack." As Jen scattered the ashes over Jack's grave, she whispered, "Oh, Gil. My poor Gil. Why couldn't you ever feel that I loved you?"

As they neared James's ranch house, Jesus darted off the porch and excitedly ran up to greet them, tail wagging in happy, hopeful anticipation, but when they all got out, he saw that James was not with them. He hung his head, turned, and slowly went back to the porch, where he lay down and rested his head on his outstretched paws. *He knows*, Jen thought.

The pickup and trailer kicked up dust as Joaquin drove on into the corral. Jen led Blaze out of the trailer, and Joaquin helped her take off the saddle and bridle. She gave them to Joaquin and said, "James wanted you to have these."

Angelica moved to his side and put her arm around his waist. Joaquin struggled to talk, "Jen, I loved him . . . he was a son to me."

She kissed his cheek and said, "I know, Joaquin. He knew that. You were a father of the heart to him, and he was always grateful. He told me so."

Jen said to all of them, "James said if he ever died to let Blaze run free on the ranch, so we're going to turn him loose." Joaquin opened the corral gate. With tears streaming, Jen slapped Blaze on the flank and yelled, "Go on, Blaze! Go on now!" They all watched as Blaze ran out of the corral across the pasture to the top of a ridge, where he stopped and turned with his head and ears up, looking at them. Jen yelled, "Go on, Blaze! Run free now. No one else will ever ride you. Go run free with James." Blaze stood for a moment, still looking at them, then he shook his head and mane, turned, and ran fast over the rise and off into the distance.

Brother Bob was standing next to Jen. She took his hand and squeezed it as they watched Blaze run, his black mane flying in the wind.

ACKNOWLEDGMENTS

I want to express a special thanks to Ava Coibion, Greenleaf Book Group editor. Her guidance, keen insights, and creative touch are manifest in these pages.

I am grateful for the people of Happy whom I knew when I was there. Their courage, faith, and humor inspired this work of fiction and taught me much about being human.

ABOUT THE AUTHOR

MICHAEL DOWNING is a writer who lives near Austin, Texas. He is a clinical psychologist and a former United Methodist minister.

www.ingramcontent.com/pod-product-compliance
Lightning Source LLC
Chambersburg PA
CBHW020139120726
47903CB00007B/2331